Wild Summer Rose

AMY ELIZABETH SAUNDERS

LOVE SPELL **NEW YORK CITY**

LOVE SPELL®

August 1993

Published by

Dorchester Publishing Co., Inc.
276 Fifth Avenue
New York, NY 10001

The name "Love Spell" and its logo are trademarks of Dorchester Publishing Co., Inc.

Printed in the United States of America.

For Mom, with love.
For Cherri and Leslie, for your belief and support.

Chapter One

France, 1788

Phillipe St. Sebastien moved quietly through the ancient halls of the château, the heels of his worn riding boots echoing in the silence. The March winds whistled through the stone corridors, a mournful sound.

Even the mellow light of his candle could not hide the decay that the once beautiful castle had fallen into—the moldering velvet drapes, the rotting woodwork, the piles of dust and God only knew what else covering the floors.

He swore quietly as a cobweb touched his face, and brushed it impatiently from his thick, black hair. The cold, damp air of the castle did little to lift his spirits, and he found it difficult to believe that this was the same château that had been his boyhood home—a warm, happy place that had seemed like an enchanted palace many years ago.

He turned the corner that led to the bedchamber of the Marquis St. Sebastien and saw his grandfather's ancient manservant, Gerard, dozing in a chair outside the door, his white wig askew over one eye, looking like a wizened old watchdog.

The old man didn't wake at Phillipe's approach, and after a moment's consideration, Phillipe coughed loudly.

"*Qu'est-ce qui c'est passé?*" the man asked blearily, opening his reddened eyes. "Is he worse, or . . . Monsieur Phillipe—is that you?"

Gerard stared uncertainly at the tall young man standing above him, trying to reconcile the sharp-featured, haughty face and glittering blue eyes with the slim, melancholy youth he used to know. But over twelve years had passed, and the slender youth had been replaced with a man's height and a hard, muscular build, and the hawklike features had acquired a fierce haughtiness.

"Yes, it's I. I take it that dear Grandpère is still alive?"

Gerard ignored the mocking tone in Phillipe's voice. "Oh, *oui*, Monsieur Phillipe. He says that he won't die until you're here. Your sister arrived yesterday, did you know? Shall I go in and tell him that you've come?"

8

"*Merci*, Gerard, but that won't be necessary. I'll just let myself in."

Old Gerard was about to argue, but he stopped when he saw the warning light in young St. Sebastien's cool eyes. This was no longer an easily cowed boy, but a man to be reckoned with.

With a scraping bow that almost caused his disheveled wig to tumble off, Gerard let the future marquis pass.

Phillipe almost gagged as the hot, fetid air of the bedchamber closed in on him, the stifling heat of the closed room a sharp contrast to the damp chill of the corridors he had just traveled.

The light of the fire danced over the red velvet that covered the cold stone walls and hung about the great dark bed of the marquis, giving the room a hellish feeling. And his grandfather, enthroned in the middle of the bed, his sunken, wrinkled face alight with perverse glee, resembled Satan himself, Phillipe thought.

Phillipe's younger sister, Christianna, sat coolly by the bed, her black curls shining in the firelight, her youth and beauty accentuated by the withered, pockmarked man next to her. She smiled with genuine pleasure at the sight of her handsome brother, who doffed his great coat and tricorn hat, tossing them easily to a waiting chair, the gesture as composed and elegant as it would have been in a Paris salon.

"The prodigal son returns," mocked the old man in the bed. "Did you come to make your tender farewells, Grandson? Or were you hoping that I had already died, that you could claim your precious château?"

"What's left of it, you mean," Phillipe answered, and he was surprised at how calm his voice was, as if it didn't matter.

He turned away from his grandfather, away from the stench of the old man's unwashed body, and moved to the window, pushing aside the dusty drapes and forcing open the heavy shutters.

He breathed deeply as the March winds rushed in, cool and clean, bringing the scent of the nearby Auvergne mountains. The draperies swayed in the wake of the breeze, the candles flickered.

"Say what you have to say and let me be about my business. I've no desire to watch your deathbed scene, as charming as it may be."

Christianna raised a dark brow at her brother's harshness, but remained silent, except for the soft clicking of her rosary beads as she slid them idly through her small white hands.

"You're very bad-tempered, Grandson. Did my sad little message force you from your mistress's bed?" The old man chuckled at his own feeble wit, the dry, wheezing sound turning into a cough, an ugly, rasping rattle. "Shut those damned windows," he barked. "That wind will be the death of me."

Phillipe sat lazily in an elaborately carved chair, stretching his long legs. "You're dying anyway," he pointed out indifferently, "and I'm sure that Satan has been planning your welcome party for weeks. You wouldn't want to disappoint an old friend, would you?"

"Phillipe," Christianna whispered reprovingly, superstitiously making the sign of the cross over her white bosom; but the old man simply chuckled.

"Such loving children. And don't try to pacify me with your false prayers, mademoiselle. I know damned well that you're over there dreaming of new dresses and balls and wondering how much longer I'm going to keep breathing."

Christianna blushed guiltily and shrugged, her mouth turning down in a petulant frown.

Phillipe almost smiled at his sister, until he felt his grandfather's yellowing eyes upon him.

"Well, boy, shall we get to business? I hear that you're very careful with your money; but I also hear that you haven't a hell of a lot. Have you found a rich wife yet?"

Phillipe laughed, a short, humorless sound. "You know damned well I haven't. My future title is small enticement, monsieur, when it's well known that you've squandered what little fortune the family had left, with your whoring and gambling."

The marquis grinned, unashamed. Without his usual wig, his hair stood up in wispy tufts, moving in the cold breeze from the window. "No wife, eh? Not even with your fine figure and handsome face?"

Phillipe sneered. "Who would marry a St.

11

Sebastien? You've blackened our name beyond redemption, you pox-ridden old fool."

The marquis lifted a spotted hand to wipe his mouth, his yellowed eyes sliding back to Christianna. "And you, mademoiselle? For two years now, you've been at Versailles, playing coy with the gentlemen. You've had no offers. With those pretty blue eyes and white tits, you could at least have become somebody's mistress."

The girl's cheeks flamed, and Phillipe lunged forward with the speed of a cat, grasping the old man by his bony shoulders, half lifting him from the bed.

"Speak to my sister like that again, old man, and I'll tear your heart out."

"Go ahead," the marquis croaked. "My time is over, and I've nothing to lose. Or perhaps you'd like to hear my plan? Would you like to save your château, Grandson? This crumbling old whore of a castle that you love so much?"

A muscle twitched in Phillipe's cheek, a flash of emotion crossed his face. He released his grandfather, who fell heavily back to his pillows, his breath coming in heavy gasps.

"I thought you might listen." The marquis's hands, twisted and knotted with age, dug beneath his heavy blankets. He withdrew a battered velvet bag, bulging with gold coins. "Here. All the money that's left. Oh, and this, if you still want it . . ." The gnarled hand held out a large emerald ring, set in a pattern of twisting gold ivy leaves.

"My mother's ring . . . I thought you had sold it." Phillipe reached out and took the ring carefully, avoiding touching his grandfather's hand. He had not seen it for twenty years, since his mother's death when he was a frightened ten-year-old, still reeling from the shock of his father's funeral; and his grandfather had come— come, taken stock of his inheritance, assigned the care of his grandchildren to indifferent servants, and gone.

"Sold it?" his grandfather echoed mockingly. "Sold the sacred ring of our dear, sainted Gabrielle? How could you think such a thing?"

Twenty years, Phillipe thought bitterly, turning the ring over in his hand, feeling its cool weight. *Twenty long years of watching you destroy my future, my happiness, my château.*

"Listen," the marquis croaked. "Listen, Grandson. Do you want your château? In the bag with the money there is a passage to England. Buy yourself some fine clothes and go there. Nobody has ever heard of us there. You can pass yourself off as a rich man. And you can marry a rich girl. Make sure that she's wealthy enough, and stupid enough, and you can rebuild your precious château."

The marquis closed his eyes, the blue veins showing plainly against the papery lids. "And you, my prissy mademoiselle," he added, waving a gnarled hand towards Christianna, "get yourself back to court and find yourself a rich man to pay for your pretty gowns. You could do well if you chose to."

13

"I choose not to," Christianna snapped. "I've met no man that pleases me."

The marquis opened his eyes, cackling obscenely. "You'll be less choosy as you age and your looks fade. By God, when I was young, when old Louis was still king, I was the handsomest man at Versailles. All the women wanted me. Noble ladies, whores, stupid bourgeois; they'd all spread their legs for me—"

"And now you're a syphilitic old fool," Phillipe interrupted, rising to his feet, "And I'm done with you. For twenty of my thirty years, you've made my life a living hell, and I'll not sit and hear you brag about how you spent my inheritance. I leave you to your memories of your golden days, monsieur—may they comfort you on your way to hell."

Phillipe bowed elegantly, turned his back, and left the room, almost knocking down old Gerard, who had been listening eagerly at the keyhole. He heard Christianna hurrying after him, swearing under her breath as she lifted the lavender silk of her skirts from the dust and mouse droppings that littered the floor of the corridor.

They walked together through hallways that had once been filled with their childish laughter, and Phillipe stopped to offer her his arm as they reached the staircase that led to the great hall, where bats now nested above the fading banners.

Christianna shivered, pulling her velvet cloak more tightly around her shoulders. "I hate this place," she whispered. "It is *dégoûtant*, horrible."

Phillipe smiled, deep dimples appearing beneath his proud cheekbones. "I know you hate it, piglet. But I don't. You just don't remember how it used to be. Why don't you go back to Versailles, if you like. I really don't mind. I've no desire to sit and watch the old goat die; but someone must."

"*Merci*, Phillipe." Christianna smiled happily. "There's a wonderful party week after next, and a private performance in the queen's theater, and I would so hate to miss it."

"But please, Christianna, try to find a husband. The money won't last much longer. Put aside your silly dreams and find a rich man. What about Artois? He seems a nice enough fellow."

"Really, Phillipe!" Christianna's laughter bubbled out, echoing under the high, vaulted ceilings. "Marry Artois! He'd really be more interested in you."

"Oh," Phillipe answered, feeling a little abashed. "I'd no idea. You seemed to get along so well. Oh, well, can't you find someone like him? Only not . . . I mean . . . Hell, Christianna, somebody has to pay for your gowns. Can't you just . . . marry someone?"

Her eyes sparkled angrily. "You sound just like Grandfather, Phillipe. So callous. What am I to do if I haven't fallen in love by the time the money runs out?"

Phillipe smiled, a sad, wistful smile. "Love

15

isn't something the impoverished aristocracy can afford. I'm sorry if I sound callous, piglet. I've forgotten what it's like to be nineteen and have your dreams intact. Go have fun—I'll worry about the money."

She kissed him happily on the cheek, standing on the toes of her ridiculous little satin shoes. "Thank you, Phillipe. I will go as soon as I can. But what will you do, Phillipe?"

"What will I do?" he repeated. "Well, Christianna, for the first time in my life, I'll follow Grandfather's advice. As soon as that old goat upstairs dies, I shall go to England. With any luck, I shall find a wife who's very rich, and very stupid, and not too ugly, if it can be helped. Then I shall come back and turn this château into what it once was. And then, Christianna, I'll dance on that old bastard's grave."

The girl shivered superstitiously as he laughed, the sound echoing mockingly in the vast emptiness of the hall.

Phillipe kissed his sister lightly on the forehead and turned to go up the stairs. "Your mistress will be very angry," she called after him.

Phillipe stopped on the staircase and smiled down at his little sister. "It doesn't matter," he told her. "For twenty years, I have dreamed of this day, and now it's here. The château matters, and you matter. Nothing else. Wish me luck, piglet—I'm off to find a rich wife."

"God keep you, Phillipe," she called, watching him bound up the stairs. She shrugged when she didn't receive an answer, and took a last look at the dark hall.

"God, I hate this place," she muttered again to the empty room, and went to find her maid, anxious to get back to Versailles.

Chapter Two

England, 1789

The roar of the old musket shattered the tranquillity of the May morning. A flock of birds scattered wildly, abandoning their perches in the sun-warmed branches of the trees, their raucous cries filling the air.

James Larkin swore as he lowered the gun, his green eyes dark with disappointment. The old wooden bucket that served as a target remained untouched.

"Better," Gareth said encouragingly to his eighteen-year-old brother.

"Much better—if you were aiming at the trees," Victoria agreed, sending her twin a wicked smile.

James glared at his sister, who was leaning

negligently against a tree, her long legs clad in his own outgrown breeches, her red hair falling in tangles over a man's rough work smock; and then he laughed at the sparkle in her green eyes.

"Go to hell, Vic," he answered good-naturedly. "I'm not planning on becoming a highwayman or a soldier, and you can't; so it doesn't much matter who the better shot is."

He offered the musket to his sister, who began reloading, biting the paper packet of powder open and carefully tapping the ball in after it.

James and Gareth smiled indulgently at her as she rose to her feet and carefully aimed the old gun. The sunlight shone on her hair, lighting the dark red with gold, and she blew the curling tendrils out of her eyes impatiently before she fired.

The musket roared, the bucket splintered at the impact of the shot, and Victoria's husky laugh rang out.

"There, Jamie—that's how it's done."

"Bloody show-off," he answered. "Why don't you go home and help with the baking or something useful?"

"Why don't you?" she retorted. They grinned at each other, and Gareth marveled at the perfect mirror images of their faces—the slightly tilted green eyes, the sharp cheekbones that lent an elfin quality to their pale faces, the thick red curls that hung around their faces.

"Why don't you both do something useful,"

20

Wild Summer Rose

Gareth asked, "and go move the sheep to the north pasture, or clean the stables? You've put it off for a week now."

"Stewart is doing it," Victoria answered, industriously reloading the gun. "He owes me, Gareth, for not telling Father that he was at the Broken Bow last week, swilling beer like a fool."

"Was he?" Gareth asked. "He's too young for that. He's only sixteen. If I'd have known he was there—"

"He's seventeen," Victoria answered with a quick smile. "And you should have known he was there, because you were there too, I hear. Stewart says that you were upstairs with Polly. We laughed about it all the next day."

Gareth's handsome face flushed red. "Good Lord, can't a man have any privacy? You oughtn't to speak of such things, Vic. Mother would turn over in her grave. Anyway, I'm twenty-nine, and what I do is nobody's business but my own."

Victoria laughed at him and fired the gun at the bucket.

"Anyway," Gareth added, when his ears quit ringing, "Stewart isn't doing your chores at all; he's coming this way like the devil was after him. Look."

They turned and looked in the direction that Gareth pointed, and sure enough, there was Stewart, his long legs covering ground with amazing speed, his thin face flushed with exertion.

21

It took him only moments to cross the green expanse of pasture, scattering sheep in his wake, and to make his way up the rough slope. He cleared the stone fence in an easy leap and rested for a moment, catching his breath before he spoke.

"You're to come to the house, Vic. Reverend Finkle's there. He's been in Father's study for the better part of an hour."

"What the devil does he want?" Victoria demanded, her eyes narrowing. It was unlike the vicar to pay a social call, and very unlike her father to request her company in the middle of the morning.

Stewart glanced at Gareth before answering. "I think we're in trouble, Vic. Geoffery listened at the door and heard him say something about sending you away."

"Father did?" Victoria cried in disbelief.

"No, jackass, Reverend Finkle," Stewart answered, wiping the sweat from his brow on the frayed cuff of his shirt.

"You'd best go put a dress on," James advised his sister. "I don't think you'll make much of an impression on Vicar, wearing my clothes."

Gareth looked suspiciously at his younger siblings, noting the worried glances that passed between their green eyes. "What in the hell have you done now, that Vicar would want to send you packing?"

"Nothing," Stewart answered, falsely bright, as Victoria climbed over the fence to join him. James offered Gareth the old flintlock and the leather bag of shot, before turning to join the other two.

"Nothing," repeated Gareth in a tone of disbelief. "Of course not."

He watched as the three made their way down the grassy slope, thinking that they looked like a pack of Irish setter pups who'd been caught in the henhouse. Except for the length of her hair, Victoria, at a distance, was indistinguishable from her brothers, both in appearance and behavior.

"What in the hell have they done?" Gareth wondered aloud, watching the three redheads close together in heated conference.

He swung the heavy musket easily over one broad shoulder and cleared the stone fence in a smooth jump, anxious to be home and see what the fuss was about.

The Larkin house had been built during the reign of Henry VIII, a sturdy structure of solid dark beams and thick plaster walls, and added on to later, so that the whole building seemed to sprawl comfortably under the surrounding oak trees.

Glossy green ivy climbed the walls, reaching up towards the thatched roof and partially obscuring the heavy leaded-glass windows. The herb and flower gardens that grew in unkempt beds seemed to thrive despite their apparent neglect, and Victoria stopped to breathe the scent of the flowering lilacs as she made her way stealthily in the back door.

There was no sign of Mrs. Hatton, the Larkin's long-suffering housekeeper, only Daniel, at twenty-six the second oldest of the Larkins, seated comfortably at the kitchen table, his dark red head bent over a book.

"Hello, Daniel. Father's fallen down the well and the barn's burning," Victoria said in greeting as she passed.

"That's nice," Daniel answered calmly, his eyes not moving from the page before him.

Victoria raced up the stairs to her room, almost falling over a long-eared hound coming down, and hastily discarded her breeches, boots, and man's shirt. She found a full-sleeved chemise tangled in the soft wool blankets at the foot of her bed, and a somewhat rumpled but otherwise acceptable skirt flung over a chair, and wriggled hastily into them. She looked frantically for her shoes, but saw no sign of them and began digging in the old chest at the foot of her bed.

"Damn, damn, damn," she muttered as the wayward shoes failed to appear. Glancing up, she saw sixteen-year-old Geoffery, the youngest Larkin, watching from the door with great interest.

"Father sent me to look for you," he announced. "What are you looking for, Vic?"

"Shoes," she answered shortly.

"There's a big stain on your front. Is that from when you bloodied your nose?"

Victoria looked down at the front of her chemise and swore again. She snatched a black wool bodice from the pile of discarded clothing on the floor and donned it hastily, knotting the laces in her hurry. There, the stain was covered.

"Better," Geoff approved, rubbing his thin, freckled nose thoughtfully. "Are you going to comb your hair? You look rather like a witch."

Victoria grabbed for the wooden comb, which stuck in her curls about halfway down. She discarded the comb and shoved her hair into a white mob-cap, arranging the lacy edges around her face.

"Very nice," Geoffery said helpfully. "You look like Mrs. Hatton, only about fifteen stones lighter."

"Geoffery, have you nothing better to do than drive me mad? Where are my bloody shoes?"

"Out here in the hall. It rather looks like Dog has been chewing at them," Geoff answered calmly.

With an exasperated look, Victoria hurried past him and stuck her feet into the soft leather slippers, which did indeed feel a little gnawed on one toe.

"Shall I go in with you, Vic? So that you don't have to face Father and Vicar alone?" Geoffery asked, following her down the stairs.

Victoria laughed nervously. "Thank you, Geoff, but no. Why don't you just listen at the keyhole as you usually do?"

Geoffery assumed a look of injured dignity. "No, I think I shan't. I really don't care to hear you defend yourself. I'd much rather go riding."

Victoria looked longingly out the heavy-mullioned windows at the warm spring morning and the delicate blossoms that fluttered on the ancient apple trees.

"I'd rather be riding, myself," she answered grimly as she approached the door of her father's study. She knocked lightly and opened the door.

Matthew Larkin's study was a cluttered jumble of books, papers, ink bottles, and dishes. The dusty room smelled strongly of pipe smoke.

The Reverend Mr. Finkle was perched uncomfortably on the edge of a battered chair, his long face arranged in carefully mournful lines, his thin hands folded calmly, looking like a watchful crow, Victoria thought.

She bobbed a quick curtsy and looked anxiously about the room, but her father was not to be seen.

"Good day, Vicar. Is Father about?"

The vicar pointed a bony finger in the direction of Matthew's desk. "He's under his desk, Miss Larkin, searching for his spectacles."

Matthew's round, rosy face appeared around the corner of his desk, his wispy gray hair standing comically on end. "Won't be a minute, dear. Why, here's my pipe . . . I was wondering where it went. Now where are my spectacles?"

"Have you looked on top of your head, Father?" Victoria asked, trying not to laugh.

"Why, there they are," Matthew exclaimed in great surprise, appearing from behind a stack of papers. He waved his missing pipe triumphantly, lowered his spectacles to the end of his nose, and took his chair.

"Victoria, dear, Reverend Finkle is a little concerned about you. It seems that some people are a little upset by your behavior lately. I'm sure it's all just a tempest in a teapot, and you can explain everything."

Victoria could feel her cheeks growing hot, and she avoided Reverend Finkle's disapproving gaze. "I shall try, Father."

The vicar cleared his throat and fixed his accusing stare on Victoria's deceptively demure face. "Well, where do we begin, Miss Larkin?"

Why don't you begin by going home and minding your own business? Victoria thought impatiently, but tried to assume a humble expression.

"I really don't know, sir. Where should we begin?"

Reverend Finkle cast his eyes heavenward, as if appealing for help from a more enlightening source. "Shall we discuss the matter of your church attendance? Can you tell us, miss, when you last attended services?"

Victoria looked down at the floor, and studied the smooth oak planks. "I . . . I don't remember."

"Oh, I do, dear," Matthew interjected helpfully. "It would have been Sunday."

Reverend Finkle sighed heavily. "Very good, Mr. Larkin. But to which Sunday do you refer?"

27

"Why, last Sunday, of course. I remember it quite distinctly, you see, because the children asked me for extra money for the collection plate, for the benefit of the London orphanage that—" Matthew broke off abruptly at the sight of the vicar's disbelieving face. "Oh dear," he finished miserably, "there probably wasn't an orphanage at all, was there?"

"No, Mr. Larkin, I'm grieved to say that there was not. There was, however, a fair in Ashby, and I have it on good authority that your children were there, mingling with Gypsies, rope-dancers, and all manner of riff-raff. You were deceived, sir, and most abominably."

Oh, bloody hell, Victoria thought, *here comes the sermon, he's getting warmed up now*.

"Mr. Larkin, the situation is very serious. Your children are running wild about the countryside like vagabonds, It is bad enough for the boys; it is even worse for Victoria. She has been seen riding wearing men's clothing. While other girls of her age are married, or preparing for their futures, she is out hunting with her brothers.

"Did you know, sir, that your daughter was seen leaving the Broken Bow, not a fortnight ago? That a young lady would even enter such an unsavory establishment—"

"I was just in there long enough to get Geoffery out," Victoria protested, but the vicar ignored this and continued his list of grievances.

"She and her brothers are responsible for all manner of mischief. Only last week, for example, I caught young Fred trying to appropriate

Mr. Harper's boat, and the young scamp tried to tell me that—"

"Who on earth is Fred?" Matthew asked, his plump face blank with confusion.

"Your son, sir," the vicar explained in a very weary voice.

"But we haven't got a Fred," Matthew protested mildly, puffing thoughtfully at his pipe. "That is, I don't think we do. Let me see . . . Gareth, Daniel, Richard, Stewart . . . it was probably Stewart, he's a wee bit of a tease."

Victoria tried not to laugh. It had indeed been Stewart, and as soon as Mr. Finkle had turned his back, the boat had been appropriated.

Mr. Finkle shot a furious look at Victoria, whose green eyes were sparkling with mischief.

"Sir, I don't really care if you named the scamp Shadrack. The point is, your children are in moral danger. If allowed to continue on their present paths, they will become cads, bounders, and ne'er-do-wells."

Matthew set his pipe down on his cluttered desk, where a stack of papers immediately tipped over and buried it. "Dear Vicar! It cannot be that bad."

"It is that bad, and yesterday's incident is the worst yet. Do you know where your daughter was, and what she was doing?"

Matthew looked longingly at his book and wished that he could finish reading it—a fascinating study of Roman bronze work. Victoria looked longingly out the window and wished that she could run.

"I shall tell you, sir. I was taking Lady Thornely's children for their botany lesson, and we happened upon your children at Miller's Pond. They were swimming, sir."

Matthew looked relieved. "Well, Vicar, that doesn't seem so dreadful—"

"They were indecent, sir."

Matthew pushed his spectacles to the top of his balding head, glancing from his daughter's red face to Mr. Finkle's outraged one.

"Oh, dear," he mumbled, "My dear Victoria . . . were you really?"

Victoria cringed. "Only a little indecent, Father. I left my shimmy on. It was the boys that were really indecent."

Reverend Finkle didn't look appeased. "It was really most unpleasant. Miss Emily fainted, and Lady Thornely had to be informed."

Emily was a bloody twit, Victoria thought with disgust, and she had certainly taken a good look at Richard before she swooned.

"Oh, dear," Matthew said, his ink-spotted fingers fumbling about his desk searching for his pipe.

"And so we come to the point of my visit," the vicar announced pompously. "Lady Thornely has reminded me that I am responsible for the moral guidance of all the inhabitants of my parish. She tells me that unless some sort of action is taken, I shall be turned out of my vicarage and forced to seek my living elsewhere."

Victoria was not able to restrain herself. "That hardly seems just. It was only a little swim, and I really don't see why Lady Thornely need meddle."

Reverend Finkle gave the girl a withering stare. "It is time, Miss Larkin, that you grew up and put aside your hoydenish behavior. As the good book says, 'When I was a child, I spake as a child, but then I put away childish things.' It is time for you to put away childish things and learn to conduct yourself as a proper young woman should. What will your future be if you continue with this shameless anarchy?"

"Oh, for heaven's sake," Victoria muttered. Shameless anarchy, indeed!

"My suggestion, Mr. Larkin, is that Victoria be removed from the influence of her brothers and go to stay in a place where she can receive the sort of education that befits a young woman. Your wife, I believe, came from a decent and gentle family. Do you have any relatives that might be willing to extend their hospitality to your daughter?"

To Victoria's horror, her father was nodding as though he might actually be considering this preposterous idea.

"Elizabeth's cousin Abigail used to write frequently. She even offered to take Victoria, after her mother died. Of course I wouldn't have considered it, at the time. But perhaps for a short stay . . ."

"You can't mean it, Father," Victoria protested. "I've never even met Mother's family. They've never wanted anything to do with us."

Matthew smiled ruefully. "That's true, dear,

but there was a time that Abigail and your mother were very close. It wouldn't be as though I were sending you to a stranger."

"It would be to me," Victoria argued, appalled at the thought of leaving her home, even if only for a while.

Reverend Finkle looked shocked that a girl would contradict her father. "It is obvious, Miss Larkin, that you have had you own way for too long. As the Good Book says, 'Honor thy father and thy mother.' Your father is acting in your own best interests."

Damn the bloody Good Book, Victoria thought blasphemously. Some of her feelings must have shown on her face, for her father sent her a soothing smile.

"Dearest Vic, there's no need to get into a temper. You know quite well that I would never force you to do anything that you didn't wish to." Matthew smiled tranquilly as he addressed the outraged vicar. "I know that my daughter is a little . . . shall we say, unorthodox. But that has never worried me. You see, in spite of her little transgressions, I'm very proud of my daughter. She is well-read, intelligent, and capable, and more importantly, she has a good heart. Victoria is kind and honorable. I would trust her with my life."

Matthew leaned back in his chair, tapping his pudgy, ink-stained fingers together, his blue eyes calm and bright. "In short, Vicar, she's hardly the sort of young woman who would

32

cause an innocent man to be turned away from his home and living simply because she was spoiled and willful and didn't want to visit her cousin."

Checkmate, Victoria thought. *Very good, Father. I can hardly refuse now*.

"I'll think about it," she allowed, not wanting to admit defeat so easily.

Matthew beamed, knowing that she would agree.

Mr. Finkle looked less sure. Since Elizabeth Larkin had died, ten years ago, the Larkin children had been a constant source of irritation to him. The older sons drank, brawled, and wenched shamelessly, and still managed (most undeservedly, to Mr. Finkle's way of thinking) to run the most prosperous farm in the community.

The younger children ran wild, indulging in childish pranks; and the long-suffering reverend was never able to prove that they were responsible. But who else would fill his church with sheep to greet him on Sunday morning? Who else would abscond with the immaculate white vestments from his clothesline and then return them the following day, dyed brilliant hues of yellow and blue?

And Matthew! Why, the man was no help at all, with his head always buried in a book. The man seemed more concerned about the state of the ancient Roman Empire than the state of his children's souls.

Victoria watched the good reverend with alarm. He appeared to be swelling up like a self-righteous toad, and she was in no mood to hear a sermon.

"May I go, please?" she asked quickly, moving towards the door.

"Of course, dear," Matthew answered, his hands already resting on his half-finished book.

"And Father?" Victoria added, unable to resist the laughter bubbling up in her throat.

"Yes, dear?"

"I believe that you've set your desk on fire."

Matthew stared at the clutter before him, which did indeed appear to be smoking.

The vicar leaped to his feet in alarm. "Good heavens, sir!"

Matthew sprinkled the smoking stack of papers with the murky remnants of yesterday's teapot, and withdrew his missing pipe, smiling calmly.

"No need to worry," he assured the horrified vicar. "Everything's quite under control."

If Mr. Finkle had any doubts as to the truth of that statement, he kept his opinions to himself; and Victoria, her slender shoulders shaking with laughter, made a hasty exit.

James and Richard were waiting in the kitchen, seated at the long oak table arguing about the best date to start shearing and trying to consume as much freshly baked bread as they could without incurring Mrs. Hatton's wrath.

Daniel hadn't moved from the other end of

the table, where the sunlight warmed his hair to a russet glow as he bent over his book.

Mrs. Hatton was waddling to and from the brick ovens, trying to unload more fragrant loaves without turning her back on James and Richard. Her round face darkened at Victoria's arrival, and she looked suspiciously at the suppressed laughter in the girl's eyes.

"There's mischief afoot," she noted darkly.

"Not I," Victoria answered, sitting comfortably next to Daniel and slipping a companionable arm around his shoulders as she looked at his book. "Omnia autem, quaesecundrum naturum fiunt . . ." she read aloud, mispronouncing the words.

"Sunt habenda in bonus," Daniel finished. "Whatever happens as a result of nature should be thought good," he translated. "Cicero."

"Cicero never had chilblains, that's what," Mrs. Hatton grumbled, slapping at Richard's hand as he reached for more bread.

Geoffery entered the kitchen, banging the thick door behind him, his thin face bright with the brisk breeze.

"Are you being sent away, Vic?" he asked, eyeing the warm bread with interest.

"Sent away where?" Richard demanded, burning his fingers on a loaf.

"Stealing like he was five instead of twenty," Mrs. Hatton observed. "Who's sending my baby away?"

Daniel finally looked up from his book. "Who's being sent away?"

"Nobody's being sent," Victoria answered crossly. "I'm going of my own will, to visit relatives."

"What relatives?" Geoffery demanded.

"A cousin of Mother's, maybe. If Father remembers to make arrangements," Victoria answered, removing her lace-edged cap and shoving it into the pocket of her skirt.

"You should leave that on," Mrs. Hatton suggested, "unless you're afraid of being mistaken for someone tidy."

"Could Father mean Cousin Abigail?" Daniel wondered.

Victoria shut Daniel's book swiftly, before he could be distracted again. "That's right, Daniel. Do you know her? I don't remember ever meeting her."

"But you did. Twice, to be exact. She was here once when you were little, and she had a daughter your age, I remember. Her daughter's name was . . . something."

"Lavinia," Mrs. Hatton supplied. "And a nicer little one I never saw. You were three, you and Jamie, and Stewart not yet walking, and you, Master Sly-boots," she added with a sharp look at Geoffery, "you were still a bun in the oven. Not a bit of trouble, and just look at you now."

Geoffery hastily removed the crust of bread that he had been about to dip in the crock of honey.

"Your mother and Abigail had words," Mrs. Hatton continued, pleased at being listened to, for once. "And that was that.

We didn't see her again until the funeral."

Victoria remembered her mother's funeral as if it were far away and in a fog. She had been nine, cold with misery and shock, itching in her new dress of heavy black wool.

She remembered how her father had seemed like a stranger, vague and lost in his grief, and how she had clutched Jamie's hand like a drowning man clutches a rope, and how tight and wounded his face was, a reflection of her own. Mr. Finkle's deep voice had droned on and on under the cold gray skies. She remembered staring at the barren branches of the trees and hearing the dead, hollow thud of dirt on the coffin.

A picture entered her mind, long-forgotten, of a very beautiful woman with a still, white face under a large hat that dripped black ostrich plumes. She had spoken to Matthew after the service, her eyes straying to Victoria as she spoke. Victoria remembered only pieces of the conversation, and the sound of the woman's quiet, cultured voice.

" . . . so like Elizabeth . . . should have a woman's care . . . all the advantages of an education . . ."

And her father's answer, bitter and clear. "She'll not be separated from James. It would be cruel, and she'd be lost. She needs her family, Abigail. I'll not send her to be turned into a hothouse flower. I intend that she grow up strong, and as healthy as her brothers. Thank you, Abigail, but I would never consider it."

Amy Elizabeth Saunders

Victoria turned to Mrs. Hatton, firmly banishing the memories that caused her so much pain. "I remember her, I think. Was she very beautiful? Blue eyes, and a soft voice?"

"That would be herself," Mrs. Hatton agreed, wiping her hands on her apron in her best no-nonsense style. "So, you're going to visit Abigail, are you? Good, it ought to have been done long ago. Teach you some ladylike ways, I shouldn't wonder."

"Not bloody likely," Richard remarked, pushing a wayward auburn curl from his eyes.

Victoria kicked at him under the table, Geoffery laughed, Mrs. Hatton made cryptic remarks about people that swore and met bad ends, and Daniel returned his attention to Cicero, who was much more interesting than his family.

Only James seemed to understand the nagging fear that Victoria felt as she looked longingly around the old kitchen with its happily mismatched chairs and gleaming oak floors, and at her kind, laughing brothers with their red hair gleaming.

He reached out and took her fingers into his, and his moss green eyes smiled into hers. "Don't think about it, Vic. It'll be a long time till Father can arrange it. And it won't be forever. Shall we go for a ride? Perhaps go fishing?"

"Nobody's going anywhere," Mrs. Hatton announced, "until somebody brings in those eggs from the henhouse. You leave them any longer, they'll grow wings and fly in."

38

"And Gareth wants everybody in the wool-shed," Daniel added, his eyes still on his book. "He says it needs a good cleaning."

This news brought a collective groan.

"Does 'everybody' mean you too, Master Bookworm?" Mrs. Hatton asked tartly, confiscating Daniel's book with a swift grab. "Or do you intend to read the day away?"

"I'm to do the records today," Daniel explained.

"Not with Cicero, you don't. There's books that need keeping, and books that can keep till later," Mrs. Hatton announced. "And somebody better see about my eggs or there'll be no custard tonight."

Victoria went obediently to fetch the eggs, stopping to admire the blue sky and bright leaves, the sweet scent of spring that surrounded her. After all, nothing was really settled yet. Abigail might not want her to come, or her father might forget about the whole mess. Honestly, Abigail hadn't seen her since she was a child, and might not want a stranger hanging about for very long.

It will most likely be for a week, Victoria thought cheerfully, her good spirits restored, or two at the most.

The May sunshine was warm and bright on her back, the breeze was moving the softly scented apple blossoms on the gnarled trees overhead, and the prospect of a good ride awaited her. Victoria moved quickly about her work, anxious to be off.

Chapter Three

Three long months, Victoria thought miserably. *For three long months I have to be amongst strangers.*

The public coach bounced and jostled its way eastward towards the village of St. Stephen's, where she was to meet Abigail Harrington. The coach was crowded and stiflingly hot, and though she had only been traveling for nine hours, Victoria felt as if she had been bouncing against the rock-hard seats for years.

Her fellow passengers were not at all interesting—a vicar, who had raised his eyebrows at the sight of a young lady traveling alone; a very fat man, who had been snoring in her ear for several hours; and an elderly widow, who kept her eyes fastened on a little prayer-book and sniffled occasionally.

Victoria, being used to plenty of fresh air and activity, thought that she might scream with frustration, and wondered what the reactions of the other passengers might be if she did. The brown traveling suit that Mrs. Hatton had so lovingly made for her was wrinkled, and damp with perspiration, and the fine wool, which had seemed so soft and fine that morning, was causing her to itch in a most unpleasant way.

Outside the coach, the passing countryside looked fresh and green beneath the brilliant sun, but Victoria had long since lost interest in picturesque fields and charming stone bridges, ordinary villages and an occasional great estate. Besides, in order to see out the dusty coach window, she had to stretch her neck past the oversized wig of the oversized man next to her.

The snoring man was leaning heavily against her arm, and she thought about giving him a good shove, but felt the watchful eyes of the traveling vicar upon her and contented herself with giving the man an uncharitable glower instead.

Victoria wished she had brought a book. She stretched her neck and wished she could give herself a good scratch. She wished she had someone to chatter to. She wished that the coach would be stopped by thieves, just to liven things up. She wished, most of all, that she was home, where nobody cared if she scratched herself or not.

Just when she thought she could bear no

more, and that her right arm, which was solidly asleep, might drop off altogether, the coach lumbered to a stop and the driver called, "St. Stephen's."

She did shove the sleeping fat man then, and the other passengers looked askance at the slender girl with the indecently untidy red curls as she clambered ungracefully over the vicar's feet and the widow's skirts in her haste to be gone. Victoria knew she should wait for the coachman to open the door for her, but felt that she would lose her mind if she had to wait quietly for another minute.

At first glance, the village could have been Middlebury. A church, a few shops, an inn, a pub, and numerous houses and cottages. Save for the fact that the inhabitants of St. Stephen's took their ale under the sign of The Three Crowns instead of The Broken Bow, the villages seemed alike in every way.

"Victoria! My dear, can that be you?"

Victoria turned abruptly at the sound of the voice. Across the innyard, a handsome, expensive-looking carriage was parked beneath the shade of an ancient oak tree, and a woman was descending gracefully from the carriage with the help of a white-wigged footman.

Victoria took a deep, steadying breath. It was Cousin Abigail, smaller than in her memory and dressed in white instead of funeral black. But there was no doubt that it was the same woman—delicate and aristocratic, her pale face held high beneath a wide hat, this one covered in white ostrich plumes and veiled in exquisite lace.

Victoria pushed a few wayward curls up beneath her own hat, which was a flat, round straw affair, and she walked forward to meet her mother's cousin.

"Cousin Abigail, it was very kind of you to have me."

Abigail stopped short and laid a delicate hand over her heart. At closer look, Victoria could see the changes that time had wrought—a few faint lines around the clear blue eyes, a softening of the jaw line—but even so, Abigail Harrington was still a beautiful woman.

"That voice," Abigail exclaimed. "You sound so like your mother. And you are just like her in looks. It's like stepping back in time."

Of course, Abigail thought privately, Elizabeth's hair would never have fallen out of its pins like that, and she never would have worn such an unbecoming frock. But hair and frocks were easily tended to, and aside from that, this girl was Elizabeth all over again; tall, and slender as a sylph, with the grace of a young doe, and those incredibly green eyes. And that voice, low and a little husky, that Matthew Larkin had said reminded him of honey, all golden and sweet.

Abigail took Victoria's arm beneath her own and led her across the innyard to the carriage, chattering all the way.

Wild Summer Rose

"We've been so excited to see you. Lavinia—
do you remember Lavinia? No? Well, you were
very young when you met. Lavinia gets so bored
in the country, so far away from London. It will
be good for her to have company. Do you play
the spinet? No? Well, perhaps lessons . . . . Here
is your cousin, darling! Won't you say hello?"

Victoria observed her cousin with interest,
since Lavinia was to be her companion for the
summer. She looked like her mother, with a
perfect oval face and a rosebud mouth, but her
cool blue eyes held no welcome. She was leaning back against the plump, richly upholstered
seats of the Harrington carriage as if she were
very tired, or very bored, her golden curls lying
in careful arrangement around her shoulders.

"Cousin Lavinia," Victoria greeted, and held
out her hand.

Lavinia looked as if she had inspected her
cousin, and found her sadly lacking. "Miss Larkin," she returned coolly, ignoring the outstretched hand.

Victoria resisted the urge to smooth her dress
and tidy her hair. She met Lavinia's eyes firmly,
until Lavinia turned away.

Lady Abigail laughed, a silvery sound. "Really, girls, you mustn't be so formal. You are
cousins, after all. Is that your only trunk, Victoria?"

Victoria turned and saw the white-wigged
footman carrying her trunk, which suddenly
looked very battered and forlorn. He gave her a

look that reminded her of the way Mrs. Hatton looked at the mice that the cats occasionally brought into the kitchen.

"Yes, that's it," Victoria answered cheerfully, wondering what on earth she was doing here, when she so obviously didn't belong.

Lady Abigail allowed the footman to help her into the carriage, and Victoria followed, noting that the footman looked at his white glove after she took his hand, as if she might have stained it.

"You will love the house," Lady Abigail chattered, "I'm sure. Your mother used to spend her summers here, did you know that? I've put you in her old room, it's so pretty. Lavinia will be happy to show you the house, won't you, Lavinia? Lavinia?"

Victoria leaned back into the comfortable seats with a sigh, and the carriage headed towards Harrington Park.

June 9, 1789

Dear James,
How I miss you! I've only been here one week, and it feels like a month. It's bloody hard work, this being good. Cousin Abigail doesn't quite know what to do with me. I don't do fine needlework, or play the spinet, or the harp, or any number of things that she thinks are amusing. She has settled on letting me read my way through the library, which is fine with me.
That's an awful way to start a letter, so let me

begin by telling you what I think of everything here.

First, the house: It is very, very large, and very, very white, with scads of columns and servants and marble and damask draperies and paintings—mostly paintings of dear departed Harringtons, horses, and dogs. Perhaps the dogs and horses are Harringtons, too. I don't have the faintest idea.

Second, Cousin Abigail: She chatters like a magpie, and means well, and says that I remind her of mother. She is a little silly about only doing what is proper. I gather that a lot of what I do is not proper.

Third, Lord Cecil: He is a very jolly man, and has a very red face, and says 'By Jove' and 'I say' a lot. He has a hound named Juno, who reminds me of Dog, and he keeps a fine stable of horses. I like him a lot. He says that I 'know how to handle a horse.' I gather that this is his highest praise.

Finally, Cousin Lavinia: I enjoy her company as much as she enjoys mine. As a result, we try to avoid each other at all costs. She says that I will 'ruin' her 'house party,' which is, I gather, a passel of her silly friends coming to visit. I dread it.

Lest you think that I am completely miserable, let me tell you that I have made a friend here. Her name is Mary Atwell, and she is the upstairs maid. She is small and dark and tidy, and she says that I am 'a caution.'

Lady Abigail has told me that my frocks will

'not do,' and so I am wearing Lavinia's things from 'last season.' Lavinia tells me that I am 'hopelessly outdated,' but I think that I'm rather elegant. I know that you hate to write, but force yourself. Tell me everything.

Victoria laid her pen down on the smooth surface of the writing desk and sighed. She had tried not to let Jamie know how really miserable she was. She had never been bored in her life, but now the days stretched before her like years. The dresses and petticoats that she wore were stiff and fussy, more cumbersome than elegant; and it was not much fun to go riding alone.

Had this really been her mother's room? It was not huge, compared to most of the rooms at Harrington Park, but it was rich with a luxury that Victoria had never known—her own fireplace, finely woven rugs patterned in vines and flowers, a writing desk of fine, dark wood, and a four-poster bed so high that it had a little stepping stool next to it, so that one could climb up easily.

On the mantelpiece above the prettily carved fireplace, a china clock adorned with cherubs ticked monotonously, and Victoria wondered what her mother had done to keep from dying of boredom.

"She fell in love with the tutor," Lavinia had said, her small nose turning up contemptuously at the thought. "Of course, she *was* a poor relation. Rather like you, Miss Larkin. Perhaps you'll find a husband this summer. But of course, that's why you came, isn't it?"

Lavinia was, Victoria decided, husband-mad. She had seen girls like that—pretty, silly creatures who found excuses to visit the Larkin farm and look at Gareth, Daniel, or Richard with dewy-eyed admiration. They came asking Mrs. Hatton the proper methods for distilling lavender, or what flowers she grew to attract bees to the busy hives; and they ended up making nuisances of themselves, and being treated with nothing more than polite contempt.

Although Lavinia was the daughter of an earl, and would never have likened herself to those rosy-cheeked farm girls, Victoria saw the same grim determination in her eyes when she spoke of her future prospects; and she would snap off their qualifications with the precision and expertise of a horsetrader.

"Too fat . . . too old . . . not enough money . . . lots of money, but no title . . . rich enough, but bookish . . . he'd do, and he has no mother to interfere . . ."

Victoria would only half-listen to this already familiar accounting, and as soon as she could, would make excuses to return to the privacy of her room, where she could read, or write to the boys, or simply look out her window at the magnificent expanses of gardens and parklands that surrounded the Harrington estate as far as the eye could see. She was bored, ill at ease, and wanted nothing more than to escape from her dainty prison and go home.

Amy Elizabeth Saunders

"Bloody hell," she said aloud to the emptiness of her pristine room, and that small irreverence made her feel better.

There was a timid knock on the door, and Mary entered, her eyes dark and round under her tidy white cap, her arms loaded with a beribboned pile of dresses.

"More frocks, miss. Would you like to see them?"

"Not really," Victoria answered candidly. "I've looked at more dresses in the past week than I've seen in my life, and it doesn't interest me much."

Mary looked enviously at Victoria, sitting at her desk by the window with the bright sunlight streaming over her glorious hair, and wondered that anybody could be so pretty and care so little about it.

"I'd care if they were mine," Mary confessed as she walked to the small adjoining room that housed Victoria's rapidly growing wardrobe. "Such pretty things . . . just look at this one, miss, just like a daffodil. So pretty."

Victoria caught the note of envy in Mary's gentle voice and immediately felt ashamed. She rose from her chair and went to inspect the daffodil-colored gown. "You're right, Mary; it's very pretty. I'm sorry for sulking, I'm just homesick and out of sorts. Do you ever get homesick, Mary?"

"Not much," Mary said cheerily. "I've been training here since I was twelve, and at home I had to share a bed with the little ones, the cot-

50

tage was so crowded. It's a good thing, being an upstairs maid. I'd like to be a lady's maid, like Daisy. But not for Miss Lavinia," she hastened to add. "She's in a temper today. The guests are arriving from London, and nothing in her closet will please her. Daisy's done her hair three times already."

Victoria laughed. "Poor Daisy. She earns her money, I daresay."

"That's the truth, miss. May I do your hair? There's lots of handsome men about, and you're too pretty to stay hidden."

" 'Stay hidden' is exactly what I'd like to do. I don't think I'd fit in well with Lavinia's friends. Are they all like her?"

Mary's round face dimpled. "No. There are three handsome men, and I intend that they get a good look at you. You never know what may happen, miss."

Victoria laughed again and, taking an armful of dresses from Mary, began to help hang them on the hooks that lined the wall of the little room. "Damn, Mary, not you, too! Cousin Abigail keeps telling me that I'm sure to be engaged before the summer's out, and Lavinia thinks that I've come to steal her admirers right from under her nose. I'm not at all interested; I just want to go home."

Mary ignored this and began straightening the room. "Lavinia's friend Rosamund Beaumont is here, and she brought eleven trunks. Imagine! And I'll tell you who else is here. The young Earl of Fairfield, that's who. Only nineteen, and already titled. Very handsome, miss, all golden-haired. And kind, too. If you want to know what I think—"

"I know what you're thinking, and you can stop thinking it. Earls aren't interested in bad-tempered farm girls, Mary; they want sweet, gentle ones, like our sweet Lavinia."

Mary sighed impatiently as she tidied the writing desk. "You shouldn't leave your ink open like this, you're sure to spill. May I do your hair anyway, miss?" she added longingly. "It looks a little wild."

Victoria smiled at Mary's diplomacy and sat obediently at the dressing table, regarding her reflection in the gilt-framed mirror. Mary was right, her hair was 'a little wild.'

Mary set happily to work with the ivory-backed brush, her small, capable hands moving gently through the dark red tangles.

"All right, I won't tell you any more about the earl, though a sweeter young man you couldn't hope to meet. And guess who came with him?"

"His mother," Victoria suggested.

"Oh, miss, you're a caution. No, he brought two friends—"

"And they're both handsome beyond praise, and virtuous and rich beyond belief, and looking for wives to grace their exemplary lives, I suppose," Victoria finished.

Mary tried not to smile at Victoria's flippancy. "Well, I wouldn't go that far. He brought Henry Winston, and he's very elegant, the son of a duke. An oldest son, too."

"Lavinia must like that," Victoria commented. "I gather that oldest sons are the desirable sort."

"He was her favorite, last season," Mary agreed. "We half expected to hear wedding bells. And I'll tell you who else is here—a foreigner, that's who. A Frenchman, miss, that Miss Lavinia met in London."

Victoria rolled her eyes. "Let me guess—is he also impossibly handsome, and eligible?"

Mary giggled, twisting Victoria's curls around her fingers. "See, miss, how pretty your hair is, when it's all brushed? There's bits of gold all through it. Where is that ribbon?"

Victoria regarded her reflection solemnly as Mary produced a length of sky-blue ribbon and tied it around the arrangement of shining curls, steeping back to admire the results.

Victoria had to admit that she looked quite fashionable. Her dress was a fine cotton, striped in light blue and white, with heavy lace dripping from the shoulders and stiff bodice; and Mary had managed to coax her usually unmanageable hair into something resembling a fashionable coiffure.

"Very nice, Mary. I look like a very presentable piece of fluff."

Mary giggled again. "As long as you don't open your mouth, you do. Now will you go below, and meet everybody?"

"That I will not," Victoria answered firmly, taking her book from her bed, and tucking it under her arm. "I'm going to go hide in the

53

gardens and read in the sunshine. And don't try to talk me out of it; my mind is quite made up."

Mary looked offended. "I was only going to say, don't forget to wear a hat. You don't want freckles." She offered Victoria a frivolous, wide-brimmed confection of a hat, covered liberally in white plumes and trailing light blue ribbons.

"Bloody hell," Victoria muttered, jamming the hat onto her carefully arranged curls. "Well, I'm off to hide, Mary, and if I happen to fall over any eligible husbands on the way, I'll invite you to the wedding."

Mary dimpled. "You are a caution, miss," she repeated, and watched Victoria make a hasty exit, the despised blue ribbons fluttering behind her.

Chapter Four

"How dreadful for you, Lavinia. There is nothing more tiresome than a poor relative—especially one that thinks she'll marry 'up.' Is she at all pretty?"

Lavinia adjusted her skirts so that they were better displayed across the marble bench where she and Rosamund sat in the afternoon sun. She tipped her dainty parasol so that it framed her face, and checked the pearl buttons of her lace mitts.

"Well, in an odd sort of way. Papa thinks she's stunning, so perhaps she is—if you like horses."

Rosamund dissolved into giggles. "How mean, Lavvy. Though I don't blame you. Poor Miss Larkin—is she really so unsuitable?"

"In every way," Lavinia answered firmly.

"Let's not discuss her anymore—she bores me. Do you like my gown?"

Rosamund's dark eyes traveled expertly over Lavinia's *robe volante* with its boned, fitted bodice, pointed waist, and full skirts. "It's dear. As sweet as can be. Did your mama make you add the fichu?"

Lavinia's eyes snapped. "No, I added that myself," she answered coldly, adjusting the delicate lawn that covered her white shoulders and décolletage. "It doesn't do to expose too much so early in the day. What on earth would the poor gentlemen have to look forward to, at dinner?"

Rosamund, whose own ripe breasts appeared to push out of the deep square neckline of her gown, didn't blush at this attempted insult. "Who cares what 'the gentlemen' think? I'm quite bored with all of them. Is it true that you've thrown Harry over?"

Lavinia nodded. "Yes, I did. I found something a little more interesting."

"The Frenchman . . ." Rosamund leaned forward, her eyes gleaming with interest. "So it is true . . ."

"Nothing's settled yet," Lavinia demurred, a secret smile on her rose-colored mouth.

Rosamund was not to be put off the scent of such an interesting item. "Oh, Lavvy, tell! Is he as beautiful as I've heard? Is he staying long? Has he kissed you?"

"Really, Rosamund! Yes, he's very dashing.

He's staying at least until my ball, which is in two weeks. And yes, he's kissed me."

Rosamund closed her eyes and fell against Lavinia's arm in a mock swoon.

"Stop it, Ros! For goodness sake, don't be silly. Look, look, here they come."

Rosamund's eyes flew open, and she sighed aloud as she saw the three gentlemen walking towards them between the lush rows of roses that led to the house.

"Oh, Lavvy, he is handsome. And so tall—you didn't tell me he was so tall. He makes Harry and Fairfield look like boys."

"They are," Lavinia answered with a wicked smile. "And Harry is getting fat."

"How mean, Lavvy. He only looks fat next to your elegant Frenchman."

Phillipe St. Sebastien was aware of the admiring eyes upon him as he approached, but he was very used to the adoring gazes of women, and it had little effect on him.

Rosamund's eyes widened as the three men drew closer, and she could see the man more clearly—tall, and broad through the shoulders, his frock coat of blue-black damask cut to accentuate his figure. Despite his height, he moved with the casual grace and elegance of an aristocrat.

Rosamund exhaled as she studied the man's face. His brows were thick and a little fierce-looking, his nose and cheekbones sharp, and his mouth decidedly sensual—the top lip as sweetly curved as a child's, the bottom lip wide and firm, set in a strong line.

Rosamund turned her head so that her face was hidden by the wide brim of her hat as she spoke. "He's a little wicked-looking, isn't he, Lavvy? I don't think you'll find him as manageable as your London beaux."

"I intend that he become so," Lavinia whispered quickly, "for I've a longing to see France. His sister lives at Versailles, Ros—just imagine."

Both girls smiled sweetly as the men walked towards them—the Marquis St. Sebastien, tall and dark and slightly dangerous-looking; Johnathon Lester, the young Earl of Fairfield, golden-haired and slender, with a gentle smile; and Harry Winston, a future duke who carried his plump body with the haughty posture of a prince, his head erect under his fashionable *ailes de pigeon* wig, two white sausage curls hanging on either side of his plump face, and the rest gathered into a neat queue.

"Lavinia," Harry called as they came within earshot. "And Miss Beaumont. Or are you two butterflies out here amongst the roses? Upon my word, I ought to have brought my net."

The two girls giggled at this, and greetings were exchanged all around. Lavinia's eyes were fastened on the elegant marquis, and her breath quickened as he bowed over her hand, his blue eyes rising flirtatiously to meet hers.

"Rosamund," she said, turning her gaze away

with some difficulty, "Have you met Monsieur St. Sebastien?"

Rosamund fluttered her dark lashes and dimpled. "To my great sorrow, no."

Lavinia gave her friend a warning glance. "Rosamund Beaumont, this is Phillipe, the Marquis St. Sebastien. Monsieur, Miss Rosamund Beaumont."

Phillipe took care not to linger over Miss Beaumont's dimpled hand and murmured a polite greeting. Lavinia's quick look of triumph didn't escape him, and he felt a pang of annoyance. She was sure of herself, this Miss Harrington.

As well she might be, he reminded himself. She was beautiful and well-dowered, the only daughter of a powerful earl, and to all reports was strong-willed, and her parents were unable to resist her wishes. And to his great advantage, he had discovered that one of her fondest wishes was to go to France and join the court at Versailles.

"I'm anxious to see the new gardens, Lavinia," the young Earl of Fairfield was saying in his pleasantly mild voice. "Lady Abigail tells us that they've taken two years to complete."

Harry Winston adjusted his heavily embroidered waistcoat. "Splendid idea, Fairfield. Nothing like a walk in the country air, is there? Lead on, Lavinia."

Lavinia offered Phillipe her arm, and she smiled up at him as the brightly dressed, chattering group strolled down the smooth, pebbled paths of the Harrington grounds. Lush roses, delphiniums, snapdragons, and sweet williams filled the symmetrical flower beds, filling the air with their warm summer fragrance, and the lawns lay like carpets of green velvet, fat bumblebees humming over them in search of clover.

Everywhere Phillipe looked, there was evidence of the Harrington wealth—money that might be his, money that could restore his beloved château, money to set the fallow vineyards back into work, money, he reminded himself, that he intended to acquire in a less than honorable fashion. He wondered what Miss Harrington would think when she first saw the crumbling castle, starkly outlined against the craggy ridges of the mountains.

She would be furious, and rightly so. But she seemed vain and flighty enough to be appeased with a position at Versailles, where she could live her own life, take her own lovers if she pleased.

Lavinia chose that moment to smile up at him, and Phillipe felt a troubling pang of conscience that he could ill afford. The other members of the party chattered on happily, and Phillipe felt like a criminal in their midst, jaded and unscrupulous in the light of their careless merriment.

"Here it is," Lavinia announced, leading her guests through a carefully constructed "natural" clearing. "Papa's new garden. Do you like it?"

The clearing was surrounded by a graceful circle of willows, their pale leaves sweeping the lush grass. A small, open-air temple of "classical" Greek design stood at the top of a grassy slope, furnished with gleaming marble benches where one could sit and admire a reflecting pool as it mirrored the brilliant blue sky and languid-looking willows. In the center of the pool, a statue of the goddess Artemis stood as if wading through the sunlit water, the graceful lines of her marble hair and robe sweeping as if caught in a perpetual wind.

"Very pretty, Lavvy," Harry said approvingly. He went immediately to the reflecting pool to adjust his waistcoat, which was, most appropriately, embroidered with peacocks.

"Is the statue Italian?" Fairfield asked in admiration as he made his way up the steps of the little temple.

"Who knows?" Lavinia answered with a careless little laugh. "It's all a little outdated, isn't it? I told Papa so, but he went ahead anyway."

"It's charming," Phillipe reassured his hostess. "Not at all outdated. If you were to ever visit Versailles, Mademoiselle Harrington, you would see many similar landscapes."

"I should love that." Lavinia's cool blue eyes fastened on Phillipe's darker ones for a moment, and then she lowered her lashes flirtatiously.

"Oh, yes," Harry interjected, a faint sarcastic note in his voice, "one hears that Lavinia is simply *mad* for all things French these days. Tell me, Lavvy, have you planned a tour of the continent yet?"

Lavinia arched a brow at her jilted suitor and started to answer sharply, but was interrupted by Johnathon as he called to her from the temple.

"Is this yours, Lavinia?" He held up a handsomely bound book that he had found discarded on one of the benches. "Titus Andronicus," he read aloud, his brown eyes alight with admiration. "Are you reading this, Lavvy? It's rather dark for Shakespeare, isn't it?"

Phillipe looked with surprise at Lavinia, wondering if she was hiding a good mind under her frivolous facade.

Lavinia's silvery laugh rang out, and she tossed her golden curls prettily. "Don't be silly, Johnathon. Can you imagine me wasting my time on dreary things like that? I'm sure that it belongs to that dreadful Miss Larkin—she's very odd, you know. Always bumbling about with her nose in a book."

"Is Miss Larkin your governess, Lavvy?" Harry asked. "I'd really thought you were past all that."

Lavinia and Rosamund burst into giggles.

"No, no," Lavinia protested between giggles. "Imagine. Miss Larkin is some charity case of Mama's. A long-lost cousin, or some such nonsense. And so dull, poor thing. I can't think why she just won't go home."

"I can," Rosamund answered naughtily, tilting her dark head as she dimpled at the men. "She's practically an old maid, and poor as a churchmouse. She's a husband hunter of the worst sort. Guard your titles, gentleman. *You* are the prey."

"Can you imagine?" Lavinia giggled.

All too well, Phillipe thought, managing a half-hearted smile.

The young Earl of Fairfield sent Phillipe a sympathetic smile. "I know just how you feel, Phillipe. Harry and I planned this trip just to get away from that sort of girl."

"I don't mind the pretty things, Johnathon," Harry protested. "It's their grasping mamas that frighten me. As soon as the gossip was out that Father was ill, I've had a never-ending line of future duchesses paraded before me. One always wonders," he added with a sharp look at Lavinia, "how far these girls will go for a title."

Lavinia's eyes shone cold, only for a second; but it made Phillipe wonder, too. Perhaps Miss Harrington was a little more sophisticated than he had thought. He hoped so; it would make him feel less guilty proposing marriage under false pretenses. He was representing himself as rich, she was representing herself as innocent. A fair trade.

Fairfield, always the peace maker, broke the tense silence.

"You look a little flushed, Lavinia. Is the heat bothering you? Would you like to go sit in the shade? I'm a little tired, myself. All that traveling."

"I'm famished," Harry added, "and it's making me a little snappish, I'm afraid. Perhaps we should head back to the house and have an early tea."

"Of course," Lavinia agreed, her calm restored. "How rude of me. You all must be exhausted; the drive from London is impossible, isn't it?"

It was quickly agreed that tea was in order, except for Rosamund, who claimed that the fresh air had exhausted her (Phillipe wondered at this, for the buxom Miss Beaumont fairly bloomed with good health) and that she would retire to her room and sleep before dinner. There was an unmistakable invitation in her dark eyes as she spoke, but Phillipe wasn't sure if it was for him or Harry, or perhaps for either of them. At any rate, as enticing as Miss Beaumont might be, Phillipe had no desire to trifle with Lavinia's affections. He already had too much time invested in this.

He declined to go back to the house with the others, electing to stay in the gardens and enjoy the air, he said; but in reality, he wanted to be away from the spoiled young things and their affected manners and veiled insults. Miss Harrington and Miss Beaumont, for all their affectations of gentility, and their healthy, English-rose looks, were apparently no more innocent than the painted, dissipated women of Versailles, who thought no more of taking a new lover than a new gown.

Phillipe watched the others as they walked

back towards the house, as bright and pretty as butterflies, their pretty manners covering their jaded, cynical thoughts.

And I, he thought, *I'm no better than them. After all these years, I am my grandfather's creature, and by my own choice.*

The thought didn't please him, and he found himself walking away from the sight of the great Harrington house, away from its white, gleaming, classical splendor, away from its lush gardens, away from the marble cherubs that seemed to mock him from the spraying fountains; and into the quiet woods, where the warm, spicy smell of green leaves surrounded him, and the affected voices of Lavinia and Rosamund were replaced by the summer sound of birdsong, low and sweet through the dense trees.

This, Victoria thought, tipping her head back and letting the dappled sunlight play on her face, *this is the happiest I've been since I left home.*

She stood in a rushing stream, her heavy skirts held over one arm, the cool water bubbling around her thighs, breathing the familiar smells of the forest—the warm brown earth, the leaves in the sun, the damp moss that covered the rocks.

It was childish, perhaps, to go wading, but it was such a beautiful place, and the water had sparkled so enticingly in the sun that she had been unable to resist, and had discarded her silly white shoes and fine stockings on the mossy bank and waded in, laughing with pleasure at the cool feeling of the water.

It was so good to be away from Lavinia and Cousin Abigail, and to be alone with her thoughts. And what an enchanted place, hidden in the woods, surrounded by bright green ferns and tiny, white, star-shaped flowers.

Victoria wondered if her parents had ever met here when they were in love. Let Lavinia look down her nose, Victoria thought it was sweet—the lovely young girl from the powerful family, hopelessly in love with the earnest young tutor, sneaking off to meet him, defying her family to marry him. She tried to picture her father, young and ardent, but she kept imagining him as he was now, with his hair all tufted up, and a crack running through the lens of his spectacles, saying, "Oh, dear," and she laughed aloud at the thought.

What were they like, her parents, when they had been young and in love? she wondered. She ran her fingers through the cold water and raised her hand to her face, letting the cool drops trickle over her face. The sunlight felt so good, streaming over her face and throat, and the water was so cool and lovely. Victoria shifted the lacy bulk of her skirts to the other arm, and wondered if she dared discard them and risk being caught in her chemise.

There was nobody about, and it was unlikely that anybody would venture onto Harrington property, she decided. And these dresses were so confining, with their stiffly boned bodices. At any rate, the petticoats were already getting wet, and it would never do to go back to the house with her skirts wet.

With a decisive motion, she reached for the back of her bodice, tugging at the tight lacings that fastened the gown from waist to neck, succeeded in untying the small, tight knot, and pulled the lace-trimmed sleeves from her shoulders, basking in the feel of the sunlight on her skin.

"Perhaps you should stop now, mademoiselle."

Victoria froze at the sound of the voice.

"Though if you wish to continue, I'll gladly watch."

The foreign sound of the voice made her immediately think that she had been discovered alone in the forest by a Gypsy, and was certain to be abducted, as Mrs. Hatton had long been threatening would happen. (Mrs. Hatton had a healthy English mistrust of all people and things foreign.)

But when she turned to confront the speaker, she saw that he was no Gypsy, at least not like any that she had seen. The man that sat on the high bank of the stream looked like an aristocrat, his dark hair unpowdered but in a neat queue and tied with a silk ribbon, white lace at his throat and cuffs, the damask of his frock coat and breeches so dark blue that they were almost black.

He sat leaning against the fallen trunk of a

Amy Elizabeth Saunders

tree, looking as comfortable as if he were in a drawing room, his long legs stretched before him. His blue eyes were fixed on her face, bright and hot, an appraising look; and something more, something that caused Victoria's cheeks to flame and her heart to race.

She quickly pulled the shoulders of her dress up her arms, and the sudden motion caused her skirts to fall from her arm and into the happily bubbling water.

"Bloody hell," she snapped, looking down at her soaking dress.

Phillipe laughed aloud at the unexpected profanity coming from this ethereal girl, who had the grace and face of a woodland sprite. He had half expected her to cry out, or faint.

Victoria felt her temper rising. This was one of Lavinia's friends from London, certainly. A Frenchman, Mary had said. Spying on her, laughing at her, intruding on her solitude. Her soft mouth began to set in a grim line, her eyes narrowed, emphasizing their tilted shape.

Phillipe stopped laughing and made an effort to look contrite. "Please, excuse my intrusion. I didn't mean to startle you. Will you come out of the water?"

Victoria struggled for words. How stupid of her to be caught in such an unladylike position. And by the handsomest man she had ever seen. And he was still laughing to himself, she could see it in his eyes. *Damned gentry*, she thought, aware of her face burning with mingled shame and fury. *Look at him, laughing. And he'll tell Lavinia, and she'll plague me with this forever.*

"Come out of the water," he repeated, gently, as if she were a startled animal, and he came forward to offer her an elegant hand, an emerald gleaming on his finger, greener than the trees.

"You should have told me you were here," she said, annoyed at the slight quaver of her voice.

"I should have," he agreed, never moving his eyes from her face. *But I was watching your hair in the sun*, he added silently, *and the way you closed your eyes and raised your pretty face to the sun, like a woman in love, and the way the lace of your petticoats was clinging to your thighs.*

The man's gaze was unnerving, she thought, looking away. Or maybe it was the quiet of the forest, and that she had been startled.

"I didn't think anyone would come here," she said, "aside from me. You frightened me out of my wits. Are you a guest of the Harringtons?"

"How remiss of me, not to introduce myself. Yes, I'm a guest of the Harringtons." He bowed, so elegantly that Victoria felt as if he were still mocking her, as she stood past her knees in the water. "Phillipe St. Sebastien, mademoiselle, lately of London and Paris, originally from the Auvergne."

He took another step forward, his hand outstretched, and Victoria warmed to his smile and the deep dimples that appeared under his haughty cheekbones.

69

Amy Elizabeth Saunders

"I'm Victoria Larkin, Lavinia's cousin," she answered. "And I believe that you're ruining your shoes."

Phillipe looked confused and glanced down to see that he had stepped into the water as he offered his hand. He had been watching the shape of her mouth as she spoke, the dusty rose softness of it, and listening to the husky sound of her voice.

"I could hardly refuse your assistance now," Victoria added, trying to restrain a laugh, "Since you've gotten wet on my account."

She reached out and laid her cool fingers in his offered hand. Victoria had grown up surrounded by the male species and had always remained unaffected by their charms, and she was startled by the warmth, the electric tremor that she felt as his warm fingers closed firmly on hers.

Her eyes flew to his face, and he smiled, a secret, knowing smile, as if he were well aware of her response to his touch. She pulled her hand away and stepped quickly to the bank, where she began wringing the water from her heavy skirts.

Phillipe watched in amusement as the girl tried to regain her dignity. She tried to coax her hair back into its pins, and he watched as it slid heavily down her back again, the heavy red curls shining with gold. His fingers itched to reach out and feel it, to see if it was as soft and warm as it appeared.

70

Victoria looked at her skirts in despair. "What a damned mess! I shall have to go in the back way. It's not very easy being proper when you're covered with mud." She knew that she was chattering, nervous and trying to fill the quiet, but couldn't stop herself.

This man, Phillipe St. Sebastien, was smiling at her, an impossibly beautiful smile, and she felt shaken.

"It's also not easy to be proper," he told her, "when your dress is unfastened and your pretty back is showing."

To his delight, she blushed, her elfin cheekbones stained a deep rose.

"Please, allow me . . ." Phillipe stepped forward and took the laces of her gown in his hands and began to fasten them. His fingers grazed her shoulders, and she shivered visibly at his touch, causing him to smile.

"And are you also staying with the Harringtons?" he asked, tying the laces with an expert touch as if it were a task he had performed often, Victoria thought. She moved away from him nervously.

"Yes, all summer. I'm a sort of cousin, and my father thought that . . . it would be nice for me," she finished awkwardly, not wanting to explain why she had been sent. To her dismay, she felt herself blushing again, and turned away, bending to retrieve her shoes and stockings from the ground. Once she had them, she was unsure of what to do with them. She could hardly sit on the ground and dress in front of this elegant man, but she couldn't very well go back barefoot.

She glanced up at him and saw that he looked very amused, as if he knew what she was thinking and was enjoying her dilemma. She must look a sight, she knew, with her skirts bedraggled and her face burning, her shoes and stockings folded tightly in her arms.

"I could turn my back," he suggested, sounding very sincere, but the dimples of his smile deepened, and Victoria thought that the twinkle in his eye looked much like her brother Stewart's when he was "up to no good," as Mrs. Hatton would say.

"Then turn it," she ordered, as if she were speaking to one of her brothers, "and if you turn around, I'll take a rock and bounce it off your head."

Phillipe raised his dark brows but turned his back obediently, and Victoria didn't take her eyes off of him as she pulled her stockings up her slender legs, tying the ribboned garters firmly, stuffing her feet hastily into her shoes.

"Would you really hit me in the head with a rock?" Phillipe asked, more amused than alarmed.

"Of course," Victoria answered, feeling much better now that she was decently clad. "You can look now."

"I'm delighted," he said, and again she blushed at the intensity of his blue gaze. "Tell

72

me," he went on, "Are you the cousin that Lavinia tells us is 'simply impossible'?"

Victoria laughed, a full, rich laugh, and decided that she liked this man. There had been a faint mockery in his voice when he spoke of Lavinia, and it pleased her. And it had been kind of him to fix her laces.

"I suppose I am impossible, to Lavinia's mind. We have very little in common."

"I can see that," Phillipe answered carefully, trying to remember what Lavinia and Rosamund had said about this Victoria Larkin. "Poor as a churchmouse" . . . "a charity case of Mama's" . . . "a husband hunter of the worst sort" . . . Was she really? Phillipe wondered. She seemed as nervous and innocent as a child, but it was hard to imagine, with that face and figure, that she was completely innocent. Her entire bearing was a study of sharply contrasting purity and sensuality—the fragile-looking cheekbones that glowed with the healthy color of a fresh peach, the earthy green eyes that tilted in an exotic way under her smooth dark brows, the lush swell of her breasts above the slender line of her ribs. She seemed as ethereal as a wood nymph, but at the same time, as seductive and earthy as a pagan goddess.

"Shall we walk back together?" Victoria asked, her heart fluttering like a bird. She felt as skittish as a colt, and just as awkward, and was anxious to return to the solitude of her room.

"If you like," Phillipe answered, and the soft sound of his voice fell on her ear like music.

He walked behind her up the path and laughed when she stopped to take her hat from the branch of a tree where she had hung it earlier.

"Stupid thing," she remarked with a wry look at the broad brimmed, beribboned thing, and she set it on her head at a comical angle.

"I think it's charming," Phillipe answered honestly. "And if you're concerned with propriety, it is *de rigueur*."

"I suppose that means that it must be done," Victoria said dolefully. "I have never in my life heard so many silly rules."

"It does seem a great shame, to have to cover your pretty hair," Phillipe said, and received a suspicious glance for his flirtation.

They walked in silence back to the tall hedges that marked the boundaries of the Harrington gardens, both of them assessing the other: Victoria almost frantic with worry about the intoxicating effect this Phillipe St. Somebody had on her, trying not to remember the feeling of his hands on the bare skin of her back; Phillipe wondering what this luscious girl was about—was she a blushing young virgin, whose eyes promised more than she knew, or, as Lavinia had said, a practiced adventuress, eager to better herself?

"Are you a great friend of Lavinia's?" she asked suddenly.

She didn't know that her face was so open,

that her eyes were so wistful, and that her suddenly awakened desire was written plainly across her face.

Phillipe wished that he could pursue her, this enchanting cousin of Lavinia's; but he was too close to realizing his goals to risk offending the haughty Miss Harrington.

"A great friend of Lavinia's?" he repeated, and his voice sounded bitter and cool. Best not to lead this little green-eyed enchantress on, he decided. Better to end this little adventure quickly, before it went too far. "Not yet, mademoiselle, but I hope to be, soon. Miss Harrington is . . . very beautiful, you know." His voice sounded cold and mocking. Victoria didn't know that he was mocking himself.

She was not sophisticated enough to hide the disappointment and shame that his words caused her, and he was surprised at how bad he felt at the sight of her wounded expression. But better to hurt her now than to lead her on.

"Cheer up," he added, sounding callous even to himself. "After all, there are other titled gentlemen at the house that you may try your wiles upon. And I'm sure that any one of them would enjoy the sight of your pretty thighs as much as I did."

He expected her to cry, or storm away insulted, but he never expected her to strike him.

She struck him hard, with a surprising strength, the back of her slender hand cracking across his cheekbone with a blow that caused him to stagger and his ears to ring.

Victoria shook with rage, and hurt, and horror at what she had done. "You bloody stupid snob," she spat, hoping that her voice was as cruel as his had been. "You're as vain and arrogant as Lavinia, and likely just as stupid. I wish you luck with your great friendship, sir. You deserve it."

By the time Phillipe had recovered his balance and pulled the lace of his cuff from the hedge that it had tangled in, she was far ahead, her red curls bouncing furiously over her slender back.

"Touché mademoiselle" he said aloud, rubbing his cheek, for her words were more true than she could ever know.

Chapter Five

Lavinia was the very picture of a fashionable young woman at dinner that night. She wore a deep rose brocade, her golden curls powdered to almost white and falling in a careful cascade over one smooth white shoulder. Pearls and rubies sparkled at her white throat, and dark red roses decorated her hair.

Phillipe found himself seated between Lavinia and the dark-haired Rosamund, who sent him reproachful glances from beneath her thick lashes. Lord Cecil, robust and red-faced, kept a bored but watchful eye on the proceedings while feeding bits of food under the table to his favorite hound. Lady Abigail sent her husband looks of disapproval from the opposite end of the table, and Fairfield and Harry sat across from Phillipe, an empty chair between them, presumably for the absent Miss Larkin.

"That's a nasty-looking bruise there," Lord Cecil commented, peering down the length of the dark table at Phillipe. "How did that come about?"

Phillipe forced a tight smile. "Very stupidly, I'm afraid. I was admiring your stables and got too close to one of your mares."

The earl seemed to find this very amusing. "Horse got the better of you, did it? Which one was it?"

"I couldn't say exactly," Phillipe answered carefully.

"Well, what color was it?" Lord Cecil demanded, oblivious to his guest's discomfort.

Phillipe set his glass of wine down before answering. "A dark red," he finally said, a wry smile forming.

Lord Cecil chuckled with pleasure. "That would be Flying Dancer. By Jove, what a horse. Too much spirit, hard to handle. Of course, Miss Larkin does well with her. There's a girl who can handle a horse." He chuckled again, leaning forward to get a better look at the dark bruise. "Couldn't handle our spunky English mares, could you?"

"Papa, that's quite enough," Lavinia said sharply. "You're making Monsieur St. Sebastien quite uncomfortable. We should apologize to him, not tease him. Why, the beast might have hurt him."

Phillipe wished desperately that someone

78

would change the subject. "Really, it was nothing. Please don't concern yourself, mademoiselle."

"Beast indeed," the earl grumbled. "No feeling for horses at all, our Lavinia. Not at all like Miss Larkin. By the way," he added with a sharp look at his daughter, "where is our Miss Larkin, Lavinia?"

Lavinia's rosebud mouth drooped, and she toyed with the rubies at her neck before answering. "I thought that Miss Larkin would be more comfortable in her room, Papa."

Lady Abigail sighed. "Oh, Lavinia, dear, don't you think she should come and meet all the young people?"

Lavinia's eyes darkened, though her voice was light and affectedly careless. "Why, it never occurred to me. She is so awkward, you know, the poor thing. I merely suggested that she take a tray in her room tonight, and she seemed so grateful."

"God knows I am," Harry murmured under his breath. "We hardly want a countrified old maid bumbling about."

Rosamund hid her smile behind the heavy linen of her napkin. "Poor Lavvy," she whispered, her warm breath tickling Phillipe's ear. "I hear that this country cousin is really unsuitable."

Cecil Harrington regarded his daughter with a stern gaze. "If Miss Larkin would rather stay in her room, I would as soon hear it from Miss Larkin." He turned impatiently to the family butler, who hovered nearby, keeping an anxious eye on the passing footmen. "Halliwell, send for Miss Larkin, please."

Lavinia's petulant frown was not unnoticed by anyone present, and when Victoria entered the room a few minutes later, it was obvious to all that Lavinia, who regarded all other females as nothing more than competition, was suffering from an extreme case of jealousy.

Victoria bore no resemblance to the "awkward and unsuitable" bumpkin that Lavinia had been complaining of; she entered the large room with the shy, delicate grace of a doe. Her gown was a simple white lawn, sashed in pale green, her slender shoulders and round breasts showing to fashionable perfection above the deeply rounded neckline. Her hair was drawn off her face in a soft, high cloud, bound with a wide ribbon of pale green, and tumbling down her back in a display of flame-colored curls that glinted with gold in the shimmering candlelight.

She hesitated for a moment in the damask-hung doorway flanked by two marble statues of graceful nymphs, and Phillipe could not resist raising a brow as her nervous gaze met his.

All of the gentlemen present rose immediately to their feet.

"Come in, come in, dear," Lord Cecil shouted happily. "Nobody's going to bite you, you know."

"But what a delicious idea," Harry Winston murmured to Fairfield. They remained standing while the white-gloved butler seated Victoria, Harry sending Lavinia a cynical grin, his broad face alight with mischief.

"So this is the elusive Miss Larkin," he remarked, beaming at Victoria. "My dear, where have they been hiding you?" He turned his white-wigged head towards Lavinia with a knowing smile. "And why?"

Lady Abigail hastily made introductions, and Victoria sighed with relief when the Marquis St. Sebastien simply inclined his dark head towards her, giving no sign of their previous meeting. She liked the looks of the young Earl of Fairfield, who was, as Mary had reported, "all gold-haired," with a smooth, high forehead and gentle brown eyes. She was less sure of the Honorable Sir Harry Winston, whose plump face looked as if he were enjoying some wicked jest, and whose mannerisms and extravagant speech she found somewhat affected. Miss Beaumont watched her with a sly, interested look; and as for Monsieur St. Sebastien, well, she would just not look at him, that's all.

She tried to devote her attention to the excellent pheasant in cream sauce instead; but all the while, she was aware of the blue-eyed man opposite her, and the way his elegant hands moved about his plate, the dark emerald on his finger shining in the light of the sparkling candelabra.

"Are you enjoying the country, Miss Larkin?" inquired the solemn young earl.

Victoria smiled at Fairfield. Even though he

bore a title, he seemed no older than she and Jamie.

"I'm doing my best," she answered candidly. "Though it's so very grand that it's hard for me to think of it as 'country,' sir."

"For shame, Miss Larkin," cried Harry Winston from her other side. "Don't you know that it's taken ten years, and a veritable army of architects and landscapers, to give us that 'country' atmosphere that we're all enjoying?"

Victoria blushed, unsure if he was teasing her or not. "It's very beautiful," she hastened to assure him. "I meant to say that it's so much more elegant than what I'm used to. You see, when I think of country, I think of a place with lots of sheep, sir."

" 'Sir,' " repeated Harry, sounding horrified. "You make me feel quite old, Miss Larkin, and I'm not yet thirty. It will quite spoil my holiday to hear that pretty voice calling me 'sir.' My friends call me Harry, or Rutledge after the family title. Won't you do the same?"

"Of course I shall, if you wish," she said, at last breaking into a merry smile.

"Really, Harry," Lavinia reprimanded, "you shall make poor Miss Larkin quite uncomfortable, behaving so familiarly when you've only just met."

"Nonsense," Harry retorted. "This is the country, and I intend to behave a little informally."

"Don't let Rutledge shock you," Fairfield advised Victoria kindly. "He does like to tease."

"I'm not teasing at all—I don't wish to be called 'sir' on my holiday, especially by such a pretty girl. And look, won't you—she blushes!"

Victoria blushed even harder at that, and Lavinia glowered silently across the table. She turned her elaborately coiffured head back towards her elegant marquis, and was further vexed to find his eyes fixed on her impossible cousin.

"And what do you like to do, Miss Larkin, while you are in the country that is not like country?" Harry asked, dividing his attention equally between his excellent pheasant and the titian-haired beauty at his side.

"I like to ride very much, and I love to read, or just go tramping about the grounds."

"I'm very fond of books, myself," Fairfield told her shyly, his brown eyes glowing earnestly.

"I am not," Harry announced, waving his napkin with a flourish. "So that leaves riding, or 'just tramping about.' Which would you prefer to do tomorrow, Miss Larkin?"

"I think I've had quite enough of wandering about for a while," Victoria answered, unable to resist a mischievous glance at Phillipe. "After all, you never know when you'll bump into an unsuitable sort of person. I think that a ride sounds wonderful. If Sir Johnathon will accompany us, that is," she added, granting Fairfield the brightness of her ready smile.

"I should like that very much," Fairfield answered. "Will anybody else join us? Rosamund, Lavvy? How about you, Phillipe? Are you up for a ride?"

"I think not," Lavinia answered, her eyes like blue ice. "Ros is still tired from the journey, and I've simply too much to do, getting ready for my ball. It's only two weeks away, and everything must be perfect. And Phillipe has already agreed to spend the morning in the rose garden with us, before the sun is too warm."

"To my delight, I have," Phillipe agreed, smiling at Lavinia, though the idea of a good ride appealed to him more.

Victoria felt relief and disappointment mingling. She thought how handsome Phillipe St. Sebastien would be on horseback with his black hair free in the wind. She wondered why his demeanor had changed so quickly, earlier in the afternoon. One moment he had been laughing and walking with her as if they were old friends, and then, at the mention of Lavinia's name, he had suddenly become cold and unkind.

She glanced up to find Phillipe's eyes on her, and for a moment she thought she saw an almost wistful look in them, but when he noticed her gaze, he simply lifted an arrogant brow and turned back to Lavinia.

Embarrassed, she turned her attention back to the pompous but complimentary Harry Winston, future Duke of Rutledge, and the shy, kind young Earl of Fairfield, until the lengthy meal was finished and she could make excuses to escape to her room.

* * *

51555

5

"What a beauty," Harry cried as soon as Miss Larkin was out of earshot. "Have you ever seen such skin? She glows like a fresh peach. And that hair . . ."

"She seems very sweet and unspoiled," Fairfield allowed. "And yes, she's very lovely."

"I suppose," Lavinia interjected, "that she seems pretty simply because she is different. You always were one to chase after a new face, Harry. I find her quite ordinary, and I've never been fond of red hair, have you, monsieur?" she inquired of the silent marquis.

Phillipe drew his eyes away from the doorway that Victoria had departed through moments before. "All the great artists and poets throughout the ages have praised golden hair above all other colors," he reassured his pleased hostess; but even as he spoke, in his mind there was a picture of a tangle of red curls, sparkling with gold in the sun, like a waterfall of flame.

"They said in the kitchen that you were a great success, miss," Mary reported, her round face glowing with pleasure. "They said that none of the gentlemen could take their eyes from you. Daisy says that Miss Lavinia will be a handful tonight."

Victoria pulled the voluminous folds of her nightdress over her head before answering. "Lavinia is always a handful. And it seemed to me that she had all of Monsieur St. Sebastien's attention."

85

"That isn't what they said in the kitchen. And if Daisy says that Lavinia's in a temper, then she is, that's what. She's used to getting all the attention, and this was a real slap in the eye for her."

Victoria laughed at Mary's figure of speech. "Good. Lavinia could use a slap in the eye," she commented wryly, climbing into bed. "And I won't pretend that I'm not happy about it."

She stretched the length of her body against the feather bed, luxuriating in the softness, thinking about what Mary had told her. So Phillipe St. Sebastien had been watching her, had he? The thought caused a pleasant tremor to run through her, her heart racing a little faster.

"It really seemed to me that he was watching Lavinia," she repeated aloud without meaning to.

Mary's dark eyes brightened with interest, and she glanced up at Victoria, her attention diverted from the pile of discarded petticoats on the floor. "So that's the way the wind blows, is it? Well, he's handsome enough, for not being English."

Victoria sat up in bed abruptly. "He is handsome, isn't he, Mary? Have you heard him speak? He has a beautiful voice, like music. Have you seen his eyes? They're the nicest blue—"

"You're smitten," Mary announced. "No mistake about it."

"For all the bloody good it does me," Victoria admitted. "For God's sake, Mary, he isn't some gangly village boy. He's a nobleman, and Lavinia has her eye on him, and that's the end of that."

Mary was quiet for a few moments, moving efficiently about the room, straightening the chair, opening the window a crack, tidying the books and papers that cluttered the desk.

"My sister Meg says," she offered after some thought, "that the surest way to drive a man wild is to ignore him. Men are odd creatures, no mistake about it, and they never seem to want what's offered them."

Victoria thought about the flocks of bright-eyed girls that followed her brothers about, and saw the sense in this.

"If I were you," Mary went on, "I'd do just what you did at dinner tonight. Ignore him. You just turn your attention to those nice young Englishmen, and you'll have him eating out of your hand like a little lamb."

"I've never seen anyone less like a little lamb in all my life," Victoria answered, laughing at the image that Mary's words evoked.

"Go ahead and laugh, if you want, miss, but that's what my sister Meg says, and she's done well for herself. Married the butcher, and has four rooms in her house, and a girl to come in and help. She could have had anyone, but she knew how to play her cards. She was May-queen two years in a row," Mary added solemnly, as if this were evidence of Meg's superior knowledge.

"Imagine that," Victoria said respectfully.

"I'd think about it, if I was you, miss. Meg says that there isn't a man in the world that can't be had, if you know how to play the game. And it would make Miss Lavinia very angry."

Victoria felt a mean, happy pleasure. "It would be nice," she admitted, "to make Lavinia angry, if nothing else."

Mary smiled. "Yes, miss. It would be nice." She extinguished the candles on the dressing table, leaving only one burning, the room darkening into a mellow twilight. "I'll be off, then, miss, unless you need anything else."

"I need a good dose of sense, that's what I need," Victoria answered with a mocking laugh. "To even think about chasing after a nobleman, for God's sake. Anyway, he's interested in Lavinia, and as far as he's concerned, I likely don't even exist."

"That's not what his eyes say," Mary returned stubbornly. "You think about it, miss."

Think about it I will, Victoria thought as Mary left the room. Was there anything to what Mary had said? And wouldn't it be fun to make him want her, and then turn her nose up. There was certainly nothing to lose by ignoring him.

She tossed and turned restlessly in her bed, thinking about all that had happened that day, and what it meant, and the clock on the mantel struck eleven before sleep finally claimed her.

Even in sleep, Victoria found little rest. Her dreams were bright and lush, with a dark, rich quality that she had never known before, and in them the Marquis St. Sebastien stood beside her in a rushing stream, the current pulling her body against his, his blue eyes sparkling, and his elegant fingers touched her face, moving warmly down her body.

She awakened in the early morning hours, the room cool and gray in the early light, her body damp with sweat, and her heart racing with the uneasy feeling that her life had changed.

During the next two weeks, while Lady Abigail and Lavinia were concentrating their combined efforts on Lavinia's upcoming ball, Victoria was concentrating on the fine art of "being charming."

Each morning she would submit to being "dolled up" at Mary's merciless hands, and, armed with second-hand advice from Mary's sister Meg (who apparently concerned herself with little else than the mysterious workings of the male mind), she set out to enchant Harry Winston and Johnathon Lester, all the while ignoring Monsieur St. Sebastien.

To her delight, she succeeded beyond her expectations.

Despite the differences in their stations, Victoria discovered that the young men were not that different from her brothers, and they were very happy to spend their time with their delightful new companion, who laughed so hard at their jokes and could ride as long and hard as a man and never cared about messing her hair or gown.

"If you're not sure what they're speaking of, ask," Mary told her. "As many questions as you can. Makes even the stupid ones feel clever, and men love to feel clever. And laugh a lot—men hate sulky girls. And don't seek them out—make them come to you. Men love girls that want nothing to do with them."

"That's the stupidest thing I've ever heard," Victoria remarked, but there was no arguing with the fact that she was getting results.

Soon, both young men were half in love. What a relief it was, they agreed, to spend time with such a pretty, unspoiled creature.

And though she didn't know it, Victoria's efforts were not unnoticed by the handsome, reserved Monsieur St. Sebastien.

Phillipe found himself strangely annoyed by the sight of the three inseparable companions who romped noisily in and out of the house, the sound of their happy laughter following them, while he himself was reduced to the less merry company of Miss Harrington, who grew more annoyed every day at the sight of her former suitors and her impossible cousin, and the equally sulky Miss Beaumont, who found her dark charms unanimously unappreciated for the first time in her life.

He told himself that Miss Larkin was nothing, simply an adventuress who had followed his advice and turned her sights towards greener pastures; but as each summer day passed, he found himself watching the red-haired girl with an annoying, increasing longing, as she made her merry way about, seemingly oblivious to his presence.

Everywhere he went, she was there first—in the library with Fairfield, bent over a book of sonnets, her red head almost touching Johnathon's gold one; in the great hall, laughing as Harry taught her the steps to the latest dances, holding her tightly in his arms as he spun her slender body over the black and white marble squares; in the rose gardens, her arm linked with both of them as they regaled her with tales of life in London.

"Have you heard what they call themselves?" Lavinia demanded one morning at breakfast, stabbing at her food with a most unladylike vengeance. "The Terrible Triumvirate. What do you suppose they mean by that?"

"I really have no idea," Phillipe answered honestly, wishing that the enchanting Miss Larkin would go home and leave him in peace, or that Lavinia would quit brooding about her.

"Who really cares?" Rosamund snapped. "Honestly, Lavvy, Harry and Johnathon are behaving like mindless children. If it weren't for your ball, I would just leave. This is the most boring house party you've ever had."

Phillipe looked at the two sour faces, and wished that he might behave like a "mindless child." He excused himself to visit the library, hoping to spend some time away from his hostess's disgruntled company.

Of all the rooms at Harrington Park, the library was his favorite. Phillipe loved the dark, masculine colors of the shining wood and the wine-colored leather wing chairs, the heavy richness of the tall, curtained windows that looked into the rose gardens. Rows of books lined the walls, carefully bound in fragrant, gleaming leathers.

He thought bitterly of the library at Château St. Sebastien, the dry rot that threatened the wood, the once priceless books mildewing on the rotting shelves. How far away it seemed from this sunny place, where everyone was surrounded by wealth and luxury, and seemed not to have the slightest care.

"I wondered where you were, monsieur. What are you doing in this dreary place?"

Lavinia entered the room, the pale pink silk of her morning gown brushing lightly over the gleaming floors, and positioned herself carefully on the windowseat where the sun touched her golden hair.

"Do you find it dreary?" Phillipe asked, looking at the shining floors, the opulent oil paintings, the imposing bust of Socrates staring blindly from the rich cherrywood table. "I find it very handsome."

Lavinia laughed, a silvery sound. "I suppose, if one likes books, that it's nice enough. But I imagine that this is nothing like the rooms at Versailles."

"Of course," Phillipe agreed, though he was rapidly tiring of that subject. Lavinia had already made her appearance at the English court of King George, and found it dull, and was hungry to move onto "better" things.

"My fondest dream," Lavinia confessed, "is that one day I might see it, but I fear that I never shall."

Phillipe took the bait and moved closer to her, taking her cool white fingers in his hand. "Perhaps your dream is not impossible, mademoiselle," he suggested silkily.

Lavinia smiled up at him, her clear blue eyes glowing. "I pray that you are right, monsieur. Will you do me the honor of calling me by my given name?"

Phillipe bowed over her hand. "The honor would be mine . . . Lavinia."

She preened with pleasure and patted the seat next to her. "Sit down, please, and tell me more. Is your castle very beautiful? Is it far from Paris, and—" she broke off abruptly, her brows knitting together as she stared beyond Phillipe, out at the gardens. "What on earth is Harry doing?"

Phillipe followed her bemused gaze.

In the center of the sunlit rose gardens stood a fountain of fine Italian marble, a quintet of cherubim frolicking under a sparkling spray. And on the edge of the fountain sat the Honorable Harry Winston, wigless, his own crinkled brown hair shining in the sun, industriously rolling his breeches above his plump white knees as if making ready to wade in.

Lavinia stared open-mouthed, and Phillipe raised his brows incredulously.

Sir Harry entered the water, letting out a bellow as the cold spray hit him.

Lavinia threw open the heavy window. "Harry," she shrieked. "What on earth are you doing?"

Harry turned towards them, embarrassment plainly written on his broad face. "My wigs," he shouted, his voice muffled by the sound of the running water.

"What did he say?" Lavinia demanded, puzzled.

"Something about his wigs, I think," Phillipe answered, and then began to laugh. "Look— look at the fountain carefully," he instructed Lavinia.

On closer inspection, it could be seen that each of the marble cherubs were sporting Harry's fashionable white wigs.

"Whoever would do such a thing, and why?" Lavinia demanded crossly. "Poor Harry—he's getting all wet."

Harry was climbing clumsily about the cherubs on their marble hillside, averting his face from the blast of the spray as he tried to retrieve his beloved wigs. Phillipe tried not to laugh.

"There, I believe, are the culprits," he said, pointing.

Victoria and Fairfield were coming around the corner of the house, their faces glowing with suppressed laughter.

"Why, Harry," Victoria called, assuming a shocked look, "what a silly place for a swim. I didn't think it was so warm."

The usually solemn young Earl of Fairfield could not restrain his laughter at the sight of his friend, his silk frock coat and fine lace limp and bedraggled, perched in the center of the fountain like an overgrown cherub.

"I say, Harry," he finally managed, "when I want a bath I usually have my valet draw one for me. It's so much simpler."

Harry let out a bellow of mock rage and, throwing his beloved wigs to the grass, began to climb down, fire in his eye. A passing gardener, his wheelbarrow full of freshly sprouted transplants, stared in shock as the future Duke of Rutledge thundered by, half running, half hopping on his tender white feet.

Victoria's laughter, rich and full like golden bells, rang across the lawn, and Lavinia shut the window with a loud bang, startling Phillipe, who had been watching the scene with great interest.

"That girl," Lavinia fumed, "has gone too far."

Phillipe hastily removed the smile from his face. "It seems a harmless enough prank. And Harry doesn't seem to mind . . . much."

Lavinia turned impatiently from the window. "Of course he doesn't. He and Johnathon are behaving just as stupidly. They're besotted with her, the want-wits. Miss Larkin should not even be here. It's an insult to me."

"How is that?" Phillipe asked curiously.

"Perhaps it's indelicate of me to say so, but I happen to know that she was sent here in disgrace, for doing something immoral. Can you imagine?"

"Yes, I can," Phillipe answered honestly, for in truth he had been imagining Miss Larkin doing a good many "immoral" things with an alarming frequency.

"And now look at her," Lavinia ranted, "working her tricks with Harry and Johnathon. She's very good at what she does, our little country mouse."

Phillipe wondered exactly what immoral thing Miss Larkin had done to inspire such scorn. Outside the window, her laughter grew louder, and Phillipe watched with interest as Harry dragged her to the fountain, ignoring her apologies and merry protestations. There was a shout of triumph from Harry, a shriek from Victoria, and she was in the water with a mighty splash.

"Just look at her," Lavinia snapped.

Phillipe was looking, hard. Victoria was climbing to her feet, helpless with laughter, her hair hanging in dark, wet ribbons around her face. The pale flowered cotton of her morning dress clung to her slender body, revealing in detail the round lushness of her breasts, the slender curves of her waist and hips. She seemed completely oblivious to the seductive picture she made. Phillipe turned abruptly away as desire flooded him, hot and quick.

"That jade!" Lavinia fairly spat with anger. "If you will excuse me, monsieur, I have borne too much. I must go speak to Mama."

Phillipe bowed as Lavinia sailed from the room. He moved towards the foyer of the mansion, his blood racing through his veins. Lavinia was right, Miss Larkin was a jade, and a sly one at that; displaying her body so blatantly to that stupid pup, Harry. He wondered if they were sleeping together. He wondered why he even cared.

Victoria pushed her dripping hair from her eyes and offered Harry her hand. "Help me out," she ordered, trying to look stern.

"Only if you say, 'I'm sorry for ruining Harry's lovely wigs.' "

Victoria tried her best to assume a contrite expression. "I'm sorry for ruining your lovely wigs," she repeated humbly, biting her lip to keep from laughing. She meekly extended her slender hand.

"Very well, I'll help you out," Harry answered after a moment's consideration and a stern glance at Fairfield, who still shook with laughter. He took Victoria's offered hand. "But I give you fair warning, Vic, if you ever—"

Her fingers snaked around his wrist with astonishing strength, she gave a fierce pull, and Harry landed in the water at her feet.

Johnathon's delighted shout of laughter and

Harry's bellow of outrage followed her as she scrambled nimbly over the fountain wall and raced towards the house, her sodden skirts leaving a dripping trail behind her, up the wide staircase and across the white expanse of veranda.

Out of breath, and trying not to laugh, she pushed open the heavy door and raced to the staircase and clattered up, casting a hasty glance over her shoulder to see if Harry was following.

At the second-floor landing, she turned sharply towards her room, and to her great horror collided with the Marquis St. Sebastien.

The impact of their bodies knocked the breath out of her, and she would have fallen if Phillipe had not caught her firmly around the waist, steadying her. Her eyes flew to his face, wide and green and with such a look of horror that he felt himself smiling at her dismay.

"My dear Miss Larkin, you seem to have the most *charmante* habit of playing in water."

He didn't loosen his grasp on her waist, and Victoria was sharply aware of the warmth of his hands against her damp skin, and the soft pressure of her breasts against his chest, the bright heat of his lazy smile.

"It's a very attractive habit," he went on, slowly. "I wonder, do you know how pretty you are, wet?"

Victoria felt as if she had lost her voice. Her pulse was racing, and she tried to move back, but the marquis tightened his grip on her slender waist. She felt her body pulling to his, as if by the current of a river, and she tried to ignore the heat that was flooding her, staining her cheeks a dark rose.

She raised her eyes to his face, intending to speak sharply to him, but her heartbeat accelerated at the sight of his eyes, glittering and hungry, fastened on her face.

Phillipe stared in fascination as a drop of water rolled down Victoria's glowing cheek and dropped to the swell of her half-exposed bosom. He raised a finger and traced its path down the satin of her skin.

"Please," Victoria whispered, and her husky voice shook slightly. "Excuse me, monsieur, I would like to go to my room. Please."

"Go to your room, Miss Larkin?" he repeated slowly. "What an excellent idea. Though I would very much like to hear you say 'please' again."

His hands were traveling up the slender length of her body, their warmth heating her through the thin, wet lawn of her frock. Victoria drew her breath sharply as they stopped, barely beneath the swell of her bosom. She stared up at him, dizzy and fascinated, at the intensity of his blue eyes, the sharp, clean line of his jaw, the way the light shone almost blue on his black hair; shocked and intoxicated by the heat that was flooding her body.

"Please," she whispered, unthinking, and Phillipe smiled hotly at her. His eyes were fastened on her mouth, on the soft, full shape, and the dark, rich rose of it; and without thinking, he bent his head and covered it with his own.

Victoria thought that she might faint at the heat and softness of it, and for a moment she gave herself up to the incredible sweetness of his mouth, and no thoughts intruded on the dark, rich feeling.

She opened her eyes only when his lips left hers, and realized with horror what she had done as she saw the hot, mocking smile on Phillipe's face.

"Please what, Miss Larkin?" he repeated, his voice as soft as she had ever heard it. "If you want more, I shall be happy to accommodate you. You say 'please' so very prettily—I would like to hear you beg a little more."

Shame and rage flooded her, and she pushed him away, backing towards the hall. She looked wildly around to see if anyone had heard, but only a graceful statue of a Roman god stood there, a mute witness with blind eyes.

"You bloody rotten bounder," she hissed, wiping her mouth with a shaking hand. "Don't you ever do such a thing again. If I had a gun, I'd blast your arrogant head off."

To her rage, the marquis looked amused. "Would you indeed, kitten?"

"I would," she asserted.

"Even after you opened your lovely mouth to me, and pressed so sweetly against me?" he asked, and his dimpled smile enraged her further.

"I would, and then I'd tell my brothers, and they'd kill you."

Phillipe laughed aloud at the sight of her, pink-faced and trembling, her wet hair dripping onto the marble floor of the landing.

"And would they kill me," he asked, "even after you had been so unkind as to 'blast my head off'? What a very . . . passionate family you must have, kitten."

Victoria uttered the foulest word she could think of, and stormed away, the marquis's laughter ringing in her ears.

"You are adorable in a temper, *cheri*," he called after her, and watched as she walked away, not dignifying his remark with an answer.

A curious kind of elation seized him despite her furious rejection. She did want him. He had seen it in her eyes, on her face, in every line of her luscious body. It had been a long time since a woman had refused him, and he was surprised at how much it intrigued him.

"Soon," he whispered. "*Bientôt*, Victoria."

"Sir?"

Phillipe turned sharply and found himself confronting Halliwell, the butler, whose perpetually worried eyes were wandering curiously from the puddled floor, down the staircase, and back to the marquis, who looked as if he had leaned against something wet and was now talking to himself.

Phillipe raised a dark brow at the concerned man.

"I was just saying, Halliwell, that the staircase is rather wet—don't you agree?"

The butler sighed as the elegant Frenchman strolled indifferently away.

"Yes, sir, very wet indeed," he agreed mildly, and set off to find a maid to deal with the mess before Lady Abigail wanted an explanation that he couldn't possibly provide.

Chapter Six

Phillipe descended the wide staircase of the Harrington house, the morning sun shining through the tall windows, reflecting brilliantly off the black and white marble floor. He stopped at the bottom of the staircase to let two gardeners pass, their arms loaded with huge bundles of flowers.

Lavinia's ball, he remembered, was tonight; and this was the night that he intended to ask for her hand. The idea left him feeling curiously empty.

Bored and listless, he wandered through the rich rooms of the estate, wondering where everybody was. There was no sign of Lavinia, or anyone else, for that matter, except for the servants that rushed past him, bearing silver trays and piles of linens. He beckoned to a passing footman and inquired where the rest of the household was.

"Miss Lavinia and Miss Beaumont are with her ladyship, going over the arrangements for tonight, I should imagine, sir. Lord Cecil is off with friends, hunting."

"And the others?" Phillipe asked. "Where are they?"

The young footman smiled happily. "Sir Johnathon and Sir Harry and Miss Larkin? They just went off to the stables. The Terrible Triumvirate, that's what they call themselves."

The beaming young man imparted this information as if it were a great witticism, which for some reason annoyed Phillipe unreasonably.

"I've heard," he said shortly, treating the young man to a disapproving stare.

A ride would be nice, he thought, a day in the sunlight. A farewell to his last day of freedom before he became Lavinia's betrothed. The thought sprang unbidden that it would be fun to spend the day with the enchanting Miss Larkin, and see how she dealt with his presence. Was she still angry, and if she was, how would she explain herself to Fairfield and Harry?

Phillipe smiled with perverse pleasure at the idea, and his step quickened as he made his way across the green lawns, still sparkling with dew in the morning sun, the air cool and fragrant with the scent of summer.

Harry and Johnathon were already astride their mounts when he arrived at the stables, and their faces registered surprise at his presence.

"Why, look, Johnathon," Harry cried. "It's our missing friend from London. Do you suppose that Lavinia has let him out for the day?"

"Good morning, Phillipe," Johnathon called, more civilly. "Will you join us on our ride, or will Lavinia miss you, do you think?"

Phillipe tried to ignore the annoyance that their comments caused him. "I think that Lavinia is far too busy with her soirée to notice my absence. And yes, I will join you."

Harry beamed from beneath his feathered tricorn. "Splendid. Boy!" he shouted to a passing stable hand., "Get the marquis a horse, quickly."

Victoria rode into the stableyard a moment later, skillfully handling her cinnamon-colored mare as it pranced impatiently beneath her. She stopped short at the sight of Phillipe, who was making ready to mount a sooty Arabian.

She felt the color rush to her cheeks. Damn him! What was he doing here? He couldn't possibly mean to come along. She couldn't bear it, after he had insulted her so wickedly on the stairs yesterday. And now, here he was, looking impossibly handsome, smiling at her in his damnably arrogant way.

"Look here, Vic," Harry called. "The Terrible Triumvirate has a guest. Phillipe has managed to tear himself away from Lavinia's side for the day."

Victoria took a deep breath, steadying her nerves. "How very fortunate for us," she replied flippantly. "But now we are four. And four can hardly be a triumvirate."

"Then we shall be something else," Johnathon answered, smiling adoringly at Victoria. "What can four be, Harry?"

Harry considered. "The Fiendish Four? No . . . Foul? Certainly not, Victoria is far too pretty. Flippant, maybe? No, we are already flippant, far too often. Phillipe has been looking rather fierce lately; what about the Fearsome Four? No, frolicsome, I think. Yes, that will do."

"The Frolicsome Four we are, then," Victoria declared, smiling brilliantly at Harry and doing her best to ignore Phillipe, who looked very bored. Her horse moved impatiently beneath her, and she tightened her grip on the reins.

"I say, Phillipe," Johnathon remarked innocently, "isn't that the mare that blacked your eye?"

Phillipe's eyes moved lazily over the frisky mare and up to Victoria's slender figure, to meet her green eyes. "Why, yes," he answered, a trace of irony in his voice. "There she is."

He was pleased to see Victoria's face color prettily beneath the delicate veil of her riding hat.

"Perhaps, sir, you made the mistake of assuming that you knew more about the horse than you actually did," she replied pertly. She turned the mare towards the front drive. "Come along. If we're going to ride, let's go," she ordered.

"Spoken like a queen," complimented Fairfield, brushing a strand of honey-colored hair from his forehead. "Shall we call you Titania? You look like a fairy queen."

Victoria frowned at him with mock severity. "I thought that we agreed not to be flippant, Johnathon. We are not flippant today, but frolicsome. Let's go frolic, for heaven's sake." She touched her heels to the horse and galloped easily ahead of the other three.

They all watched her with admiration, graceful and slender in her black riding habit, the little veiled tricorn pinned securely to the shining masses of her ruddy curls, moving down the graveled, tree-lined drive as if she and the horse were one creature.

"Damn, she's beautiful," Harry breathed admiringly, and nobody thought he was talking about the horse.

"The fairest flower of June," agreed Fairfield poetically. "She makes the London girls seem . . . well, almost jaded."

"I wish I could take her to London, for the season," Harry added longingly. "She would set society on its heels. She is so frank and amusing."

Phillipe glanced sharply at the young man. "Have you asked her? I would think that a girl in Miss Larkin's position would be happy to be your mistress." Even as he spoke the words, he felt a pang of jealousy at the idea.

Both young men looked shocked.

"My dear fellow," Harry replied in an incredulous tone, "she would never consider such a

thing. I offered to have her up for the season—
very respectably, of course, to stay with my
Auntie Augustine—and she wouldn't even consider it. She can't wait to get back to that silly
farm of hers and her countless brothers."

Phillipe thought about that as the horses
walked slowly down the shaded drive. "Are you
sure about that, Winston? Or is she perhaps
waiting for a better offer?"

Fairfield looked appalled and started to
speak, but Harry interrupted with a noisy
laugh. "Do you mean that she hopes to get married? To catch herself a rich man? My poor
friend, you've been spending entirely too much
time with Lavinia and Rosamund, I think. No,
our Vic has no desire to join 'the ton,' to my
great sorrow."

Phillipe looked down the drive to where Victoria waited impatiently.

"Come on," she called, "move your lazy . . .
horses."

This time, Phillipe laughed with the others.

They ventured far into the countryside, laughing, arguing, breathing the fresh clean air, and
Phillipe felt more relaxed than he had in weeks.

Victoria sang them a barroom song about a
man who drank so much that he thought his
horse was his wife, and made them all laugh.

Johnathon quoted a poem about the beauty
of nature, and Harry rolled his eyes and expressed a preference for Victoria's performance.

At noon they reined into a shady clearing where small butterflies floated over the tall grass and foxglove grew in purple clusters, showing their spotted throats. Victoria threw her hat to the ground, collapsed in exaggerated exhaustion next to it, and pronounced it the perfect place to rest.

"It's damned hot for June," Harry complained, settling his ample body beneath a tree.

"Take off that stupid hat if you're so hot," Victoria suggested.

Harry looked horrified. "My dear, what can you be thinking? A gentleman never goes riding without his hat."

"Even if he's sweating to death?" Victoria asked. "How very stupid. *Monsieur le marquis* isn't wearing a hat. Is he sensible, or just not a gentleman?"

She darted a quick look at Phillipe, who looked a little taken aback at her teasing. He wasn't wearing a hat, and the sun shone on his thick dark hair as he tied his horse to a low branch.

Johnathon settled happily on the tall grass next to Victoria and produced a bottle of wine from beneath his coat. "Here, Harry, this should help the heat. Save some for the rest of us."

Phillipe sat across from the two, reclining with his back against a gnarled oak tree, where he had a good view of Victoria, who looked, he thought, particularly charming, sprawled in the grass like a child, her wayward curls shining around her glowing face. She sat up, leaning on one arm, and removed Johnathon's hat, tossing it disdainfully to the ground.

"There, now Johnathon is sensible as well. You don't mind, do you, Johnathon?"

"I don't mind anything you do, Vic. Take my heart too, if you like." Fairfield's smile was gentle and happy, his words only half joking.

"No, thank you," Victoria answered briskly. "I've already got one of my own, and it's no end of trouble."

"How cruel she is, our Circe," Harry remarked, sipping lazily from the wine bottle.

"Circe!" Victoria echoed with a hoot of laughter. "Isn't she the sorceress that turned men into pigs?"

"It's already working with Harry," Fairfield teased. "He's not only hogging the wine, he's dribbling down his shirt."

Phillipe laughed along with the rest of them as Harry swore, looking down at the ruby stains that decorated his snowy shirt front.

"My valet will be quite cross," Harry protested, holding the bottle out to Fairfield, who drank heartily before passing it to Phillipe.

"Don't fuss about your clothes, Harry," Victoria ordered, tilting her face to the sun and breathing the scent of the sun-warmed grass.

"If we wanted to hear that, we'd have invited Lavinia," Fairfield added, with a mischievous smile. "Oh, sorry, Phillipe," he added hastily. "Didn't mean to be rude. After all, we can't expect every girl to be as jolly as Vic."

The marquis smiled, an honest, happy smile that caused Victoria's heart to flutter like a bird.

"No," he agreed softly, "they cannot all be as jolly as Miss Larkin. It's a great pity."

Victoria looked away, confused at the sad note in his voice. He seemed so different today, so happy and kind, and not at all cold and snobbish, as she thought him.

"But you cannot say 'Miss Larkin,' Phillipe," Harry said. "That is the first rule of the Terrible Triumvirate. No titles or formal names. Here we are simply Harry, Johnathon, and Victoria, or Vic, if you prefer."

Phillipe smiled again and drank from the bottle of wine. It slid down his throat, cool and fruity, tasting of lazy summer days. Lavinia, the château, his rapidly diminishing funds, they all seemed far away from this peaceful place. He offered the bottle to Victoria, who shook her head.

"Thank you, no. I prefer water."

"Water suits you very well . . . Victoria."

Her cheeks flamed, but Phillipe looked so kind and jolly, as if they were sharing a private joke, and she smiled back forgivingly.

Harry leaned back, surveying the endless expanse of blue overhead. "What a sky," he shouted happily at nobody in particular.

It was a beautiful day, Victoria thought, surveying the landscape before her—green trees covering gently rolling hills as far as the eye could see, the steeple of a church in the distance, the dusty road curving by gentle meadows and away into the distance like a brown ribbon.

Phillipe shed his coat and rolled up his sleeves, leaning comfortably against the gnarled tree trunk. Victoria watched his arms, strong and dark, and tried not to think about them around her waist, holding her against him. She wondered what it was that made him so devilishly attractive. Maybe it was his hair, thick and black, and the way it was falling out of the ribbon that bound it at his neck, just like Johnathon and Harry, but somehow, so much more attractive. She stared, fascinated, at the shape of his mouth, and shivered as she remembered the heat of it on her own. She was admiring the bright blue of his eyes and how thick his dark lashes were when she noticed him watching her back. She blushed at how silly she must look, and turned away.

"Why do you call yourselves the Terrible Triumvirate?" he asked suddenly, leaning forward and resting his arms on his knees.

Wary glances passed between the three companions.

"Why . . . because there are three of us," Johnathon offered.

Phillipe raised a disbelieving brow. "The 'triumvirate' part I understand. But what have you done to earn the title 'terrible'?"

"Shall we tell?" Harry asked, lazily opening one eye.

"No, we shan't," Victoria announced firmly, "or Phillipe shall think us . . . well, terrible."

Phillipe thought how pleasant his name sounded in Victoria's husky, pleasant voice, so different from Lavinia's clipped, precise speech.

"You must tell me," he said to her, "or I won't dance with you tonight."

Victoria's heart skipped a beat at the thought of dancing close to him, and for the first time, she thought that Lavinia's ball might not be such a dreadful experience.

"Tell, then," she capitulated.

Harry roused himself and cleared his throat importantly. "It all began the day after we arrived. We went for a ride, and then stopped at The Three Crowns for a pint of good ale—"

"Several, for some people," Victoria put in with a disapproving look at Harry.

"Hush up, Vic, or I shan't dance with you either. At any rate, there we were, and the most unsavory fellow was there, and he kept bothering us. He smelled like the devil and was really annoying—"

"He's the town drunk," Victoria interrupted, "and Ethel says—"

"Who is Ethel, please?" Phillipe asked her, a dimple showing in his lazy smile.

"Ethel is the innkeeper's wife, and Ethel says that this fellow will rot in hell. He married an honest, hard-working woman and drank all her money away, and beat her, and then . . . she died."

"He killed her?" Phillipe asked, horrified.

"Well, no," Victoria admitted. "It was pneumonia. But after she died, he found a lot of money hidden under the floorboards that she had hidden away, and he's been drinking it up ever since, and having a laugh at his poor, dead wife's expense."

"I like the way that I'm telling this story," Harry remarked, but Victoria went on.

"We all agreed that he was a real toad, and went on our way. And when we were riding home that night, we saw him passed out cold against a fence by the road. What do you suppose was sitting next to him when he woke up?"

"I can't imagine," Phillipe answered, watching the dappled sunlight play on Victoria's hair. "Tell me."

Victoria's eyes sparkled. "His wife's gravestone. Sitting right at his side, as if it had walked from the churchyard."

The three friends burst into merry laughter at Phillipe's incredulous face.

"However did you manage that?" he asked.

Victoria laughed again, the husky sound falling pleasantly on his ears. "It was simple. We could see the churchyard from where we were, and Harry said he was surprised that the fellow's wife didn't rise up from the grave and give him what he deserved; and we thought, wouldn't it be funny . . ."

"So we took the gravestone and moved it," Harry interjected. "After all, it was a very small stone—"

"It was not," Victoria argued, pelting him with grass. "It was very heavy indeed."

"I'll witness to that," Fairfield agreed. "At any rate, Harry, all you did was tiptoe about and hush us, while Vic and I did all the work."

Phillipe tried to picture it—the serious young earl, the arrogant future duke, and the delicate-looking young woman dragging a headstone from the churchyard, and the image set his blue eyes dancing, and the dimples beneath his sharp cheekbones deepened.

"I cannot believe that you went into a church-yard and stole a gravestone," he said, shaking his head. "What if you had been seen?"

Harry took umbrage. "You needn't make it sound so . . . so . . ."

"Terrible?" Phillipe suggested.

"There it is," Harry answered with a chuckle. "We are terrible, indeed."

He sounded not the least ashamed, and Victoria laughed.

"The odd thing is," Fairfield confessed, "as silly and childish as it sounds now, at the time it seemed the funniest thing in the world. I've never done such a thing in all my life."

"I've done far too many such things," Victoria admitted with a rueful smile. "That's why I was sent here. Cousin Abigail was supposed to teach me some fine manners, and Lavinia was supposed to influence me with her ladylike ways."

"They're failing miserably, thank God," Harry announced, holding up the empty wine bottle to

115

the light and peering sadly at the few remaining drops.

"Go to hell, Harry," she answered in a good-natured tone. "I shall be so proper tonight that everybody will fall over in shock."

"Please, don't even consider such a thing," Phillipe implored, flashing a white grin at her. "How dull things would be if you decided to behave."

Victoria thought there had never been such a beautiful day, and wondered why she had ever wanted to go home.

"This has been the jolliest summer I've ever had," Fairfield announced, echoing her thoughts. "I have never laughed so much in my life."

Harry struggled to his feet. "We've lolled long enough. Don't you need hours to prepare for a ball, Vic?"

"How the devil would I know? I've never been to a ball before, and I likely never will again."

Harry rolled his eyes in exasperation. "Do you even know what you're wearing?"

Victoria stood and began dusting the grass from her skirt. "Something that Lavinia has cast off, I shouldn't wonder. I'm letting Mary, the upstairs maid, decide."

"What a trusting soul she is," Harry remarked to Phillipe and Johnathon. "Can you imagine Lavinia trusting the maid to pick out her dress?"

Victoria blushed as the three men laughed. She noticed that Phillipe seemed especially amused, and her heart sank a little. *Probably comparing me to Lavinia*, she thought, *and thinking what an uncouth little bumbler I am*. For a minute she wished with all her heart that she were a lady, poised and elegant, languishing her days away over her petit-point and Italian lessons.

Phillipe was comparing her to her cousin, but not in the way she thought. He was thinking how honest and unspoiled she was, and how he laughed in her company, and he was thinking of how Lavinia had been fretting about her ball, and her gown, and what jewels she would wear, and what flowers should garland the ballroom, and if the musicians would arrive from London early enough, until he thought he would go mad.

He watched as Victoria untied her horse, laying her cheek against the animal's muzzle, speaking softly to the mare in her soft, husky voice. Harry and Johnathon were mounting their steeds, arguing about which was the better animal.

"Leave off your bickering," Victoria ordered, "and race to the bridge."

"Done," Fairfield agreed, and the two nobleman set off, their horses' hooves kicking up clouds of dust from the road.

Victoria looked nervously at Phillipe as he rose to his feet and walked towards her across the clearing. He looked very different today, divested of his fine coat, his white shirt unfastened at the throat, his dark hair tousled by the day's ride. She was very aware of his height and strength, and the graceful line of his well-muscled body.

She mounted her mare hastily, avoiding his clear blue gaze as he stood next to her, and gathered the reins in her hand.

"Please, Victoria," he implored swiftly. "One moment."

Surprised at his gentle tone, she looked down from the height of her horse. Her green eyes fastened on the finely chiseled features of his aristocratic face, and he smiled at her cautious expression.

"I owe you a great apology, mademoiselle," he said simply. "I misjudged you, and I regret it. I have treated you very rudely, and wrongly. In truth, you are as sweet as springtime, and I cannot remember a day that I have enjoyed more." He laid his hand gently over hers, the emerald on his finger sparkling in the sun, and the soft touch was as intoxicating to her as the heated embrace of the day before.

Phillipe looked up at her, his expression open and tender. "Am I forgiven?"

Victoria searched his eyes, and saw only the truth. She looked down at the hand covering her own, and wondered at the heat that his touch sent through her body.

"Of course, you bloody booby," she answered, the soft laughter in her voice covering her nervousness. "Forgiven."

He gave her a smile so sweet and bright that she shivered despite the sunlight that streamed over her. Unthinking, she lifted her hand, her fingers moving to his cheek as if possessed of their own will.

Phillipe turned his face into the softness of her palm and pressed his lips silkily against the feather-soft skin.

Victoria was shaken at the dark heat that raced through her body, and pulled her hand away.

For a moment they were still, the only sound the hum of the bees and the warble of birdsong, their eyes locked together.

Victoria wondered if he could hear the beating of her heart as it thumped wildly against the tight bodice of her riding habit.

Phillipe stood in silence, hot desire plainly written on his face, seeing his feelings reflected in Victoria's honest, open countenance.

She took a deep breath. "Shall we go, monsieur?" she asked lightly, trying to control the slight tremble in her voice.

Phillipe turned towards his horse. "As you wish, sweet Victoria," he answered, and the careless endearment caused her heart to race anew.

"I wish that I didn't have to go to Lavinia's ball tonight," she exclaimed suddenly, trying to fill the silence with her chatter. "I'm sure I'll be perfectly miserable."

Phillipe swung his long leg easily over his horse's back and laughed at her discontented expression.

"Shall I tell you something?" he asked. "*En secret*, of course. I shall be perfectly miserable too. I despise that sort of thing."

Victoria sent him a warm smile as they moved towards the road. The brilliant sunlight and green fields seemed brighter and sweeter than they had before, and she breathed the scent of summer joyously.

"Let's race," she suggested, looking down at the empty road before her, and her heart sang as she kicked her horse to a gallop and the hooves thundered on the road beneath her.

Chapter Seven

"Almost done, miss," Mary announced, adding a final hairpin and stepping back to admire her work. She smiled at Victoria, her round face glowing with pleasure. "There—what do you think?"

"It's hard to believe it's me," Victoria admitted, staring into the gilt-framed mirror. She didn't look at all like the girl who had sprawled in the grass earlier that day. A stranger stared back at her from the mirror.

Mary had done well, she thought. She had dressed Victoria's hair in the fashionable *chiens cochants* style, drawn high and puffed off of the forehead, gathered into a shining twist in the back, with a cascade of ringlets hanging over one shoulder.

Lavinia's cast-off gown was a dream of a

dress, cut very low in the bosom and off the shoulders, the tight waist plunging to deep points in front and back, the sleeves tight to the elbow and then dripping with shining white lace over her slender forearms.

The fabric was white silk, as light as a feather and ethereal as smoke, with a pattern of roses and vines embroidered over it all in sparking gold thread. The skirt moved like a cloud in the wind, full and swirling, held out by eight layers of gossamer petticoats that rustled like leaves when she moved.

For the first time in her life, Victoria thought she was beautiful, and her cheeks glowed with excitement, her eyes were wide and sparkling.

"It doesn't look like me," Victoria repeated. "Oh, Mary, I don't look like a damned Irish setter. I look like a lady."

"As long as you don't open your mouth, you do," Mary agreed, her dark eyes shining with delight. She laughed as Victoria danced around the room, delighting in the motion of the full skirt and the way the gold threads sparkled in the candlelight.

"You look like our little Sally showing off a new Sunday dress," Mary scolded.

Victoria made a prim face at the mirror and said, "Now I look like Lavinia." The sight of the décolletage once more unnerved her, "Oh Mary, it's too low! I feel like I'm in the bath."

Mary sighed. "Oh, miss, let's not go through that again. This is a ball gown, and that's how they're made, that's what."

"Are you sure? I am so afraid of looking silly."
Especially in front of Phillipe, she added silently.
She wondered what he would think when he
saw her, if he would find her beautiful.

Mary was holding out a white box tied with
yellow ribbons.

"This was sent up earlier, miss."

Victoria seized it as eagerly as a child and
opened the note that lay beneath the ribbons,
unfolding the thick white paper.

" 'To the dearest and most jolly of friends, a
small token of regard, and hopes that your first
ball will bring you happiness.' It's from Harry
and Johnathon," Victoria cried. "What can it be,
Mary?"

"I'm not saying," Mary answered primly, but
Victoria already had the box open and was sigh-
ing with delight.

A confection of cream roses, lace, and gold
ribbons lay on the a bed of damp moss. It was
as enchanting and sweet as a butterfly's wing,
and Victoria laughed with pleasure as she lifted
the beribboned frippery out of the box, its gold
ribbons trailing airily.

"It's beautiful," Victoria pronounced. "What
is it?"

"It's for your hair, miss," Mary explained, "because you haven't any plumes or jewels." She
held the nosegay to the side of Victoria's head,
demonstrating. "Like so . . . and there should
be something else in there, if you don't trample
it."

Victoria rescued the discarded box and

pulled out a fan. Its sticks were carved of ivory, as delicate as lace, and the silk covering was painted with a pattern of golden roses, sprinkled with brilliants that sparkled like dewdrops.

"Oh, God, I'm happy," she cried. "Never mind the ball, Mary, I think I'll just sit in front of the mirror and wave my fan at myself."

Mary giggled, steering Victoria back to the dressing table, where she began pinning the roses and ribbons on the side of the thick red curls, so that the sparkling ribbons trailed through the cascade of ringlets.

"I'm glad I don't have plumes and jewels. This is much nicer, isn't it, Mary?"

Mary gave the confection a sharp tug, testing the hairpins. "Done. Now, if you remember to watch your language, nobody would ever know that you're not a princess. You'd better get it moving, miss, and you just remember, you're as beautiful as any lady in there."

Victoria threw her arms around Mary, hugging her close. "Whatever would I do without you, Mary? You're the only girl that's ever been my friend, and it will break my heart to leave you at the end of the summer."

Mary blushed and hung her head, pleased and embarrassed. "It will break my heart to see you go, and that's a fact, miss. Life has been much better for me since you came. Now leave off and get out of here before you make yourself late. I've got extra work tonight, with all the guests."

Victoria sailed to the door, her heart racing with excitement. "Just wait, Mary, you'll never believe how proper and elegant I'm going to be."

Mary folded her small hands over her spotless apron and smiled knowingly. "I'd wish you luck with your Frenchman, miss, but I don't think you'll need it. He'd have to be blind not to notice you tonight."

The Harrington ballroom was a glittering tableau of sparkling candelabra, swags of lush summer flowers and ivy, faceted crystal and gleaming silver, and Victoria caught her breath in delight.

The ceiling soared two stories high, shining with the light of six enormous chandeliers, and the sparkling light was reflected off the elaborately carved moldings that curved their gilded way around every possible corner, window, and doorway.

All along the length of the great room, tall French doorways opened onto the terrace, showing the moonlit green lawns and flagstone paths of the garden. The warm, sweetly scented air of the June night filled the room, refreshing the throngs of brilliantly attired guests.

Victoria was dazzled by the sight, her eyes drinking in every detail. "It's beautiful," she whispered, her voice trembling with excitement as she clutched the plum brocade sleeve of Harry's frock coat.

"Don't wrinkle me," he ordered, beaming at his bemused companion. "My valet is cross enough."

Victoria pointed at the musicians who were filing into an alcoved balcony above the room, identical in their pale blue velvet coats and white wigs.

"Look at them, Harry, look, Johnathon—I've never heard a full orchestra before, only Miss Eagen on the church organ."

"Perish the thought," Harry muttered.

Johnathon smiled indulgently, patting the slender hand that clutched his sleeve. "You're in for a real treat tonight, Vic. I heard them rehearsing earlier, and they're very good. Listen . . ."

Victoria stood spellbound as the violinists took up their bows and the sweet sound of the strings filled the air, floating high and clear above the room, the full, rich sounds of the cellos singing beneath them.

Victoria fairly trembled with delight. "Oh, just listen. Isn't it glorious? Have you ever heard such music?"

Harry laughed aloud. "Many times. Calm down, you silly child, it's just a simple polonaise. Do you think you can gather your wits together long enough to dance?"

"Oh, yes," Victoria assured him hastily. "And then I must dance with Johnathon, even if he looks far too grand in his wig. I feel as though I should call him 'Lord Fairfield' tonight." She dropped a mocking curtsy.

"You must do no such thing," Johnathon answered, with his gentle smile. "And I'd be happy to dance to real music for a change. Harry's humming is atrocious, though it does well enough for practice."

Victoria clutched Harry's hand as he led her across the smooth flow of dark green and white patterned marble, her eyes scanning the crowd, looking for Phillipe. Would he dance with her, she wondered? She shivered deliciously at the thought of his hands touching her.

"Don't be nervous, Vic. Just don't trample my new shoes and you'll do fine."

Victoria laughed as they took their place among the dancing guests, with their rainbow-hued finery, powdered hair, and glittering jewels. Harry led her easily in the rhythmic pattern of the polonaise, and she relaxed as she saw the admiring glances that came her way.

She was turning gracefully, enjoying the sweep of her almost gossamer skirts, when she saw Phillipe enter the room.

He was magnificent in an emerald green velvet frock coat, white lace frothing at his collar, his black breeches fitting tightly to his muscled legs.

And at his side, her arm wrapped possessively around his, was Lavinia, cool and aristocratic in ice blue satin and white lace, her elaborate coiffure powdered white, diamonds and sapphires around her swanlike throat and sparkling in her hair.

Victoria felt immediately miserable.

"What on earth is wrong with you?" Harry demanded, following her gaze. "Oh, I see, Lavinia's here. Don't let her bother you, Vic, she'll be far too busy to torment you tonight. And she should be as happy as a lark. I understand she's finally won the marquis's heart, and that he intends to propose tonight. Of course Cecil and Abigail have some reservations, but Lavinia will have what she wants . . . ."

Victoria barely heard the rest of his words. She felt as if her blood had turned to ice. A moment ago, she had been delighting in the crush of the glittering society around her, feeling almost as if she belonged; but suddenly she felt like an outsider, a duck that had stumbled into a flock of peacocks. She struggled to regain her composure.

"Really, Harry? Where did you hear that? Your valet?"

"Don't be rude. Though, to be perfectly honest, I did. I have to admit I'm a little surprised. Not that Lavvy isn't pretty, and certainly she has enough money, and she stands to inherit a good deal more. But Phillipe didn't seem that keen on her, last season in London. At least no more fond of her than he was of the others."

Victoria was beginning to understand why Reverend Finkle lectured so vehemently against the sin of envy. She felt as if it were choking her, consuming her stomach like a biting ulcer, and it took all her effort to keep her tone light and careless.

"What others?" she asked. "Were there lots of them, Harry?"

"Oh, yes, lots of women. They were flocking around him. Ladies are always mad for a handsome new face, especially a titled, unmarried one. Lavinia in particular. Watch your feet, Vic."

Victoria forced her attention back to the steps of the dance.

"And what do you think, Harry? Will Lavinia get her wish and go to France?"

"Who knows? France is awfully unsteady, one hears. Like a keg of gunpowder waiting for a match. Lord Cecil may not want Lavinia going there when things are so unsettled, the General Assembly and all that."

Victoria was less than interested in the state of the French politics. "Do you think your valet is right, Harry? Will the marquis ask for her hand tonight?"

Victoria's eyes followed Phillipe through the crowd. He did not look her way but continued through the throng, Lavinia at his side, stopping to chat with her many friends.

"Turn, Vic. You're not paying attention. As for Phillipe, who knows? He didn't seem to care for her, last season, but he's certainly being very biddable now, where she's concerned. Not at all like he was with the women in London. He didn't seem to have time for any of them. Oh, occasionally a barmaid or a little serving wench for a quick tumble, but—" Harry broke off abruptly at the sight of Victoria's horrified face. "Pardon me, Vic. How indelicate of me. There, the music's stopping. Shall we go rescue Johnathon? It looks as if those horrid Percy sisters are boring him to death, and he's too kind to say so."

Two hours and three glasses of champagne later, Victoria felt much better. Or at least she thought she did. She told herself very sternly that she did. She laughed and flirted recklessly with Harry and Johnathon and their innumerable London acquaintances that flocked to meet her. She dismissed their extravagant compliments with easy laughter, teased them when she felt they needed teasing, rapped them with her fan when they behaved too familiarly, and let them bring her little plates of food and sparkling glasses of champagne.

Harry watched her with pride, Johnathon with bewilderment; and underneath her sparkling bodice, her heart swelled with misery. She felt as brittle as crystal, as lost as a lamb separated from the flock, but she forced herself to smile and chatter about the weather and recklessly accepted every invitation to dance, her satin, gold-buckled shoes clicking carelessly over the shining floors.

She was miserable.

It isn't fair, she thought, *not at all. It's only because Lavinia is rich, and I'm not.* She had never seen Phillipe laughing and high-spirited in Lavinia's company, only impeccably mannered and politely gallant, with his handsome face a closed, unreadable visage.

Perhaps, she thought, *he thinks I'm like a barmaid, a serving girl for a quick tumble*. Even while she blushed at the thought, she was sick with envy, knowing that Lavinia would sleep with him, that he would kiss her and make love to her.

Victoria drew herself up sharply. *Don't think of it*, she told herself firmly. *Think about what this nice young man is saying to you. What in the hell is he saying, anyhow?*

Harry appeared at her side at that moment, his face flushed with drink. "This dance is mine," he shouted happily, whirling Victoria from the arms of her astounded partner.

"Cheer up, Miss Vic," he cried merrily. "You're the most beautiful woman in the room, and you're taking the ton by storm!"

"You're drunk, Harry, and making a fool out of me," she scolded, laughing despite herself. Harry pulled her into the dance, and they were enveloped in the glittering, perfumed crowd.

Lavinia floated by in Phillipe's arms, her oval face looking adoringly up at him, pink-cheeked and delicate. Phillipe looked briefly towards Victoria, his expression a careful blank, as though she were a stranger.

Desperate that he not know how miserable she was, Victoria moved closer to Harry and tilted her head back flirtatiously.

131

Amy Elizabeth Saunders

"Am I pretty, Harry? Tell me again."

Harry lifted his brows, momentarily surprised by this new, coquettish Victoria.

"My darling girl," he exclaimed with pleasure, "I shall sing your praises all evening, if you'd finally like to listen. And tomorrow too, if you like. Come drink champagne with me, and let me introduce you around."

"Of course, Harry," she murmured. She smiled up at him, unaware of how completely devastating the effect was, and let him lead her from the floor.

"Look, Lavvy—do you see that hoyden, Miss Larkin? You'd think that she was *somebody*, the way those stupid men are following her about." Rosamund covered her rouged mouth with her fan as she spoke, her dark eyes glinting with mischief.

"I'm trying not to look," Lavinia snapped. "She really makes me quite ill. I suppose she thinks that one of them will marry her, but they won't, you know. They'll just take what they want and be on their way. She does lend herself to that sort of thing. Farm girls are like that. They're given to fits of lust, like animals."

Rosamund giggled. "How wicked, Lavvy. Do you really think that she . . . does?"

Lavinia tossed her carefully arranged curls, diamonds sparkling. "Don't be an idiot, if you can help it, Ros. Of course she would. Look at how she's flaunting herself. And that swine Harry is practically drooling in her bosom."

132

"Isn't that your dress from last season, Lavvy? I don't remember it fitting you like that," Rosamund remarked cattily with a pointed look at Lavinia's meager bosom.

Lavinia bristled, and she and Rosamund glared at each other.

"There's a good deal more to interesting a man than simply displaying one's overstuffed bodice," Lavinia said, her nostrils flaring with scorn.

"Oh, really?" Rosamund drawled, fanning herself languidly. "Then pray don't look across the room now, Lavinia, because your handsome marquis is over there, and he's looking at your little cousin as if she's something good to eat."

Phillipe watched Victoria, trying to ignore the jealous feeling that nagged at him. She was surrounded by a crowd of society's most eligible young bachelors, her face alight with merriment, or champagne, he thought. Behind her, Harry leaned heavily on her chair, gazing down at the white swell of her cleavage as he drank thirstily from a crystal glass. Phillipe didn't care for the lustful expression on the florid face, and he felt his temper rising.

Victoria seemed completely oblivious to the interest her friend was showing in her well-exposed breasts, and was listening to Fairfield, who sat contentedly at her side, speaking to the neighboring squire's son.

"She sits a horse as well as you, Lawrence, and can outrun both Harry and me."

"Really?" the young man answered with obvious approval, and turned to Victoria, "Then I shall have to challenge you to a race. Will you be staying long, Miss Larkin?"

"All summer," Victoria answered recklessly. "And thank you, I accept your challenge." How kind everyone was being, she thought, and what a nice invention champagne was.

She held up her glass, watching the light sparkle through the faceted crystal.

"D'you want more, Vic?" Harry asked, his voice slightly thickened.

"No, and I don't think you do either, Harry. I'm feeling a little light-headed, and I've promised far too many dances to risk looking like a fool."

"Then perhaps I should claim mine now," Phillipe suggested, stepping into the circle of admirers that surrounded the slender girl, "before you've promised all your dances away."

He took her hand and pulled her to her feet, leading her almost roughly on to the dance floor. Victoria shot him an offended look as the first sparkling notes of the minuet sounded.

Phillipe looked down at her as their hands touched in the opening steps of the dance. "Well," he said, and Victoria thought his voice sounded cynical, "you have certainly charmed the London crowd *tout à fait*, haven't you?"

"I've no idea," she replied crossly, "and I don't speak French. But I do think that it was rather rude of you to haul me out here as if I were a sack of potatoes."

"A sack of potatoes," Phillipe repeated, smiling despite her angry tone. "What a way you have with words."

Victoria tried not to smile back but couldn't help herself. "You did," she insisted. "Look at Harry. He looks quite put out."

"He looks drunk," Phillipe said bluntly. His blue eyes searched her glowing face, her glittering green eyes. "And you look a little lightheaded, yourself, mademoiselle."

"So what?" Victoria asked carelessly. "I've seen my brothers much drunker, and they haven't died from it."

Phillipe laughed aloud at her candor. "How shocking of you to say so. You must remember not to say such things to the good aristocracy of London. It would not be *comme il faut*, not done, you see. And remember, please," he added seriously, "that Harry is not one of your brothers. You should have a care."

Victoria tilted her head and smiled mischievously up at him as she dipped a graceful curtsy. "Do you honestly think I couldn't defend myself?"

"You may be able to," he agreed, bowing in perfect rhythm to the dulcet tones of the minuet. "I must admit that you can deliver a nasty blow."

Victoria laughed, unashamed.

"All jesting aside, Victoria; be careful around drunken men. Silly flirtations can become ugly scenes, and you don't want one of your innumerable brothers to fight a duel in your honor, do you? I should be very put out if I ever had to fight a duel for my sister."

"Do you have a sister?" Victoria asked curiously. "Where is she?"

"At Versailles, ordering more new gowns than she could wear in a year. She is what you English call a lady-in-waiting, I think. She attends the queen."

Victoria digested that. It reminded her of the great gulf dividing them. She had brothers who drank at the Broken Bow, he had a sister who was an intimate of Marie-Antoinette.

"Harry tells me that things are quite dangerous in France. Is that true?"

Phillipe's face darkened. "It may be. It's hard to say. One hears so many rumors. The government has called together a General Assembly, something like your Parliament. I hope that will put everything to rights. The rich are ridiculously rich, and the poor are so damnably poor. There is much injustice in France."

Victoria saw the worry plainly in his eyes. "Aren't you worried about your sister, Phillipe? You must love her dearly."

He smiled, his dimples deepening. "Christianna? She's the most spoiled, selfish little minx I've ever had the misfortune to meet. And yes, I love her dearly."

Victoria laughed at his contradictory answer. "She can't be that bad."

His hand clasped hers tightly as she moved in a graceful circle.

"But she is," he protested. "You see, our parents died when she was just a baby. It was an epidemic, I'm not sure of the English word. A sweating sickness. Christianna was so little, and so pretty, that we all spoiled her abominably after that. The nurses, the servants, myself. We could deny her nothing. Even my grandfather, when he came to the château, which was not often. He treated her like a spoiled lap dog."

Victoria saw the dislike on his face when he spoke of his grandfather. "So you had nobody? Just servants?"

Phillipe smiled at the compassion in her voice. "It was not that bad," he lied. "I had Christianna, and the château. They were enough. They are my only true, constant loves."

He stopped abruptly, surprised at himself for revealing so much. It wasn't like him.

Victoria regarded him solemnly, her green eyes dark. "My mother died," she confessed, "when I was nine. So you see, we have a pain in common."

Phillipe smiled, changing the subject. "What funny expressions you use. 'A pain in common.'"

Victoria laughed at herself, truly happy for the first time that night. How nice he was when he was happy and joking. She thought of how boyish and carefree he had seemed earlier that day, riding through the gentle countryside. Unbidden, the image entered her mind of his mouth, warm and soft, pressed against the skin of her palm.

She blushed and, glancing up at Phillipe, saw

137

a knowing smile on his mouth. He bowed over her hand as the dance ended, and she felt his warm breath tickle her skin. His eyes rose to meet hers, sparkling with mischief, and something more.

Victoria averted her eyes hastily as a shiver of pleasure ran up her spine. "There is Lavinia," she said quickly, "and she looks very cross. You should go speak to her."

His dark brows lifted. "But I'm speaking to you. Are you so anxious to be rid of my company, to return to your new admirers? Is my company so dull?"

Victoria's cheeks flushed even pinker, but she met his eyes, directly and honestly.

"No, monsieur," she answered, and her voice was so low that Phillipe had to lean forward to hear her answer. "To be honest, I like your company very well. Too well. It makes me very . . . uneasy. I've no desire to make a fool of myself, getting all starry-eyed about a man whose heart belongs to another."

Victoria hung her head, aghast at her own bluntness. *I should never have touched that champagne*, she thought. *I should have listened to Mary, and acted as if he didn't exist.*

"Victoria," he said firmly, and lifted her chin with a gentle hand. She met his clear eyes hesitantly, shame burning in her cheeks. All around them, people were leaving the floor, talking, laughing; but she saw nothing but his clear blue eyes, heard nothing but his gentle, melodious voice.

"Listen to me, *chéri*, and listen well. Lavinia does not have my heart. I may dance attendance on her, I may walk by her side, I may, for reasons of my own, marry her. But she does not have my heart."

Victoria was shocked, as much by the fierce intensity in his eyes as by the words he spoke. The hand that held her chin seemed to burn her flesh, and she was painfully aware of his closeness, the heat of his breath, the faint, spicy smell of sandalwood that rose from his velvet coat.

"I don't understand," she whispered.

"*C'est fini.* We need not speak of it again." The cool, unreadable mask that she had begun to dread descended over his features, and his hand dropped from her face.

Harry's exuberant voice broke in, startling Victoria out of her reverie.

"I say, Phillipe, you've kept Vic to yourself long enough. It's time to give another fellow a chance."

Victoria allowed Harry to take her hands and lead her back into the powdered, perfumed throng, but the ball had lost its charm for Victoria. She mechanically followed Harry's unsteady lead in the dance, her thoughts buzzing in her head like a swarm of bees.

If Phillipe did not love Lavinia, why would he marry her? It made no sense. *And you*, she told herself angrily, *you're stupid for caring*.

Her head was aching, a tight, painful throb; the lively air that the instruments sang was jangling her nerves; and would Harry never shut up? His babble was buzzing in her ears, strings of words that meant nothing. "London," he buzzed; " . . . beautiful . . . St. James Square . . . the King's Theatre . . ."

Victoria nodded mechanically, her eyes far away across the room where Lavinia was laughing at something Phillipe said, reaching out to touch his shoulder with a possessive gesture that broke Victoria's heart. Next to them, Rosamund, resplendent in deep pink and rubies, caught Victoria's eye and smiled, a knowing, pitying smile, a look of pleased condescension in her dark eyes.

Victoria wondered in horror if her feelings were so obvious, if everyone knew, if Lavinia was laughing. The swirling patterns of the dancers around her made her head spin, and she tried to focus on Harry's babble.

She seized on the end of his sentence like a cat pounces on an unsuspecting mouse. "Outside? Of course, what a splendid idea, Harry. I should love to go outside, and the sooner the better. Right now."

Harry's broad face went still with shock, and then a brilliant grin shone across it.

"Magnificent," he breathed, and he grasped her arm tightly through his, leading her hurriedly through the French doors and into the cool, moonlit gardens.

Chapter Eight

Victoria breathed the cool air in relief as she walked at Harry's side, their feet crunching over the graveled path. The sounds of the crowd and the music grew fainter, the sparkling lights farther away.

Victoria saw a stone bench in a leafy alcove and sank weakly onto the cool, hard surface with a sigh. Harry staggered a little as he collapsed beside her.

"Please, Vic," he whispered, his voice thick. "When?"

"When what, Harry?" Her eyes were blank as they turned to him. "I'm sorry, Harry, I really wasn't listening. When what?"

"London," he crowed. "When will you come? You'll be a smashing success, I'll be the envy of everyone. Can you see it, Vic?" He lifted a heavy hand to her bare shoulder, and Victoria sighed in exasperation as she pushed it away.

"Oh, Harry! Will you never stop? London, indeed. And how would I live in London? You know damned well that I haven't a penny." Victoria rolled her eyes towards the star-sprinkled sky, wondering at the apparent idiocy of men, with the exception of her own brothers.

Harry's drunken face brightened. There it was, just as he'd thought. It was always a matter of price, with girls. And such a girl. He had almost choked on the dance floor when he had asked her, for the hundredth time, to come to London, to forget her silly farm, to be his, and she had nodded, her green eyes bright and dreamy, and then followed him into the garden so decisively, no coyness or delaying.

He gazed at her in rapture—that hair, he thought drunkenly, all that wonderful hair. And that glowing skin, and those beautiful white breasts, half exposed in her shimmering ballgown.

He pulled her suddenly to him, crushing her breasts against the stiff embroidered front of his vest, his burly arms tightening across her back.

"I'll give you money, Vic," he whispered hotly, and she pulled her face away from the brandy-soaked scent of his breath. "I'll buy you a house, if you wish, a carriage, pretty clothes . . . ."

Victoria was horrified as his mouth sought hers, damp and eager, and she pushed him away, striking his shoulder forcefully with the heel of her hand.

"Damn you, Harry! You're drunker than I thought. Leave off!"

To her surprise, Harry merely laughed. "Oh, Vic," he slurred, "I didn't take you for a tease. You've been flirting with me all night, you led me out here. Tell me what you want."

Victoria pushed at his chest, fury rising in her chest. "I want you to turn me loose, you booby. Good God, Harry, have you lost your mind?"

She was struggling in earnest now, trying to escape Harry's suffocating grip. She tried to stand, but he held her tightly. She heard her skirt tearing and kicked at him, trying to dislodge him from her side, where his weight was settled on the white silk of her gown.

She pulled her head back as Harry tried to kiss her again, and she felt her teeth scrape her lip beneath the force. She swore furiously, trying to work her arms loose from where they were trapped between them, but Harry was undaunted. Victoria began to panic, kicking at his shin, the heel of her shoe catching in the lace of her cumbersome petticoats.

She felt his heavy hand fumbling at her breast, his rings scratching her skin.

"Damn it, Harry, don't do this, please," she begged, trying to push at his hands, clawing at them. She shuddered at his drunken laugh as her struggles upset their balance.

She tumbled to the ground beneath his weight, the hard edge of the stone bench hitting her shoulder with a sharp pain. Her breath left her with a sickening gasp as she hit the ground, Harry's bulk pressing on top of her.

He seemed oblivious to her terror, and Victoria cried out as she felt him fumbling at her skirts. She fought blindly as she felt the fabric of her bodice give way, felt the cool night air on her breasts and legs.

She writhed wildly, hot tears of fear and fury flooding down her cheeks, felt his mouth, his teeth sharp against her lip. She worked a hand loose and struck blindly at his face, over and over.

"God damn you, Harry! Damn you, get off! Oh God, Harry, please, please, leave me alone . . ."

And suddenly he was gone. There was the sickening crack of a fist against flesh, and the sound of breaking branches as Harry spun drunkenly into the hedge. Relief rushed through Victoria as she saw Phillipe standing above her, his stark profile silhouetted against the dark sky.

Victoria pushed herself to a sitting position, her hands shaking wildly as she tried to gather the torn fabric of her bodice over her breasts.

Through her hot tears, she saw Fairfield, his youthful face whiter than his wig, bent over Harry's inert form.

"Good God, Victoria," he asked her shakily,

"are you all right?" He looked hurriedly away from her disheveled clothing, her pale legs.

Trembling, she nodded, looking down at the grass.

"Get that drunken pup out of here before I kill him," the marquis ordered, his voice cold with rage.

"I think you may already have," Johnathon answered anxiously, shaking his unconscious friend. "Harry . . . Harry, wake up, you jackass."

Harry moaned as Johnathon pulled him heavily to his feet, staggering beneath the weight. Victoria turned her head away as she saw the dark glint of blood on Harry's face.

"Take him in the back," Phillipe ordered, "and if you're seen, say that he fell. He's drunk enough; you'll be believed."

With an anxious look at Victoria, Fairfield began steering his inebriated friend towards the house.

"Will you be all right, Vic?" He called back uncertainly.

The marquis's voice shook Victoria like a clap of thunder. "Of course she'll be all right, you idiot. Get that souse out of here before there's a scandal."

Fairfield hurried to obey, Harry staggering heavily at his side.

Phillipe knelt down and raised Victoria's face to the moonlight. Fury was evident in every taut line of his face, and his eyes glittered like blue ice. Victoria closed her eyes against the sight and tried to still the shaking sobs that were rising in her throat.

His fingers were examining her face gently. "Are you hurt?" he asked.

Ignoring the throbbing pain in her shoulder and her scraped mouth, she shook her head, trying to ignore the sick feeling in her stomach, the way her limbs were shaking.

"No," she managed to choke out. "Just frightened."

"You're lucky," Phillipe told her, the sharpness of his voice contrasting with the gentle touch of his fingers on her face. Glancing down, he saw the bare skin of her white thighs glowing in the moonlight. He pulled her skirts down to cover her legs, and Victoria cringed at the bitter anger in his face.

"Can you stand?" he asked, his voice harsh.

Victoria wiped the tears from her eyes and drew a deep, shaking breath.

"Of course," she lied. She glanced up at Phillipe, and the sight of his stern, hard face made her want to cry anew.

"Go away. Please, just go away. You were right, and I was wrong, and Harry was awful. Drunk and horrible. And I couldn't defend myself, and I'm sorry."

"Don't be stupid," Phillipe ordered shortly. "It isn't your fault that Harry was drunk and behaved like a swine. Let me help you up." He grasped her arms firmly, and Victoria rose unsteadily to her knees. The torn silk and lace at her breast fell open, and Phillipe averted his eyes from the sight of her round, white breasts. Alarmed by the surge of desire that seized him, he pulled her to her feet, almost rough in his haste.

"Cover yourself, mademoiselle," he said, turning his back abruptly. "And in the future, try to remember that when a man asks you to join him in a secluded corner at night, he's usually not interested in conversation."

Victoria swayed on her shaking legs. She felt sick with shame, and her shoulder ached where Harry had tumbled her to the ground. She wanted to go home, away from these people. And Phillipe was so angry.

She stared at his back, struggling for words as she saw the tense line of his shoulders, the elegant emerald-colored bow that tied his thick black hair, the snug fit of the black breeches along his long legs, the shining buttons that fastened them at his knees.

From far away, she could hear the violins singing sweetly and innocently through the night air, and she wondered at this beautiful night that had turned so swiftly into a nightmare. Unhappiness welled up inside her, and for the first time in her life, Victoria thought she might faint.

Curious at her silence, and with his heated blood now safely under control, Phillipe turned around just as Victoria began to collapse towards the grass, her hair spilling over her face.

His strong arms caught her firmly, pulling her against his chest, a soft hand at the back of her neck. She fell against him, trying to fight the roaring in her ears, the red-black darkness that was pulling her down.

She heard Phillipe's voice as if through a fog, murmuring softly against her hair. She didn't understand the foreign words, but the tender, comforting sounds fell soothingly on her ears, and gradually the darkness subsided and her senses began to focus.

She was acutely aware of the feeling of her cheek pressed against the fine lawn of Phillipe's shirt front, the warm scent of his skin beneath the soft fabric, the comforting rhythm of his heartbeat, and the soft, spicy scent of sandalwood that clung to his velvet coat.

She felt his warm hands moving gently through her tangled hair, stroking her neck soothingly, gently fondling the silky curls that Mary had arranged so carefully only a few hours before. At the thought of Mary, who had held such high hopes for Victoria's first night amongst the fashionable nobility, and who would be so disappointed when she discovered the disastrous reality, Victoria gave in to a fresh flood of tears, shaking in Phillipe's arms.

"Oh, Victoria," he whispered. "Don't cry, *petite*. I should have stopped you when I first saw you leaving, but I thought you were trying to anger me, to make me jealous." And so she had, he added silently, and a good thing too, or the ugly scene he had interrupted might have gone too far. His arms tightened around the slender girl in his arms as he remembered the sight of Harry pawing her.

Victoria leaned into the warmth of the embrace, and a slow, soothing languor began to move through her body. She wondered at the feeling of safety and comfort that she felt, and closed her eyes, abandoning herself to the soft warmth, and gradually her tears subsided.

"You see?" Phillipe asked softly as he felt her trembling ease. "Everything will be well. We can take you in the back door, and you can reach your room without being seen."

Victoria nodded, stepping back and trying to arrange her torn gown, despite her shaking hands. "But what shall I tell Cousin Abigail?" she asked pathetically. "She's certain to notice that I'm missing and ask me about it."

Phillipe was hastily removing his coat, and he settled it around her bare shoulders, covering the all too intoxicating sight of her exposed skin. "You will tell her that you drank too much champagne and went to your room with a headache." He placed his arm around her slender waist, trying to ignore the exposed skin where the stitches had given way, and the soft warmth of it against his hand, and began guiding her to the path that led to the back of the house.

Damn Winston, he thought furiously, *he had gone too far. If it was not certain to cause a scandal and make everyone miserable, I would call him out*. He glanced down at Victoria, and his temper increased at the sight of her unusually pale face and the teardrops that still trembled on her thick lashes. He tried not to think about the closeness of her, the sight of her ripe, round breasts above the ripped lace of her exposed chemise, the clean soft scent of her hair and the way it felt in his hands.

"You should never have come here," he said aloud, and the roughness of his voice startled Victoria. "You don't belong amongst these *cynique* aristocrats, these spoiled pups. You are far too innocent for their jaded little games, and nobody bothered telling you the rules. They will always judge you by their own standards, they will think you are seeking to better yourself, honorably or not. Every man who spoke kindly to you tonight, who danced with you and flattered you, saw you as a potential mistress, a new toy. If you stay, you will either be hurt or completely corrupted and spoiled. I think you were much safer on your little farm, *petite* Victoria, with your innumerable brothers to protect you."

Victoria stopped abruptly in the path and a wave of homesickness washed over her. She thought with longing of the old, cluttered house, and the fresh green fields, and her absentminded father, and her noisy, troublesome brothers.

"I want to go home," she whispered. "You're right, I shouldn't be here, and I said so from the beginning." She looked around at the dark, lush gardens and over at the great mansion, ablaze with sparkling lights, noisy with the distant sounds of the merry guests.

"I hate all this. It's stupid, and I hate all these people. I want to see Jamie, and Gareth, and even Geoffery, for all that he's a little monster. I'd even be happy to see Reverend Finkle," she confessed with a hard catch in her voice. "Do you know that once, Jamie and Stewart and I joined the church choir and sang badly on purpose just to make poor Reverend Finkle unhappy and see him turn red and wave his arms about? Oh, and now I'm so sorry. I wish I could go home."

To Victoria's great dismay, tears began flooding her eyes again, and she dashed them away angrily with the back of her hand.

Somehow she was in Phillipe's arms again, and he was wiping her tears from her hot face, and she was pressing her face into his shirt-front.

"Don't cry," he whispered, and his gentle voice made her cry harder. "Please, Victoria."

She felt his lips press softly against her forehead, felt his warm hands on her hair, and a sweetness, a gentle glow filled her at his touch. She shivered lightly and moved closer into his embrace.

Softly, almost hesitantly, his warm kiss touched her forehead again, and then feather light on her damp cheeks. Instinctively, she turned her face towards his, and with a melting, velvet softness their lips met.

For a moment, Phillipe moved his mouth

across the soft fullness of her yielding lips, tasting the sweet, luscious flavor of her unpainted mouth, clean and sweet, like wild strawberries.

He drew back and looked down at her face.

She stared back, her eyes huge and dilated, in innocence and desire, her mouth slightly open, her breaths swift and shaky.

Victoria knew that she had never felt like this in her life. The hot, teasing kiss he had given her on the staircase had shaken her, had aroused her, but it had not been a kiss like this, rich and warm and honey-sweet, moving like wine through her veins.

She gazed in wonder at Phillipe, as if to commit the sight of him to memory—the bright, intense blue of his eyes, the deep shadows that the moonlight cast beneath the high cheekbones, the sharp, almost arrogant shape of his nose and jawline. A gentle breeze moved a strand of dark hair across his forehead, and Victoria reached up to brush it back. The simple intimacy of the gesture caused her heart to race with joy, and in that moment she loved him, fiercely, and with all her honest heart.

Phillipe's hand moved to her neck, and he pulled her face towards his again. He traced the outline of her mouth with gentle kisses and then with the soft heat of his tongue.

Heat rushed through her veins, flooding her body with a sweet, warm hunger, and her hands moved to Phillipe's dark hair, the heavy silk of it moving through her fingers as she pulled his mouth closer to her own. She moaned softly as she felt the satin of his tongue against her own and the warmth of his hands moving along her waist, pulling her closer to the hard length of his muscled body.

For a moment, their lips parted, and she felt his breath mingling with hers, quick and hot.

"Sweet," he whispered. "So sweet, Victoria."

His words sent thrills chasing through her, his voice husky and dark with desire. He buried his mouth in the tender hollow of skin behind her ear and tightened his grip as she cried out softly at the sensation. She felt as if she were floating, lost in a dream.

She wanted to cry with the sweetness of it, feeling Phillipe's lips against her neck trailing across her collarbone. His ragged sigh sounded like a benediction, like a gift, the sweetest sound she had ever heard.

He bent his head to the soft curves of her breasts, rubbing his cheek against the satin curves, inhaling the soft fragrance of her body.

Victoria's back arched against the strength of his arm as she felt the wet heat of his tongue through the rough, torn lace that covered her aching nipples. He brushed the fabric easily aside and let his tongue travel slowly over each dusky rose-colored bud, before he closed his lips over one and sucked so gently that she almost fainted at the poignant rapture of it.

He was pulling her hips to his, and she rocked against him, instinctively wanting him closer. She had no maidenly thoughts of modesty. Her hands pulled him towards her hungrily, lost in the honey-sweet call of their need for each other.

Phillipe pushed away the torn lace that covered her shoulders, and his hands moved softly over the slender line of her back. He lifted his head from the silken skin of her breasts and was about to take her mouth again when he saw the bruise on her shoulder, dark and ugly against the pale skin, and he froze.

His hands were on her shoulders, and with the greatest difficulty he stepped back, away from her eager body, away from her hungry eyes that glowed like stars at him.

Good God, St. Sebastien, he thought bitterly. *You are your grandfather's creature, aren't you? You rescue an innocent from a lecherous drunk and dry her tears so that you can ravish her yourself. And all on the same night that you intend to ask her cousin to marry you, so that you can line your pockets with gold.*

"Make yourself decent, mademoiselle." The words did not come easily to him. His hands dropped from her shoulders, and he looked away from her disbelieving eyes.

Victoria felt as if someone had dashed a bucket of cold water on her. Her heart was beating wildly, and she felt more confused than she had ever been. Frantically, she tried to rearrange her dress, shame burning in her cheeks as she thought how wantonly she had behaved. Was that it? Was that what had disgusted him, caused him to turn away from her and his voice to turn to ice?

"Please, Phillipe," she whispered, her voice plaintive in the dark night, trembling with passion and confusion. "What did I do?"

Phillipe turned back to her, his face settled into its usual cool, unfathomable expression. The only sign of his previous passion was his dark hair, loosened from its beribboned queue and hanging in disarray over his broad shoulders.

"What did you do, kitten? All too much, I'm afraid. I told you that you didn't know the rules of the game. You are far too innocent for me to take advantage of your . . . shall we say, eagerness? And I'm not such a swine as to take you in the grass like an animal, when your pretty body still bears the bruises left by the last swine that tried to corrupt you."

Victoria watched as he picked his coat up from the grass where it had fallen. Her head was swimming. She wondered if he would have continued if he hadn't seen the bruises. She wondered if he ever kissed Lavinia like that. No, she decided, her cousin would never behave with such fevered lust. And Phillipe would never treat Lavinia like that, would he? Only a peasant, a meaningless wench. He was no better than Harry, when you came right down to it.

"I understand," she said, her voice low and cold. "Perhaps I'm learning the 'rules of the game,' after all. Damn you, and damn Harry, and damn Lavinia. You bloody aristocrats— we're not real people to you, are we? You

155

wouldn't treat bloody Lavinia like this, would you?"

Phillipe smiled, a bitter, humorless smile. "To my great misfortune, I have no desire to 'treat bloody Lavinia like this.' I wish I did, it would make my marriage so much more pleasant. But I'm sure that Lavinia will not be half so amusing."

"Amusing," Victoria repeated, and the word felt ugly in her mouth. "Is that what I am, monsieur? A toy for Harry to buy, or you to use, as you see fit? And you are twice as bad as he, for Harry was honest, at least, and offered to pay me outright; while you, you kiss my hand and smile at me as if you truly care for me, and make me think I love you."

Phillipe's face paled, he flinched as if she had slapped him.

"Please, Victoria . . ."

"Please be damned! Don't use your pretty voice and your sad eyes on me. I'm not a toy for you to pick up and put down as it amuses you. The next damned time that you start something with me, you'll finish it, by God."

Victoria regretted her hasty words the second she spoke them. And he laughed. He had the nerve to laugh, hard and loud.

"What a terrifying threat," he finally answered, wiping his eyes on the back of his sleeve. "But perhaps you should worry, because the next time I 'start something,' as you so charmingly put it, I probably will finish it. You have no idea how much I long to. I would love to take you in my arms this very moment and make you writhe against me."

Victoria sputtered with fury, trying to find a curse, a word vile enough to wound him, to wipe the dimpled smile from his arrogant face. What had Stewart shouted at Richard last year that had almost caused them to come to blows?

"You can bloody well kiss my ass," she finally managed, her face red with fury. She turned away with what she hoped was icy scorn, satisfied at having the last word.

Phillipe's deep laughter rang out behind her. "That, mademoiselle, is something I shall await with pleasure."

Chapter Nine

"Things are funny around here, no mistake about it," Mary observed suspiciously as she brought Victoria's dinner tray to her room.

Victoria was lying among the rumpled blankets and sheets of her four-poster bed where she had spent most of the day, dressed in an equally rumpled riding habit. She looked at Mary over the top of the book she was reading and tried to assume an indifferent expression.

"Whatever do you mean? I have a nasty headache, Mary. Too much champagne last night, I suppose."

"You and everybody else around here," Mary answered, setting the tray on the little marble-topped table by the windows. "Miss Lavinia is in a real snit today, says she has a 'headache.' Daisy says it's because her Frenchman didn't 'speak' last night, and Lavinia was all ready to announce her engagement. The Frenchman, he has a 'headache' and has been skulking about like an ogre. Lord Fairfield is looking like he lost his best friend, all worried-like. It wouldn't surprise me if he had a 'headache,' too."

Victoria closed her book with a sharp bang and looked at Mary with a resentful glower.

"There was a lot of champagne last night, Mary."

Mary's round face wore a look of disbelief. "And Sir Harry," she went on sagely as if Victoria hadn't spoken, "he was up and gone with the dawn. Left a note saying he had business to attend to in London. Funny sort of business, if you ask me. Things are funny around here," she repeated, "no mistake."

"Perhaps he had a headache, too," Victoria retorted, sounding a good deal more cross than she intended to.

Mary assumed an injured air. "Fine. If you don't want to tell me anything—"

"I don't," Victoria interrupted sharply.

Mary raised her dark brows. "And no appetite? Just look, miss, cook has made the loveliest soup, and the lamb is so tender tonight . . ."

Victoria looked dolefully at the steaming tray.

"And you lumping about in bed all day," Mary added. "And torn ballgowns, and more headaches in the house than I could shake a stick at. Things—"

"Yes, I know. Things are funny around here," Victoria finished in exasperation.

"Of course," Mary added, "I could give you this letter that's in my pocket and see if that didn't cheer you up a little, but perhaps you're too cranky to care."

Victoria sat straight up, pushing her wayward curls from her face. "What letter, Mary? From whom?"

Mary withdrew a folded piece of paper from the pocket of her starched white apron, and offered it to Victoria, whose eyes were fairly crackling with interest.

"Read it yourself," she answered testily. "I don't make a habit of prying into other people's affairs."

"Since when?" Victoria muttered, snatching the paper eagerly and unfolding it.

She knew the instant she saw the heavy, sloping writing that it was from Phillipe, and she held her breath as she read.

Victoria—It is necessary that I speak to you. Meet me at the reflecting pool, at eight. Phillipe.

That was all. No apology, no explanation, not even a proper greeting, Victoria thought. And not "would you," or "if you please," just "meet me," as if he were sure that she would.

"God help me, Mary, what am I to do?" She looked helplessly at Mary, whose brown eyes were alight with curiosity.

"Don't ask me, I didn't read it. What does he want?"

"He doesn't say. He just asks . . . no, he demands, almost, that I meet him in the garden. He doesn't say why. What should I do?"

Mary considered this at some length.

"What you *should* do and what you *will* do are two different things. What you should do is eat your dinner and mind your temper, and ignore that note." Mary heaved a sigh. "But I know you, miss. And I know what you'll do. Wild horses couldn't keep you in your room, so you'd better change your dress and let me do your hair. It looks like something tried to build a nest in it."

Victoria looked at the mirror in alarm. "You're right. Oh, bloody hell, Mary, what shall I wear?"

"Something sweet and demure," Mary answered tartly. "And maybe a proper corset, for a change. They said in the kitchen that some of the gentlemen at the ball last night were taking bets, as to whether you were wearing one or not."

"It's too warm. I can't breathe with those fool things on."

Mary sighed, lifting her small shoulders in a helpless gesture. "Very well, I'll not fight you again. Here, your white dress with the green sash should do. And, miss—don't let Lavinia see you. She'd be in a proper pet if she knew you were off to the garden to meet her beau."

Victoria's eyes narrowed dangerously as she felt the all too familiar stab of envy that pained her every time she heard Lavinia's and Phillipe's names spoken together.

"Lavinia," she snapped, "can go to hell."

Mary raised her brows at the language, but simply smiled and helped Victoria into the white dress, and offered sweetly to do her hair. She prayed with all her heart that the handsome Frenchman would marry Miss Victoria, and that she herself would leave with them, in the exalted position of lady's maid.

The sun was sinking over the wooded hills in a glorious display of rose and gold when Victoria entered the garden, her heart fluttering like a caged bird.

The marquis stood by the reflecting pool, every line of his tall body showing his impatience, a heavy gold timepiece in his hand.

"You're late," he announced abruptly. "I was beginning to think you weren't coming."

"I almost didn't," Victoria admitted, annoyed at the faint tremor in her voice. "Your note was a little rude, you know. It read like a command, and I don't take orders."

"But here you are," he said, smiling.

"My curiosity got the better of me," she confessed grudgingly.

Phillipe smiled again. "I thought that perhaps it might."

She reminded herself that she was angry with him, and that he had insulted her terribly, and that he had no right to stand there with his dimples showing and his blue eyes sparkling as though everything were fine.

She turned away and watched the pool of

water, the gold and rose and crimson reflection of the sky on the water, the graceful black shadows of the surrounding willows.

Phillipe watched the light on her hair and saw the confusion on her face.

"Perhaps, since my note was rude, we should start anew," he suggested. "Rudeness was hardly my intent. Why don't you forget that I sent the letter, and pretend that you just happened upon me?"

Victoria laughed aloud. "That's the silliest thing I've ever heard."

Phillipe tried to look humble, which was not in his nature, and the sight of his sorrowful expression made her laugh harder.

"Oh, all right. Just quit looking like that. You remind me of Dog."

Phillipe looked confused. "Of whom?"

"Dog. That is, my dog, Dog. Never mind." Victoria assumed a surprised expression. "Why, *Monsieur* St. Sebastien! What a surprise to bump into you at the reflecting pool at eight o'clock. What on earth are you doing here?"

Phillipe sighed in mingled exasperation and humor. "That was hardly a convincing performance, mademoiselle. I hope you never intend to become an actress."

"Not a chance," she assured him. "Get on with this, and get it over with."

"Oh, of course. Actually, Miss Larkin, I came here hoping that you might happen by, and that I could persuade you to spend some time in my undeserving company." He bowed elegantly.

164

"And," he added, the joking light gone from his eyes, "I wish to speak to you. I feel that I owe you an explanation. Will you walk with me for a while? I'd be more comfortable away from the house."

Victoria considered his words. "Against my better judgment, I will," she agreed wryly.

His eyes sparkled merrily at her sour tone, and he offered her his arm. He looked down at her with a fond expression as they left the garden, strolling through the twilight towards the path that led to the green woodlands.

"Look," Victoria said happily, gazing at the darkening forest.

The golden-rose rays of the setting sun moved in slanting beams between the trees, and the winding trail ahead beckoned like an enchanted path in a fairy tale. "Isn't it beautiful?"

"Very beautiful," Phillipe agreed, his eyes on Victoria's face. "The sunlight makes your skin glow in the most delicious way."

Victoria returned the compliment with a suspicious glance. "I hope that isn't what you ordered me out here to tell me, because if it is, I'm going right back to the house. I don't want to hear a bunch of twaddle about my skin and my hair. It makes you sound like those fools at Lavinia's ball."

"God forbid," Phillipe murmured. "You really are a very exasperating young woman, you know. Most women love to hear compliments. They eat them up like so many pastries."

"Good for them."

Phillipe sighed. "No, Victoria, I didn't ask you out here to shower you with pretty words. I'd like to speak to you seriously, if I may. Will you come sit with me by the stream? What I have to say is very important to me, and I don't wish to be rushed."

Victoria wondered at the wistful sound in his voice. "Of course," she answered swiftly, curious as to what he could possibly have to say.

Phillipe followed her down the sloping path to the mossy bank, watching the way her white dress clung to her graceful back, and the way the wide sash of heavy green satin accentuated her tiny waist. She settled herself comfortably on the ground, heedless of her dress, and gestured at the ground beside her, covered in green moss, starred with tiny, white flowers, lush ferns growing over the fallen log at her back.

"Is this good enough?"

"It's perfect," he answered honestly, watching the gold sunlight play along the ripples and bubbles of the stream as it rushed by. He sat next to her, reclining against the fallen log. "I very much like the sound of the water. It's like music, is it not?"

Victoria smiled. "You're right, though I never thought of it before."

Perhaps it just seemed like it, she thought, but the woodland had never been as beautiful as it was tonight. The sound of the stream, the spicy smell of the leaves, the golden light on the opulent greenery, the sound of the crickets singing, and the sweet smell of the summer evening—it all seemed too perfect to be true, as if it had been touched by magic.

They sat in silence for a few moments, listening to the throaty gurgle of the stream and the evening calls of the woodland birds.

"Well," Victoria announced bluntly, "spit it out."

" 'Spit it out,' " Phillipe repeated, his dimples showing. "Where do you learn these charming expressions?"

Victoria had to smile back. "My brothers, I suppose. I've never really spent time with anyone else until I was sent here."

Phillipe heard a wistful sadness in her voice when she spoke of her family.

"You miss them, don't you? Exactly how many of them are there? I asked Lavinia once, and she said, 'An indecent amount.' "

Victoria laughed at his imitation of Lavinia's proper voice. "There are six of them. Gareth is the eldest, he's twenty-nine, and he runs the farm. Daniel is three years younger. He's very bookish and works as a tutor, like Father used to. Richard is twenty, and Jamie and I are twins; we turned nineteen past November. Stewart and Geoffery are eighteen and seventeen, and that's all of us." She smiled shyly. "I suppose that does seem rather a lot, but I wouldn't say it's 'an indecent amount.' Maybe I'm just used to it. I was terribly lonely here until Johnathon and Harry came."

"No wonder you were so comfortable with them," Phillipe remarked. "And so trusting."

"I'll not make that mistake again," Victoria observed bitterly. "Harry would have to wear a hair shirt, feed the poor for a year, and crawl seven miles on his knees over rocks before I'd even consider speaking to him again."

Phillipe tried not to smile at the unlikely image that her words evoked. He said nothing, merely sat gazing silently through the trees at the darkening sky, watching the indigo night moving towards the crimson horizon.

Victoria watched his face, marveling at the elegant contours of his proud cheekbones, the slightly long, patrician-looking nose, the sweet curve of his upper lip and the firm line of the lower one, and the way the light shone in his clear blue eyes. When he noticed her staring, he gave her a quiet smile.

"Were you wondering when I would 'spit it out'?" he asked softly.

"No," she answered candidly. "I was thinking that you're very lucky to be so rich and beautiful."

Phillipe laughed again, delighting in her artless honesty.

"Beautiful? Isn't that the feminine word? Shouldn't you say handsome, rather?"

"No," she replied with a slightly abashed smile. "I meant beautiful; that's why I said it. And I think it's lovely when you laugh. You look nicer." She bowed her head so that her hair fell across her face, and plucked at the moss beside her, embarrassed at her own candor.

Phillipe was watching her carefully, as if he

were studying her, and when he spoke, his voice held a sad note, a longing.

"I have never laughed so much in my life as I do when I am with you. Perhaps that's why I have come to care for you so much."

For a moment, Victoria thought she had misheard; and then a wild, sweet joy rose in her heart. Her throat seemed to swell with happiness, and for a moment she was speechless. She raised her eyes almost fearfully, afraid that she had misunderstood, afraid that he was joking.

Phillipe was smiling, a gentle, tender smile that shook her to the depths of her being.

"I . . . I care for you, also," she confessed, her voice low and almost trembling. She felt as if her soul were exposed to him, her heart lying in front of him.

He looked away from the brilliant glow of her green eyes. When he spoke again, his voice was low and quiet. "That, Victoria, is why it shames me to say what I must say to you."

He paused uncertainly for a moment, unsure of where to begin. "When I was ten," he began at last, "my parents died, within days of each other. This I've already told you. We lived in the Auvergne, far from Paris, in an ancient castle high in the mountains. It is not much like Harrington Park. We were not rich, like most of our friends, but we were very happy.

"When my parents died, everything changed. My grandfather arrived from Versailles, took stock of our inheritance, and left. He did not care for children. We saw him once or twice a year after that, and the rest of the time we were left to our tutors and nurses.

"Christianna was a very beautiful child, like a cherub with black curls, and she was petted and spoiled and made much of by the servants.

"I, on the other hand, was a very sullen and rude little boy, and I was left alone, to amuse myself."

"I'm sure you were a beautiful little boy," Victoria interrupted hotly. "It sounds as if you were left to a pack of jackasses that knew nothing about children."

Phillipe smiled at her vehement defense of the boy he had been. "Perhaps. I think, though, that my tutors would disagree with you. Do you know how I amused myself?" he asked lightly. "How I passed the lonely hours of my youth? I shall tell you—I fell in love."

Victoria's heart skipped a beat. "With whom?" she asked, trying to sound indifferent and failing miserably.

"Not with whom," he corrected gently, "with what. I fell in love with my home, with the Château St. Sebastien. I fell in love with every room, every window, every stone. There was not an attic or cellar I did not explore, not a courtyard whose stones I did not know by heart. Each dusty room, each overgrown garden, each worn step in every ancient staircase. I adored every dusty painting, every fraying tapestry, every piece of rotting wood."

He smiled, a faraway smile, and reached out to tug on the hem of Victoria's dress. "How can

I possibly make you understand? You are so innocent, and you've seen so little of the world. I grew up in these decaying rooms, but I saw only the beauty, the splendor that they had once had. And as *Grandpère* drove us deeper and deeper into debt, and blackened the St. Sebastien name with his depraved whoring and gambling, and the very walls around us were starting to crumble, I made plans.

"I swore to myself that when I became the marquis that I would restore my home, that I would set the vineyards to work again, that I would redeem my family's name. With each passing year, my love for the castle became fiercer, and stronger. My dream fed me, consoled me through my youth. And that, *chéri*, is my curse."

"Why?" Victoria asked, alarmed by the raw emotion on his face, the bitter longing in his voice. "Why is that a curse?"

Her hand touched his, her cool fingers lying over the great emerald on his finger, and he hated to answer her honestly.

"Because, little innocent, great castles consume great amounts of money, and my bastard grandfather left almost none. Oh, I have enough to live on, enough for a set of rooms in London or Paris, and I've invested in a shipping company owned by a friend, but it may be years before I see a return. And even then, it will not be enough. And so you see, my poor little Victoria, I came to England for the sole purpose of acquiring a rich wife. One who had never heard of the sad state of the St. Sebastien family."

"Lavinia," Victoria said aloud, and the name felt like broken glass in her mouth.

"Lavinia," he concurred quietly.

Victoria swallowed hard, unable to speak. She stared straight ahead, thinking about what he had told her. Unfair, she thought, it's all so bloody unfair. She remembered her own mother's death as clearly as if it were yesterday, and she could picture Phillipe at the same age, alone and uncared for in his grief, focusing his love and affection on the cold stone walls of a castle that would never love him back.

The sun sank a little lower behind the inky shadows of the trees, a slash of crimson beneath an expanse of violet blue. The stream bubbled past, sounding cheerful and indifferent.

"It's not fair," she said aloud. "None of it. You don't care for Lavinia a bit, but you intend to marry her anyway, don't you? No wonder you walk around with a look on your face as if . . . as if you had a thorn in your bum."

"I don't," he protested, half laughing.

"You do," Victoria argued. "You do, and I would too if I was going to marry someone as awful as Lavinia. It *is* unfair, don't laugh. Oh, how I wish . . ."

"What do you wish, kitten?" he asked softly, his face solemn, his eyes fixed on her face, bright and clear in the darkening shadows.

"I wish I were rich," Victoria answered, and her voice was bitter. "I wish I were as rich as a king and had diamonds to wear in my hair and ropes of pearls around my neck, like Lavinia. I wish I had enough gold to buy ten castles, and then you'd marry me for my money." She blushed, but didn't flinch from his gaze. "Would you, Phillipe, if I were as rich as Midas? Would you marry me for my money?"

He reached out and gathered her hands into his, stroking her clenched fists. "Sweet Victoria, I would have thought myself the luckiest man in the world. From the moment I first saw you, standing in the stream with your skirts around your thighs, I wanted you. More than I have ever wanted any other woman. I told myself not to think of you, but as each day passed, I found myself wanting you more. And Lavinia with her diamonds and pearls cannot compare to you. You are like a breath of fresh air, like spring incarnate.

"I cannot bear the thought of leaving you behind when I return to France; and I must return, soon. I've told myself that it's inevitable, and to forget you, that you will marry an honest man and live a happy life. And I find that I can't stomach the thought."

He took a deep breath, and his hands tightened over hers.

"I can't leave you here. I want you to come with me when I leave."

Her heart soared like a bird, his words were like music in her head. She had dreamed of hearing this, and the heat of his hands over hers was as intoxicating as the champagne she had so giddily consumed last night. For a moment, the word "yes" rose to her lips, but she stopped herself as an unanswered question intruded on her joy.

"But what of your castle? What of Lavinia?"

Phillipe turned his head away, his hair blacker than the shadows that fell over them.

"Lavinia, I believe," he answered quietly, "will go too, as my wife. I'm asking you, my poor innocent, to be my mistress."

For a moment she felt only shock, as if her blood had turned to ice. Then a cold, ugly fury overcame her, such as she had never known before.

"God damn you," she whispered, her voice shaking. She swallowed hard. "Damn you," she repeated, her voice gaining strength and clarity. "You bring me here and smile sweetly at me and tell me that you care for me, and ask me to be your whore. How can you!" She struggled to her feet, trying to pull her hands from his grasp, but he hung on tightly.

"Please, Victoria, just think—"

"You think!" she cried wildly, her face stark and white in her rage. "You think, *Monsieur le Marquis*! Will you buy me a little house, a pretty carriage, with my cousin's money? Will you come and rut with me before you go home to your wife and children? May I stand with the villagers, with the other peasants, and watch when the great lord of the manor goes by with his lovely wife?"

She drew a deep, painful breath. She hated

him, hated him and his beautiful face and sweet voice, and oh, how she hated Lavinia.

"Will that make you happy?" she asked with a bitter laugh, "To make me love you, and make me your whore, and have me watch my cousin sitting in your damned castle at your side, where I long to be?"

Phillipe's eyes met hers, dark with pain. Each of her words struck him like a blow.

"No, Victoria. It shames me. But even more, I cannot bear to live without you."

Victoria pulled her hands from his and dashed the hot, angry tears from her cheeks. "I will not be your whore," she said fiercely. "I cannot. I love you too much."

Phillipe's face was white and still with shock. "You don't," he whispered. *"C'est impossible.* You're very young, Victoria, you don't know what love is."

"I do," she cried, "I know that I do. I would do anything to prove it."

"Anything," he repeated softly. "Anything but live as my mistress. You say you love me, but you love your virtue, your honor, far more. I suppose I would not care for you so much if you were different. I'm very sorry, mademoiselle, I've insulted you grievously, and I never meant to."

He rose to his feet, his face carefully arranged in the cool, composed mask that Victoria had begun to loathe. "Let us go back to the house, Victoria, and forget this. I'll not insult your honor again."

"The devil take you," she snapped. "You're as thick as a brick. It has nothing to do with my damned virtue, or honor. I love you, that's all. I love you too much to share you."

Phillipe's eyes were dark with sorrow, his features carefully composed. "Again, I'm sorry. I never meant to hurt you. Will you accept my apology?" He took her hand and bowed gracefully over it, and the touch of his cheek on her hand was as sweet and painful as anything she could imagine. He straightened, and turned to go.

Victoria had heard of people dying of broken hearts, but she had always dismissed it as an expression. Now she knew better. Her heart felt twisted with pain in her chest, and she wondered if it might indeed shatter. She thought of him marrying Lavinia, and giving Lavinia the pleasure that she herself longed to know, and the idea was too awful to be borne.

And he'd be gone, she realized. He'd return to France with Lavinia, and she would go home to Middlebury and her brothers, and it would be as if these bittersweet summer days had never existed.

A wild, reckless heat seized her.

"Wait," she said aloud. Her heart was thumping loudly, her eyes felt hot and dry, but her voice was steady.

Phillipe turned quickly at the sound of her voice, and was startled by the sight of her.

She looked like a wild creature, a wood nymph, standing in the darkening night. Her face was pale and glowing, her eyes huge and bright, sparkling with a wild intensity, one slender hand extending towards him through the darkness.

"Please," she whispered, and the word seemed to hang in the air between them, husky and sweet. "You can't leave me with nothing. It would break my heart, I know it would. And I know that you'll marry Lavinia, but . . . I would like to steal from her." Victoria drew a shaking breath and closed her eyes for a moment. "One night. Please."

Phillipe stood as if frozen. "Do you know what you ask, *chéri*?"

"Yes." The word was poignant, a whisper in the dusk.

For a moment they stood silent in the indigo night. A faint breeze rustled the leaves, a bird sang a warbling note. Then Phillipe moved forward slowly, moving towards the white-clad figure in the darkness as if drawn by the force of her need.

He stared into her eyes, searching, curious. His hand touched her hair softly, almost reverently, and came to rest feather-light against the warmth of her slender neck.

"God help me," he whispered plaintively, "for I cannot help myself."

His hand moved to her face and tilted her head back, and his mouth covered hers, his lips moving slowly, languidly over her mouth, his tongue melting against hers; and Victoria's hands moved instinctively to the thick silk of his dark hair, pulling him closer as she melted into the velvet softness of the kiss.

She pressed willingly into the warm length of his body, drowning in the feeling of his hands on her back pulling her tightly to him, pressing her hips closer, moving against her.

Their mouths met eagerly, again and again, slowly and smoothly at first, then with a fevered, demanding rhythm.

Victoria wanted to cry with joy as her hands explored the broad, taut lines of his back, the heat of his skin through the fine fabric of his shirt, the shape of his neck beneath her hand. She tasted the salty taste of his skin, breathed the scent of it.

She became aware of an ache, a deep throbbing pulse, a trembling thrill that radiated from the most secret places of her body. With a hungry instinct, she moved her hands to the firm flesh of his buttocks, pulling him closer to her body, feeling as if she could become part of him; and she felt a hot surge of triumph at the sound of his sigh, ragged and low.

He pulled the ribbons and pins from her hair, rubbed the ruddy silk of it against his cheek, smelled the soft fragrance of it, like lilacs in the sun.

"Sweet Victoria," he whispered, and his hot breath stirred near her ear, thrilling her.

The filmy lace of her fichu fell silkily from her shoulders to the forest floor, baring her shoulders, and she felt Phillipe's hands in the hooks and lacings of her gown. He slid it deftly from her shoulders, and with a tug of her sash, it fell to the ground with a silken whisper, like the rustling of leaves.

His blood raced at the sight of her, pale in the moonlight, clad only in the gossamer lawn and lace of her chemise and the white silk of her stockings, the thin fabric hiding nothing from his eyes. He moved his hands over the taut, slender lines of her ribs, and filled them with the softness of her breasts, warm and round beneath the delicate fabric.

"Victoria, if you wish to turn back, you must do it now; for in a moment I will not be able to stop myself. Are you sure this is what you want?"

Victoria was beyond thinking, beyond caring. All that existed now was the white-hot fire that raced through her veins. She tilted her head back to meet his eyes, her own glowing with a fevered brightness. "I couldn't stop now," she whispered, her husky voice rich and dark with desire.

Without a word, he guided her back to the soft bank of the stream and, stripping off his coat and shirt, he spread the garments on the ground and he laid her down on them.

She moved her hands across the bare warmth of his chest, over the dark down that covered it, and she rubbed her cheek against it like a cat.

Their hands explored each other's bodies, hungry, seeking, intoxicating. Victoria moaned at the feeling of his mouth at her breast, his tongue moving like hot satin over the dusky buds of her nipples, his hands traveling the length of her legs, removing her stockings. She arched against him, unabashedly reveling in her desire, aching with need of him, delirious with the touch of his skin, the scent of his hair.

The rest of the world ceased to exist, there was only Phillipe, his beautiful mouth taking hers, his warm hands caressing her, his whispered words of passion, words that she didn't know but which were no less sweet to her ears; and the stars that sparkled in the dark sky above her, and the lush grass and ferns that sheltered her.

Her chemise she cast aside eagerly, hungry for the feeling of his skin against hers, and Phillipe sighed at the sight of her, pale and slim, her body glowing in the moonlight, the dark, curling ribbons of hair that moved over her full breasts and tickled her slender waist. She smiled tenderly at him, her eyes glittering with a fevered brightness, and held her arms out to him.

"Beautiful Victoria," he whispered, looking at her with eyes so bright they seemed to burn. He rose to his knees, his eyes never leaving hers, and unfastened the buttons of his breeches, pushing them down over his slender hips.

He lay over her, and Victoria felt, for the first time, the velvet smoothness, the hard, hot length of him against the soft curve of her thigh. His hands sought the soft down between her legs, and Victoria cried out at the heat of his fingers, moving softly and firmly in her. She wondered if anyone had ever died of pleasure, and when his mouth took hers again, it was with a hunger and intensity that made her quiver.

"My God," he whispered when their lips parted. He raised himself up and gazed at her, drugged by her beauty, by his own need for her body, by the warm scent of her skin. His hand continued moving at the hot, damp center of her, his hand moving like satin through the soft, velvet folds.

"Do you know what you make me think of?" Phillipe asked, his voice soft and uneven.

She arched against him, aching, unashamed. "A trollop. I don't know. What?"

His laugh was soft. "No. Never a trollop. But here . . ." His hand moved over the damp heat of her. "Here, you remind me of a rose, a dark, sweet, summer rose. Sweet and pink . . ."

His words inflamed her as much as the touch of his hand, and when he took her hand, showered it with kisses, and guided it to his shaft, she touched him joyously, marveling at the smoothness, the hardness and length of him, rejoicing at the groan that her touch wrung from him.

"Are you ready?" he asked, his voice low and shaken.

Victoria couldn't speak. She reached for his shoulders and pulled his body to hers; and he entered her with one swift, hard thrust.

Victoria was shocked by the clarity of the pain, brief and hot, and for a moment they both lay perfectly still, and she listened to the murmur of the stream, and the song of the crickets, and the sound of Phillipe's quick, ragged breaths. She moved her cheek against his, felt the silk of his hair against her face; and then slowly, smoothly, he began to move in her.

The hot, sweet rhythm of his movement pulled Victoria into its current, and she exulted in her possession of his body, the feeling of melting into him.

She felt as if they had become one, as if they were fused together by the friction of their joined bodies, and her body sought his strength as he filled her completely, again and again.

"My own," Victoria whispered against his hair, and the words felt sweet on her tongue, and right. Her hands sought the firm skin of his strong thighs, his hips, pulling him deeper into her body, and she began to move desperately against him.

Phillipe did not expect the unbridled passion that engulfed her, he did not expect the unabashed frenzy with which she moved against him, or the wild, keening cry that sprang from her throat, rising through the branches of the moonlit trees.

He forgot his resolve to be gentle, and half-lifting her off the ground, he began to plunge into the hot, tight grip of her with a fierce, quickening rhythm.

Victoria was lost, drowning in the dark, blood-hot drumbeat of her pulse, drowning in the feeling of his hands, in the salt taste of his skin and the hot, damp flow of his breath against her throat.

The drumbeat of her pulse seemed to burst within her veins, wave after wave of blazing sensation pulling her to Phillipe's body. She heard herself crying out, like a wild creature under the stars, but she didn't care.

She felt Phillipe shudder over her as he plunged deeply into her, clutching her to him; and for the first time, she felt the hot, primitive triumph of a woman as he exploded deep within her body, and she knew that he had found the same joy in her body that she had discovered in his.

Afterwards, they lay together in the cooling night, her head over his heart, his fingers twining languidly through her hair, and he kissed her face gently and reverently, as if she were something fragile.

Victoria was silent as the soft night breezes moved across her bare skin, and a feeling of well-being, a magical languor, soothed her body. She didn't worry about the future; she cared only that she was here in Phillipe's arms, and she loved him, loved him more deeply than she ever could have imagined.

She studied the indigo and black sky above her, marveling at the beauty of the stars and the black shadows of the trees in the light of the half-moon. She wished that time would stop and that she could stay here forever.

"What are you thinking of, kitten? Are you sorry, now that the awful deed is done?"

Victoria laughed. "No. No, I shall never be sorry. I was thinking about the stars, actually. Do you see the constellation of Andromeda?"

Phillipe glanced briefly at the sky where she pointed, then turned his attention toward her arm, slowly trailing a delicate line of kisses over her soft, bare skin.

"Do you see?" she repeated. "That great star is her head, and the two lower stars arching out on either side are her arms."

"I adore arms," he answered, and Victoria shivered deliciously at the touch of his mouth on the inside of her wrist.

"I love you," she said unexpectedly. Their eyes met, and even in the dim moonlight she could see the sorrow in his eyes.

"Don't. Don't love me, Victoria, because it will only cause you unhappiness when we part."

He brushed the thick curls off her forehead, his hands lingering in the softness of it. "Unless, of course, you've reconsidered my offer."

"I think not," Victoria answered after a long pause. "But my offer to you, I'll reconsider."

He raised himself to one elbow, arching a quizzical brow. "My beautiful girl," he said lightly, lowering his head to her breasts and kissing each one slowly, "I believe it's a little too late to reconsider."

She laughed softly. "I meant the part about doing this only once. It seems such a hasty decision."

His laughter mingled with hers, surprised and delighted. "You may be right, *chéri*," he agreed warmly. "Perhaps we should try again, just to be sure. Of course, if you're still not decided, I think that I might help you reconsider again . . . and again."

Her smile was bright and hot as he bent over her breasts again, the satin of his tongue and his warm fingers tantalizing her already erect nipples.

The sound of her husky laughter mingled with the throaty murmur of the stream, and they turned to each other again.

Chapter Ten

The next morning, Victoria found Mary in the music room industriously polishing the gleaming spinet with a combination of beeswax and lemon oil, her sleeves pushed up over her small forearms.

"Thank heavens," Victoria exclaimed, looking about to make sure that they were alone. "Listen, Mary, I need your help."

"I'll say you do," Mary agreed, with a sharp glance. "Anybody that isn't in their own bed at dawn is likely to need some serious help. Things are—"

"Yes, yes, I know," Victoria interrupted. "Never mind that. Just listen; it's this. He can't marry Lavinia, he can't. I couldn't bear it. So we have to stop it, and—"

"I like this 'we' business," Mary interjected

with a mournful sigh. "Just what do you suppose 'we' might do?"

Victoria looked over her shoulder. The morning sun streamed between the damask draperies, falling on the delicate armchairs and Persian carpets; the harp stood silently behind her, but no one was in sight.

"Make me beautiful," Victoria said, her words quick and sharp. "I've fought you on it, I know, but I never will again. Do your worst, bring out the paint and perfume and the fans and ribbons, if you must. Lace me up, every day if you want to. Then I shall stick to Lavinia like glue, and he'll never get the chance to propose. It's simple, really."

Mary folded her small arms and contemplated Victoria's glowing eyes, the bright flush in her cheeks. "Mmm-hmm," she responded after some deliberation. "And if that doesn't work, are you planning to stuff him into a bag and take him home with you?"

"If I must," Victoria replied, taking the cloth from Mary's hand, and tossing it to the floor. "Please, Mary, come and help me decide what to wear, and lace me. Please."

Mary allowed herself to be pulled from the room, hurrying to keep up with Victoria's quick stride. She heaved a sigh at the sight of Victoria's room, a mountain of discarded frocks and petticoats piled on the patterned carpet.

"You see," Victoria cried, shutting the door firmly, "I just don't know what to do."

Mary examined the discarded finery. "This

white here is nice and virginal," she remarked wryly. "Why not that?"

"God rot white and virginal," Victoria answered blasphemously. "It's a little late for that. Just help me choose whatever will make him want me most, without being too obvious."

"I'm glad to see we have a little modesty left," Mary said, digging busily through the clothes. "Here, just look at this pink. And it has the prettiest rosebuds embroidered all around, and the same rosebuds on the underskirt—where did it go? There. And it should fit you like a glove. You'll look like an angel."

Even if I'm not, Victoria thought, her conscience poking at her. *Don't think of it. Think of Phillipe.*

She discarded her simple dress and pulled a corset around her already slender waist, offering Mary the tapes with the grim determination of a soldier preparing for battle.

"Tight," she instructed as Mary laced the stiff garment. "I may look like an angel when you've finished, but the angel wants a good display of cleavage."

Mary laughed at last, and Victoria could not help joining her. "God help us," Mary exclaimed, giggling. "One day, God will strike you down, miss, for your wicked tongue."

Victoria pulled the dress over her head and regarded her reflection with satisfaction. Mary found a fichu of transparent lace and covered Victoria's exposed shoulders, tucking the ends into the deep, square neckline. The filmy fabric did little to cover the swelling curves of her half-exposed breasts, but it was enough to be proper.

"I want to be beautiful," Victoria repeated firmly. "I want Lavinia to fall down and die of envy."

"That would solve everything," Mary agreed happily. "She'd fall down dead on the spot, and all your troubles would be over."

Victoria looked at herself in the mirror and felt another troubling stir of conscience. Reverend Finkle had always lectured on the sins of envy, vanity, and lust, and here she was, damning herself to perdition, and happily, too.

"God help me," she said aloud, "I love him, Mary."

Mary laid her small, warm hand over Victoria's.

"I know you do, miss. And if I have to, I'll help you stuff him into that sack and send him with you when you go."

Both young women lost their solemn expressions, and their laughter mingled happily in the quiet room.

"Bless you for that, Mary. You're a true friend."

Mary smiled sweetly, picked up the silver hairbrush, and went to work with a vengeance.

"Victoria?"

Johnathon looked across the library at Victoria, his high, smooth forehead wrinkling in concern. She sat nervously on the window seat, her slender fingers clutching a volume of sonnets, her eyes fastened anxiously on the window. She looked exceptionally pretty today, but also nervous and distracted.

"Victoria," he repeated patiently, "have you heard a thing I've said?"

Victoria started, and glanced quickly at Fairfield, who was settled calmly in a large wing chair, his brown eyes fixed on her curiously. Behind him on a gleaming table, a bust of Socrates seemed to regard her with equal suspicion.

"Of course I'm listening; what did you say?"

Fairfield smiled, a little confused. "I asked if you wanted to go for a ride, maybe stop at the inn for some gossip."

"Oh," she replied, her gaze wandering to the window. She leaned back on the wine-red cushions of the window seat, staring out at the rose garden. Where were Phillipe and Lavinia? They always came this way, every morning. Perhaps, she thought frantically, it was too late. Perhaps he was proposing to Lavinia at this moment, perhaps he was kissing her—

"Well, would you or wouldn't you?" Fairfield asked, absently flipping through the pages of a book.

"Would I or wouldn't I what?" Victoria asked in alarm, a guilty blush racing over her cheeks.

Johnathon sighed in exasperation and raked a hand through his heavy gold hair. "Really, Victoria, are you all right?"

Victoria wondered what the original question had been, and finally offered an innocent smile.

191

"Sorry," she said, hoping that her answer would suffice.

"Victoria," he cried in frustration, "are you quite awake? I asked if you wanted to go for a ride. For heaven's sake, are you sure you're all right?"

"Oh, Johnathon," she exclaimed in dismay, "I am sorry. I just can't help thinking . . ."

"Thinking what, Vic?" he asked seriously, leaning forward. "Are you still upset about Harry? I hate to bring it up, but I know how awful it must seem—"

"Oh, dear, no. Please, Johnathon, don't speak of it. No, I wasn't thinking of that at all. I was thinking of what it will be like when I go home, and if the boys will find me much changed, and how much I shall miss . . . all of this," she finished weakly, waving a vague hand at the room with its handsomely paneled walls, rich oil paintings, and beautifully bound books.

Johnathon looked around as if he expected to see something different.

"I thought you didn't care for 'all this,' " he reminded her.

"Well, I don't. That is, I didn't. What I mean is . . . Oh, bloody hell, I don't know what I mean. I don't know what on earth is the matter with me. Come on, let's go for a walk in the gardens."

Johnathon smiled gently, thinking how extraordinarily pretty Vic was today, if a bit muddled. "I really don't think that you want to walk in the gardens right now," he said. "Because there go Phillipe and Lavinia, and who wants to walk about with them?"

Victoria abandoned the window seat with the speed of a pistol shot, and Johnathon found himself being pulled from his chair and dragged to the door.

"I do, that's who. Come on, Johnathon, let's catch up to them."

"I say, Vic, are you sure you're feeling all right?" Victoria was already ahead of him, her curls bouncing energetically down her back, her heels clicking across the marble floors as she hurried into the sunlight.

Fairfield shrugged and quickened his step. "Wait, Vic," he called, and hurried to fall into step beside her. "What on earth are you up to?" he demanded. "Since when would you rather stroll about with Lavinia than go for a good ride? Is this some sort of a joke?"

Victoria whirled and grasped his forearm, her eyes bright and glittering, as light and clear as jade. "Yes, that's it—it's a joke, and a damned good one. We stick to them like burrs, and he won't have a chance to be alone with her, and she'll be furious. Isn't it funny?" Her smile was quick and bright. "Come on, let's go."

He's looking at me as if I've lost my mind, Victoria thought. *Maybe I have.*

Johnathon shrugged again. "If you like. Though it's so easy to make Lavinia angry that I can hardly see the joke."

"I can," Victoria answered grimly. "Now be

agreeable, here they come." She tried to ignore the sinking feeling in her stomach when she saw them together, looking as if they had been created only for the purpose of complementing each other's looks—the elegant marquis, tall and dark and sophisticated in his dove gray coat and breeches, and the earl's daughter, golden and languid and delicate, her face a perfect oval beneath the lace of her parasol, her white skirts trailing prettily on the dew-covered grass.

"Good morning, Lavvy," Johnathon called agreeably, "Phillipe. Do you mind if we join you? it would be such a shame not to enjoy the gardens on a day like this."

"Yes, it is rather pretty, isn't it?" Lavinia returned, sounding very bored.

"Rawther," Victoria could not resist echoing, and Johnathon smiled behind his hand.

"I'm surprised you're not out riding," Lavinia said, a pointed suggestion in her words.

"We felt that we needed a change, didn't we, Johnathon?" Victoria said swiftly.

"Oh, oh, yes, nothing like a change, I always say."

Phillipe looked suspiciously at Victoria, who smiled back, radiant and lovely. It was a disarmingly sweet look, and he thought how lovely she was, even more enticing in the morning sun than she had been in the moonlight, if that were possible, blushing and bright. He wondered if that was a new dress she was wearing. He'd have remembered if she had worn it before, he would have remembered the way the waistline made her seem so incredibly slender, and how the tight bodice pushed her soft breasts up—

"Phillipe," Lavinia snapped, "are you listening to me?"

"Of course," Phillipe lied quickly. "I was just thinking that perhaps we should walk to the reflecting pool, or to the fountain."

"That's exactly what I just said." Lavinia's voice was cool, and her eyes glittered like blue ice.

"Forgive me," Phillipe apologized smoothly. "I confess that I wasn't listening at all. Of course, we shall go to the pool, if you wish." He took Lavinia's arm, turning his back on Victoria's disturbing beauty.

"I wonder," Johnathon murmured under his breath, "if it's something in the food that's making everybody so absentminded."

Victoria glanced at him in alarm, relaxing at the sight of his gentle smile, a teasing sparkle in his soft brown eyes.

"Go to hell," she whispered back with a quick, wicked grin.

Their eyes met, and Fairfield nodded, understanding. "So that's the joke, is it? Lavinia will be angry, won't she?"

Not nearly as angry as I, Victoria thought. She hadn't expected the hard, ugly bite of envy that she had felt when Phillipe had taken Lavinia's arm and turned his back to her. This was damned easy for him, wasn't it?

195

Lavinia was chattering gaily now, something about gardens, and Victoria wished she could step on the trailing white skirts in front of her.

"What I really long to see is the orangery at Versailles," Lavinia was saying, gazing up at Phillipe as though he were personally responsible for the glories of France. "Is it really as beautiful as they say?"

"It's staggering," Johnathon broke in before Phillipe could reply. "Simply astonishing. That's where Phillipe and I first met, on my tour of the continent last year. What was it you said about Versailles, Phillipe, that amused us so much?"

"I really don't recall," Phillipe answered uncomfortably.

"Oh, yes," Johnathon said with an amused laugh. "You said that the whole place was a colossal waste of money and time, and that you could hardly stand to spend even one day there. That it reminded you of a gluttonous, over-painted old—"

"I must have been in a very foul mood that day," Phillipe interjected, coloring at Lavinia's puzzled stare and Victoria's mischievous laugh.

"That's very odd, Johnathon," Lavinia remarked contentiously, "For Monsieur St. Sebastien has always spoken very highly of the place. Perhaps you're confusing him with somebody else."

"Absolutely not," Johnathon asserted pleasantly. "I remember the conversation quite distinctly, don't you, Phillipe? We were in the hall of mirrors, with your pretty sister and her friend; Artois, wasn't it? You said that the court was a disgusting, ostentatious waste of time and money, a vulgar display of overindulgence, and that you much preferred the simple country life."

Lavinia looked appalled. "I'm sure you're mistaken, Johnathon. Phillipe is very impressed with the place, I know, and he would never—"

Victoria almost felt sorry for Phillipe. Almost. "Perhaps we should change the subject. Isn't it a pretty day? Did you see how very clear the stars were last night?"

Phillipe shot her a look of alarm, and she smiled sweetly.

Lavinia looked annoyed that Victoria would dare to suggest anything.

"Of course you would want to change the subject, Miss Larkin," she remarked with apparent indifference. "You've grown up in the country, and really don't understand, do you? Great art, great buildings, court life . . . it's all a little beyond you, isn't it? I daresay you've never even seen London."

Johnathon looked a little shocked at Lavinia's rudeness, but Victoria smiled.

"That's very true, cousin. I have no experience with 'great' buildings, and grand places, and perhaps I am a little simple about such things. I would be much happier in a cottage with people I respected and admired, than in . . . say, a castle with people I found stupid and tiresome."

Lavinia didn't know how to answer this, so

she simply walked ahead, tossing her blonde head indifferently.

Phillipe smiled coolly at Victoria, a warning light in his blue eyes. "Your philosophy is a great credit to you, mademoiselle—if a trifle naïve."

Did you think I'd make this easy for you? Victoria thought, lifting her chin. *If so, you may think again, Monsieur le Marquis.*

Phillipe was alarmed at the mischievous smile that played around Victoria's soft, pink mouth, at the dangerous sparkle in her tilting green eyes. Damn her, if she weren't so incredibly lovely . . .

Victoria shivered deliciously at the glowing heat in his blue eyes. "I believe, sir, that your lady-love is growing impatient," she said sweetly, nodding in the direction of Lavinia waiting impatiently down the graveled path.

Johnathon and Victoria exchanged smiles as Phillipe hurried to take Lavinia's arm, and followed them happily to the shaded grove that enclosed the reflecting pool.

The water reflected the bright summer blues and greens of the day. The marble Artemis stood, still frozen in the pool's center, in her sheer, windswept robes.

"Such a marvelous work," Johnathon said admiringly. "Is it by Canova, do you suppose?"

"I really don't know," Lavinia replied impatiently. "I think it's a little indecent, myself. Almost unclothed."

"Then we should certainly move on," Victoria

suggested, "for I'm sure that nobody here would want to stand about gawking at half-naked women standing in water."

The marquis raised his brow at Victoria. She looked infuriatingly angelic with her red curls shining in the sun and wearing that very feminine pink color. Only the sparkle in her eyes gave lie to the seeming innocence of her words. In spite of himself, Phillipe felt an amused smile forming on his lips.

"According to legend, Artemis could be quite cruel to the poor mortals that dared to disturb her woodland baths," Phillipe remarked wryly.

"Oh, yes," Victoria agreed with a brilliant smile. "She turned them into animals, didn't she? Common, rutting animals."

Johnathon laughed aloud, and Lavinia gasped.

"Really, Miss Larkin," she sputtered, "that is hardly the kind of remark that one should make in front of gentlemen. It is . . . indelicate."

"Nonsense," Victoria replied with infuriating good humor. "It is simple mythology. There are far more shocking things in Hesiod's *Theogony*. You should read it sometime, cousin."

"I had no idea that you could read Greek, Lavvy," Johnathon remarked pleasantly.

Lavinia drew a deep breath. "I don't," she answered, and the words were clipped and sharp.

"Sorry, Lavvy," the young earl replied with a pleasant smile. "Didn't mean to be rude."

Lavinia turned her back to the two intruders

and strolled stiffly to one of the heavy stone benches that sat in the shade of the willows. She sat primly, with a disdainful glance at her impossible cousin, who had settled herself comfortably on the grass.

"I am so looking forward to the Lawrences' musicale tonight," she said to Phillipe, looking away from Victoria's blazing curls. "It's rather a tiresome drive—half an hour by carriage. Don't tell me you've forgotten, Phillipe! It ought to be quite a crush, everyone shall be there. Perhaps even his highness, the Prince."

"Of course," Phillipe murmured. "The Lawrences' musicale."

"It's too bad that you weren't invited, Miss Larkin," Lavinia went on, "but the Lawrences are very fond of art and music and that sort of thing, and I'm sure they prefer to invite guests that have been exposed to the finer things and can converse comfortably about them. I'm sure you'd feel most awkward."

"Being the Philistine that I am," Victoria agreed, "you're probably right."

"But she was invited," Johnathon protested. "Young Lawrence was quite taken with her at your ball, Lavvy, and he made quite a point of insisting."

Victoria smiled radiantly at her cousin's outraged face. "You see, Lavinia, your sympathy was quite misplaced, though it was *so* kind of you to think of me. I hope that the carriage won't be too crowded, with four instead of two."

Lavinia looked as if she might choke, and Victoria wished she would.

"I really don't think you'd enjoy yourself, Miss Larkin. Wouldn't you rather stay here and read a book?"

"And miss an opportunity to be exposed to 'the finer things' that I'm so sadly lacking? Not a chance."

"Of course not," Lavinia answered, her tone barely civil. "How very unlike you that would be, to miss an opportunity."

Victoria turned from where she sat and coolly regarded her cousin, sitting so prettily in the shade, her swanlike grace and careful poise at odds with the furious glitter of her eyes.

Victoria met Lavinia's condescending stare, and held it.

How right you are, cousin, she thought, *for I've had my opportunity, and taken it, and I would do it again, gladly.*

Johnathon's pleasant voice broke the strained silence.

"I say, Lavvy, you look a little flushed. Is it too warm for you?"

Lavinia smiled, a strained, false smile. "Why, yes, it is rather warm. Phillipe." She beckoned, turning to him, "I would dearly love to go somewhere cool. Will you walk with me to the stream? It's so shady and tranquil there."

Phillipe's careful composure faltered, and he was visibly dismayed. His eyes met Victoria's, and she had to cover her mouth to keep from laughing at his panic-stricken expression.

201

"What a wonderful idea," Johnathon said smoothly, as though he and Victoria had not been pointedly excluded from the invitation, and offering Lavinia his arm. "Let me help you up, Lavvy. We don't want you to faint on the way."

Lavinia took his arm with ill-concealed anger, her rosebud mouth tightening with displeasure as Johnathon tucked her arm firmly beneath his and led her towards the path, seemingly oblivious to his hostess's rising anger as he chatted about how hot it was, so early in the summer.

Lavinia shot a venomous look over her shoulder at Victoria as Fairfield led her away.

"Very clever, Miss Larkin," Phillipe said mockingly, raising a dark brow at her. "What will you do next?"

Victoria met his eyes squarely, and the memory of the night before was bright and hot in her eyes. The air between them seemed alive, full of unspoken words.

She wasn't aware, when she stared up at him, of the softening of her expression, of the gentle sorrow of her smile, the longing glow in her dark green eyes.

"I'm sorry," she said simply. "I really didn't know that Johnathon would do that. As to what I shall do next, I have no idea. I've never been in such a position before, and I had no idea it would be so very . . . uncomfortable, to be near you."

Phillipe laughed softly and rubbed his chin

thoughtfully. " 'Uncomfortable.' That's a good word for it. And now we have to go sit by the stream with your dear cousin. That will be even more 'uncomfortable,' won't it?"

He offered her his hand and pulled her gently to her feet. The touch of their hands made Victoria shiver with delight.

"I wish we were going there alone," she confessed. "I wish Lavinia would drop off the face of the earth."

Phillipe touched her face gently, his sharp features softening. "Do you know what I wish?" he asked softly. "I wish I could tumble you to the ground right here and tear the lace away from your pretty breasts, and push your skirts up around your waist, and take you, right here on the grass, until you cried out with pleasure."

Victoria felt heat rush through her body and drew a shaking breath.

"As it is," he continued, tracing the shape of her soft mouth with one finger, "we had better join Lavinia and Fairfield, or they will wonder why."

Victoria stepped back, away from the heat of his breath and the sandalwood scent of him, spellbound by the fevered glow in his blue eyes. "You're very wicked, you know," she told him, her voice husky and shaken. "And very hard to resist. But you know that, don't you? I imagine that you do this a lot, don't you? You've probably left a hundred women behind you just like me."

"A hundred women, perhaps," he admitted,

his dimples showing, "but none like you, or I'd be dead of exhaustion. You've started a fire, *chéri*, that will be very hard to put out."

"We had better join the others," Victoria said as the sound of Lavinia's petulant voice floated back to her through the air.

He walked silently beside her down the woodland path, and they were both thinking of the night before when they had made this walk in the twilight, and what it had led to.

"Victoria," he said suddenly, and she stopped in the path, unable to meet his eyes.

"Think about my offer," he said, his voice gentle, almost wistful. "Please."

"I'll think about it." The words sprang unbidden to her lips. "I make you no promises, but I'll think about it." Unnerved at the longing that shook her, she hurried ahead, her heart hammering against the stiff bodice of her gown.

Phillipe stood, momentarily stunned by the fierce pleasure that gripped him. She was considering his offer, she might accept.

He imagined showing her the ancient towers of Château St. Sebastien, the wild beauty of the surrounding forests and mountains. He imagined making love to her in the massive, dark bed that had graced the bedchamber of the marquis for at least three hundred years; imagined her white body glowing in the firelight, in the dark splendor of the room.

Oblivious to the beauty of the day around him, Phillipe hastily composed his features as he approached the stream, and Lavinia's voice floated through the trees, high and petulant.

" . . . not fond of rough places. I usually have one of the servants come ahead with a carpet to sit upon. It makes it so much nicer."

"Really?" Victoria responded, her eyes flashing up at Phillipe as he approached. "I think this is lovely just as it is. As a matter of fact, this moss is quite as comfortable as a bed. I could very happily stay the entire night here."

Lavinia sighed in annoyance. "What odd things you say, Miss Larkin. Though I daresay you probably do find it comfortable. I'm just not accustomed to the rough sort of life that you lead."

"How very sad for you," Victoria answered briskly, tossing a pebble into the stream and enjoying the small splash. "You really have no idea what you're missing."

Chapter Eleven

At least the Lawrences' musicale was not as
crowded as Lavinia's ball, Victoria thought to
herself, looking around the spacious drawing
room. And the music had been beautiful, the
haunting, sparkling notes of the harpsichord
filling the room with their baroque sounds,
raining on her ears like kisses, making her
shiver with delight. At one point, the music had
moved her so much that her eyes filled with
tears, and Johnathon, sitting beside her, had
patted her hand approvingly.

When at last the music ended, the other
guests abandoned their delicate needlepoint
chairs and gilded settees immediately, the air
filling with chatter, with the whisper of silk
gowns and fluttering fans.

Victoria remained seated, a little dazed as she

watched the others with their powdered hair and gleaming jewels, still hearing the last poignant notes quivering in the air, until Phillipe approached her, leaning on the tapestry-covered chair next to hers.

"There is punch, or champagne, if you like."

Victoria laughed, a little startled. "No, no, thank you. I feel as if I'm drunk on music."

Phillipe smiled appreciatively. "You have an ear for music, I think. A love for good music cannot be taught. You're very lucky. I would wager that half of these fools here tonight barely even listened—they were too busy admiring each other's clothes."

"I can't blame them," Victoria replied, coloring at his praise. "I feel terribly underdressed, like a milkmaid."

Phillipe smiled at her, his eyes moving over the simplicity of her white gown and the wide sash of lavender silk that bound her slender waist. Her only ornaments were a spray of sweet peas woven through her shining curls, the soft fragrance of them wafting with every movement.

"Nonsense," he murmured, in a voice meant only for her ears. "You're easily the most beautiful woman in the room."

Victoria blushed and dropped her eyes. How stunning he was in his evening clothes, the rich plum velvet of his frock coat echoing the deep violet and emerald embroidery of the waistcoat beneath, his thick, black hair fastened with a dark ribbon of plum silk. He was the most elegant man in the room, and she was about to tell him so when Charles Lawrence rushed to her side.

"You came," he exclaimed in delight. "I cannot tell you how happy we are." He bowed to Phillipe. "Excuse me, monsieur, of course we're delighted to receive you, as well, but I'm afraid that my good manners quite desert me in the face of such loveliness."

"Of course," Phillipe murmured graciously, but he didn't care for the way young Lawrence's puppy-dog eyes traveled surreptitiously over the glowing skin of Victoria's cleavage, or the eager way he took her hand.

"Our temperamental musician is demanding to meet you," Lawrence continued. "Everybody is quite taken with you. How clever of you not to powder your hair."

"I tried," Victoria confessed with a self-deprecating laugh. "It looked very pink, so I abandoned my attempts at being fashionable."

"Even better," Lawrence proclaimed, "you're original." He waved a beckoning hand to the blue-coated musician hovering impatiently across the room. "Aristotle . . . Aristotle Hamilton, come meet Miss Larkin."

Phillipe tried not to glower as the sharp-featured young man bent over Victoria's hand a little longer than necessary.

"My dear young woman," the musician announced, "you were my muse this evening. I played each note as an ode to your loveliness. Am I mistaken in thinking that you are an aficionado of music? What did you think of the second fugue?"

Victoria noticed nervously that a small crowd was forming, waiting for her reply, and somewhere behind her she heard Lavinia's spiteful murmur, " . . . doesn't even know what a fugue is."

She lifted her chin proudly, and, as was her policy, spoke honestly.

"I'm sad to say that my cousin is right, sir. I don't have the faintest idea what a fugue might be—I'm completely ignorant of the language of music. It seems to me that the music itself is a language. But I can tell you that I've never heard anything so beautiful. There was such sadness, such sorrow in the sounds; and I've never thought of sorrow as beautiful, yet you made it so."

"Well said, my dear," Lady Lawrence said, nodding her powdered head approvingly, and there was a murmur of assent around her.

Aristotle Hamilton bowed dramatically. "I am indeed triumphant. I wish I could have captured the tear you shed, for it was the sweetest compliment I have ever received, and I value it more than Solomon valued all his treasures."

Phillipe rolled his eyes at these overblown dramatics, and Victoria laughed merrily.

Phillipe watched as Victoria was led away by the posturing artiste and the enthralled Charles Lawrence, and her easy laughter floated back to him. He was not even aware of Lavinia standing beside him until she spoke.

"Trust Miss Larkin not to miss an opportunity. She tries so obviously to gain attention that it's quite sickening."

Phillipe glanced impatiently down at her, and he found no pleasure in the small, oval face, in her pale, even features.

"I believe," he answered coolly, "that it is because she does not seek attention that everyone finds her so attractive."

Lavinia was startled and furious at his ungallant reply, he could see it in the tightening of her rouged mouth and the cold sparkle of her eyes. Her fingers moved idly through the pearls at her throat.

"I'm afraid I don't feel well," she announced after a moment of consideration. "I'm going to have the carriage brought around, and if you care to accompany me, you may. Or if it pleases you, you may stay and join that crowd of idiots gathering around that stupid girl. I don't really care."

Lavinia turned, and left the room, unnoticed by anyone, her rose-colored silk skirts hissing.

Phillipe's eyes traveled longingly across the room, through the powdered, perfumed throng, until he saw Victoria, her ruddy curls shining like a sunset, her lovely face glowing with laughter as she listened to that popinjay Hamilton sing her praises.

As if she felt Phillipe's gaze, she turned and gave him a brilliant smile and an easy shrug, as if to say, "Isn't this bloody silly?" before turning back to her admirers.

Phillipe sighed heavily before joining Lavinia in the foyer, where she was haranguing a servant for not locating her wrap quickly enough.

"So you decided to join me," she snapped. "How very fortunate for me. I suppose I should consider myself lucky that at least one man here has the intelligence to prefer my company to that of that . . . that little trollop."

Phillipe found that he wanted to slap Lavinia's spoiled, petulant face. *Good luck, St. Sebastien*, he thought, *you have at least forty more years of this to look forward to.*

"My dear Lavinia," he said coldly, "please don't lower yourself to such undignified remarks. It is so . . . *déclassé*."

Lavinia grew very quiet and cold, and Phillipe wondered if he had gone too far. She did not object, however, when he helped her into her cape; and she allowed him to accompany her home, sulking silently all the way.

He sat alone in his room later that night, reading through the mail that had arrived from London—a letter from his friend Etienne urging him to return to France, and a hastily scrawled missive from Christianna, full of nonsensical gossip and copies of her bills, including one for an ermine-trimmed cape that made him swear, and a ridiculously high amount owed to her hairdresser that made him grit his teeth.

Are you married yet, Christianna wrote in her careless hand, *for I'm afraid that my bills are a*

*little out of hand, and I don't know what to do.
Etienne writes that you are as good as engaged,
and that there will be lots of money. I hope she
isn't too awful . . .*

"Ah, but she is," Phillipe whispered, and he
wondered again what it would be like to be
married to Lavinia. He crumpled his mail in
disgust and poured himself a glass of brandy,
gazing out the windows at the vast lawns of
Harrington Park, dark and shadowy in the
moonlight. He wondered what Victoria was doing, if she was thinking of him, if she had decided to go to France with him when he left. He
couldn't delay much longer, he knew.

He tried to imagine her face when she first
walked up the ancient staircase in the great hall
of the château, imagined her hair shining in the
light from the high, stained-glass windows. He
could see children, their children, running
through the brambles and overgrown hedges of
the gardens, racing up and down the staircases
of the towers, filling the ancient halls with their
happy laughter.

Almost immediately, the image faded, to be
replaced by one of Lavinia, furious and miserable, twenty long days away from Paris, trapped
in the cold, craggy mountains, and in his mind
he could hear her voice, high and piercing. "I
thought I would see Versailles, why am I not at
court, Phillipe? I didn't get married to rot in
this backwater . . ." and he could see children, at
least seven of them, regarding him with pouting

rosebud mouths, golden-haired hellions whining at him for ponies and parties and trips to Paris and tours of Italy and . . .

"Good God, I'm losing my mind," he said aloud, shaking his head. This was ridiculous, this schoolboy fantasizing, and completely pointless. If the château was to survive, he must marry Lavinia, and that was that. He had been perfectly contented with his choice of brides, he reminded himself, until Miss Larkin had interfered.

Damn her, anyway. What kind of wife would she make? She wades in creeks, and throws as well as a man, and reads Greek, and can shear a sheep, and cries at the sound of Bach, and swears like a sailor, and makes love like a lioness; and if that wasn't enough to frighten a man, what was? She was upsetting his plans in the most annoying way, and it had gone far enough, he decided.

Tomorrow, he swore, he would tell her that he was sorry, but that he wanted nothing more to do with her.

Twenty minutes later, all resolution vanished, he was dropping an unseemly amount of coins into the hands of a tired-looking footman in exchange for the directions to Victoria's room.

"I really shouldn't say, sir," the young man protested, his eyes looking nervously around the darkened hall. "Halliwell would have my job if he knew."

Phillipe sighed, and added another coin to the pile.

"Up the stairs, through the gallery and the music room, and the fourth door on the right," directed the young man, pocketing the coins.

"You're too kind," Phillipe murmured, turning to go.

"And sir?"

Phillipe turned impatiently. "Well, what now?"

"I was going to say, be careful, sir. I've heard that she can throw knives."

Phillipe raised an incredulous brow. "Can she, really? God help us."

"Exactly, sir."

Phillipe took the stairs two at a time, stopping to steal a bouquet of roses from an arrangement in the music room, and made his way silently down the dark hallway. He took a deep breath before knocking softly on the door.

"Now what?" Mary demanded within, pulling the hairbrush through Victoria's curls and looking suspiciously towards the door. "As if things weren't lively enough around here without midnight callers. And you in your nightdress . . ."

"Go ahead, answer it," Victoria replied, her heartbeat accelerating.

Mary crossed the darkened room and opened the door to reveal the marquis, looking slightly disheveled in his white shirt, without his coat, a tired-looking bunch of roses clutched in his hand.

Victoria wanted to sing with joy, but she remained seated at the dressing table and spoke calmly.

"Let him in, Mary, it's all right."

Mary raised a brow, as if to say that she doubted that, but she opened the door, dropping a grudging curtsy.

Victoria didn't move from her chair and offered him a cool smile over her shoulder in the mirror.

"Please, come in, monsieur. I was afraid you'd been taken ill. You disappeared so suddenly tonight."

Phillipe felt as awkward as a schoolboy in the feminine room, with the small, dark-haired maid looking daggers at him from beneath the ruffled edge of her mob-cap, and Victoria seated in a glowing circle of candlelight, with her beautiful hair loose and shining, as poised and calm as a princess in her white nightgown.

"Actually, Lavinia insisted that we leave," he finally answered.

"And what Lavinia wants must be done," Victoria exclaimed lightly. "It's really too bloody bad. I had a very interesting evening. Tell me, what do you think of this?" She lifted a sparkling pendant from the shining surface of the table and held it out to him, the chain dangling from her slender finger.

Phillipe, caught off guard, crossed the room and took the pendant, examining it curiously. "It's a diamond, I think. Where did it come from?"

"It was tucked in the pocket of my cape, with a letter. Just hear this. 'Dear Miss Larkin. This is to replace the teardrop which you so carelessly lost. I hope that I will see you again, soon. With warmest admiration, Charles Lawrence.' What do you make of that?"

"That pup," Phillipe exclaimed indignantly. "He hopes that you will become his mistress. You must send it back without delay. What nerve he has. The spoiled creature."

Victoria felt gratified by Phillipe's show of temper, but managed not to laugh. "I see," she replied. "Really, this is bloody funny, isn't it? Harry, Lawrence, you ... Only Johnathon seems to have the good manners not to ask me such a thing."

The marquis sputtered furiously. "Don't mention me in the same breath as those ... bounders," he ordered. "It's a very different thing."

"I'll say it is. They don't have fiancées, and Lawrence sent a diamond, whereas you have only brought me those sorry-looking flowers."

Phillipe glanced down at his hand, remembering the roses, forgotten and a little sad-looking. He felt very foolish.

"They are for me, aren't they?" Victoria went on, and a teasing smile danced around the corners of her mouth. "Or are they for Mary?" she asked, indicating the disapproving-looking little maid.

"Of course they're for you," he replied impatiently. "*Bon Dieu*, Victoria, you really do have the most aggravating sense of humor."

She smiled up at him with a brilliant smile and took the roses from his hand. "Thank you. I'd rather have your sorry-looking roses than a crown of diamonds from Charles Lawrence. You're right, he is a pup."

"Victoria," he said suddenly, "I need to speak to you. Alone," he added, casting an impatient glance at Mary, whose eyes widened nervously.

"It's all right, Mary. You can go."

Mary looked unsure, but gave Victoria a tremulous smile and nodded as she left, closing the door softly behind her.

Phillipe rested his hands on Victoria's slender shoulders, standing behind her, studying her reflection in the mirror. Without Mary's comforting presence in the room, Victoria felt her self-assured poise vanishing, and the warmth of Phillipe's hands on her made her heartbeat quicken, brought a flush to her cheeks.

"I need an answer," he said quietly. "I can't put Lavinia off much longer. The situation in France is becoming treacherous, and I can't abandon my sister, or my home. Already, Christianna owes more money to tradesmen than I see in a year, and the servants at the château must be paid, or it will be a ruin. I need to know if you will come with me when I go."

For a few moments Victoria didn't answer, just sat listening to the silence of the sleeping house, the ticking of the china clock on the mantelpiece, the distant bark of a dog somewhere in the summer night outside the open window. The light of the single candle reflected with a golden warmth off the mirror before her, the soft light shining on the sharp planes of Phillipe's face, casting shadows beneath the curve of his lip and the line of his cheekbones.

"I don't know what to do," she answered. "How should I know, Phillipe? How would it be different to be your mistress, from being Harry's or Lawrence's? Even if I love you, it's the same thing. Do you think of me as they do? Do all rich men just marry for money and then buy themselves a poor girl for pleasure? I don't like it, not at all, and I bloody well don't want to be part of it."

"Is that your answer, Victoria?" His voice was low and soft.

Victoria looked down at the table before her, her eyes coming to rest on the wilting roses lying on top of a letter she had written to James . . . *Dear Jamie, everything is very boring here . . . Nothing unusual has happened at all* . . . the first time she had ever lied to her brother.

"Yes. I'll stay until your betrothal is announced, and then I'll go home. I'll not leave my family—it would break their hearts."

How funny, she thought, that her voice could sound so calm, so resolute.

Phillipe drew a deep breath, and his eyes focused on some invisible point in the room. He looked very tired, and far away.

"I'm sorry," he said at last. "Very sorry. If I could take back what I've done, I would, because it was monstrously unfair. Of course, you're doing the right thing. You can't break your father's heart, or your brothers'." His fingers moved softly against her neck, touched one shining curl.

"I'm not sorry," Victoria said. "Not about what I've done, anyway; but I hate to end it. I do love you, you know." The touch of his hand was like silk in her hair, the warmth of his fingers gentle against her throat, and she turned her face to his palm and pressed her lips against it.

"Kiss me," she whispered, rising from the chair; and she turned to face him, her hands moving hesitantly to his shoulders, feeling the warmth of his skin beneath the fine linen.

Her eyes glowed green in her pale face, her body pressed against him with a soft, welcoming warmth, and he bent to kiss her mouth, tasting the sweet softness of her lips, the melting heat of her tongue against his, hot and gentle.

Her skin was warm beneath the light fabric of her nightgown, and he stroked the length of her back, his hands following the curve of her spine, feeling her nakedness beneath the thin cotton.

"Oh, God, Victoria," he murmured when their lips parted, his breath warm against her hair as he held her to his body. "Do you have any idea what you do to me?"

She was shaken, violent waves of heat washing over her body, feeling him against her, her back pressing against the dressing table, the hardness of him firm against her, his hands tracing the curves of her bosom, her nipples stiffening almost painfully at the touch.

Wantonly, she pressed against him, lifting herself to the surface of the dressing table and wrapping her arms and legs around him, pulling him to her body, feeling the hard length of him pressed against the very core of her. Her hips rocked against him, and he sighed, a ragged sound, before dropping his mouth to the tender skin of her neck, trailing hot, soft kisses to her collarbone.

His fingers teased her nipples through the thin cotton of her nightdress, his hands filling with the soft roundness of her breasts, and her spine arched back at his touch. She knew that his mouth would follow, and longed for it; she pushed her nightdress from her shoulders and let it fall to her waist.

Phillipe felt his blood race at the sight of her, her slender torso and round breasts glowing like satin in the golden candlelight, her hair spilling over her back, the filmy white fabric of her nightdress falling across her lap, her slender legs wrapping tightly around his hips, pulling him towards her. Behind her, the mirror on the dressing table reflected the soft glow of the candle, the pale skin of her back, the sweet curve of her derrière, like a ripe peach, he thought, and his hands curved around her back to stroke it, his palms caressing the round curves.

Once more, she thought, leaning into the strength of his body with a bittersweet longing, and she whispered the words against the warm skin of his throat, her breath moving through the clean black silk of his hair.

She lifted her mouth to his again and fed hungrily on the warm brandy taste of it, her body melting against his. He pulled his shirt off impatiently, eager for the feeling of her silken curves against his chest, and his hands moved up the length of her legs, stroking the skin of her thighs, parting them and moving in the damp petals of her. She trembled at his skillful touch, and writhed shamelessly against his fingers, her head tossing in fevered desire.

She reached for the pressing, hard length of him, her hands trembling as she felt the heat through the strained fabric of his breeches, and Phillipe groaned low in his throat at the touch of her hand.

His breeches went the way of his shirt, and Victoria moaned with delight as he entered her, slowly filling her with the hot, throbbing length, his hands around the backs of her thighs, opening her wider to his possession, almost lifting her off the table.

Their eyes locked together in the moment of possession, hot and bright with fire, echoing the age-old need that drove them towards the heat of each other's bodies.

For a moment he pulled back, his eyes drinking in the sight of her, naked and gleaming in the candlelight, her breasts rising and falling with her rapid breathing, the soft, pink petals of her most intimate places shamelessly open to his gaze, the sight of his throbbing shaft still half buried in the tightness of her, the gleaming curtain of her hair spilling over her shoulders, and the whole scene reflecting back from the mirror behind them.

Intoxicated by the sight, he moved into her, held her against him, and began to rock into the sweet velvet of her grip.

She writhed against him with the grace of a seasoned courtesan, yet blindingly beautiful in her innocent desire. She was lost in the call of her body, in the feeling of him as he filled her again and again, swiftly, with an intensity that she had never dreamed of. She gripped the strength of his shoulders, pulling herself against him, and his mouth plundered hers, burning her very soul, the rhythm of his tongue echoing that of his hips.

Her legs tightened around his waist, his hands were gripping the curves of her haunches, lifting her against him, filling her completely, the very core of her tightly against the heat of his root.

Mindless with passion, she rotated against him, her hips moving in fevered circles, and the flooding heat that spiraled through her half-maddened her.

His mouth covered hers as she cried out, the sound disappearing into the heat, the taste of him, summer wine taste, melting into her. She rode him wildly, the friction of their bodies plunging her into a light-sharded blackness, brilliant spasms racking through her body, through her soul; and she heard his low, fierce cry of triumph through a blinding flash of sensation as he exploded in the pulsing heat of her body.

He held her tightly, rocking her gently as the throbbing pulse of their passion faded, her heartbeat slowing. She leaned her head weakly against his shoulder, damp with sweat, and she drew a shaking breath as the world came back into focus.

She felt the warmth of his breath against the top of her head, and he rubbed his cheek against her hair.

"Good God," he muttered, sounding more than a little dazed. "Good God, Victoria. I could have at least taken you to the bed."

She laughed softly. "The bed? Is that where this should be done?" She stretched her legs languidly, like a cat.

They untangled their limbs, laughing softly at their own passion, their voices soft and quiet, the sound of contented lovers, and he carried her to the bed and lay next to her.

They touched each other's bodies softly, exploring with quiet tenderness the curves and hollows of their forms, their eyes bright and soft.

"You're very beautiful," he told her, his fingers playing along the taut skin of her stomach, his voice soft in the summer night. "I was mad with jealousy tonight."

"Jealous of whom?" she asked curiously, stretching deliciously beneath his touch, basking in the warmth of his body.

"Every man at Lawrence's. Every man in the world who may offer you what I cannot—a home, an honorable life."

Victoria laughed, without bitterness, just at how funny it seemed. "They don't offer me anything honorable at all. It seems that honor is reserved for members of their own station, and we lowly poor are for . . . amusement. To keep them from being miserable with their wretched wives, I suppose."

Phillipe felt slightly ashamed. "You make it sound very stupid and sordid."

"It is," Victoria agreed, tracing the sharp line of his profile with a finger, stopping on his firm mouth for a kiss. "Except for us. We're very different, you know."

Phillipe examined her face carefully, but there was no mockery in it, just pleasure; and she gave him a smile so radiant that it shamed him.

"Because you love me," she added, laying her cheek against the soft, dark hair that covered his chest.

Phillipe sat straight up. "I *what*? I've said nothing of the sort," he objected.

Victoria smiled lazily, planting a kiss on his

shoulder. "That's all right," she said airily, dismissing his objection. "You needn't say so. I can tell."

He laughed quietly, running his hands through the wild tangle of her hair, smoothing it away from the soft skin of her face. "Oh, you can tell, can you? You, with your vast experience of men."

Victoria met his eyes, the teasing light gone from her own. "I know enough to know when somebody truly loves me, and when they don't. Harry didn't, you do. That's what."

"But I have not said so," Phillipe said feebly, helpless in the face of this logic.

"No, you 'ave' not," she answered, mocking his accent. "But that bothers me not a whit."

She felt his exasperated sigh, but he didn't argue again; he simply lay beside her, stroking her body and playing in her hair while the sweet languor of the quiet night stole over her and she lay in his arms as if asleep, listening to the sounds of his heartbeat and breath, smelling his skin, wishing that she might sleep this way every night, forever.

After a while, he sighed heavily, his breath warm against her hair, and she heard his whisper.

"Sweet Victoria. *Je t'aime*."

He started at the sound of her sleepy laughter.

"That much French I do know. You see—I told you you loved me."

He felt a mingling of amusement and annoyance, and kissed her almost roughly, feeling the laughter bubbling on the lips beneath his. With a growl of mock annoyance, he disappeared beneath the covers, burying his face between her thighs, moving his tongue against the soft, seashell taste of her, until her mingled laughter and protestations turned to soft moans, floating into the dark, quiet air.

Chapter Twelve

July rushed in, hot and brilliant days of roses and hollyhocks, of shimmering fountains under cloudless skies. Warm breezes carried the country scent of warm hay through the air, and purple foxgloves grew in showy clusters next to dusty roads, showing their spotted throats beneath their glossy petals.

And Victoria was in love, for the first time in her life. She understood for the first time why a drunkard would seek out more drink even as he knew that it would hurt him, for in just such a way she thirsted for Phillipe, longed to be close to him. She waited with longing for the stolen kisses in the stables, the notes passed beneath the table, the silently mouthed *"Je t'aime"* that he would send her as they passed each other in the hall.

And most of all, she longed for the nights, when she would leave her bed and spend moon-lit nights in his arms, beneath the ancient cano-pies of oak trees, or in the cool sheets of his bed that smelled intoxicatingly of his warm skin and sandalwood. She told him that she liked the smell, and the next day he gave her a fan, its delicate spokes carved of sandalwood. When she waved the ivory silk of it, the scent would waft around her face, transporting her thoughts to the waiting night.

Victoria was no longer bored in the least. Oc-casionally, she felt guilt, and sometimes (not often) pity for Lavinia, who waited with grow-ing dismay for Phillipe "to speak." There were mornings when Victoria blushed with horror at her own wanton behavior, and Mary would look at her flaming cheeks and kiss-reddened lips, and offer to say a few prayers for her soul.

She laughed at Mary, and asked if she thought that God would forgive her if she low-ered the neckline on the white gown, and the yellow, and why not the sky-blue striped as well?

As each day passed with no news of Phillipe's and Lavinia's betrothal, Victoria allowed her-self to hope.

Johnathon was troubled by Victoria's behavior. He was very fond of her, happy with their easy friendship, and though they never spoke of it, he knew what was happening, and it troubled him. Not that he ever said a word, but Victoria could see the worry in his dark brown eyes, and the uncomfortable silences that passed between them made her feel uneasy and, worse, guilty.

Their rides through the countryside were less and less frequent, and Victoria was often distracted and nervous when they went. Johnathon, in turn, was unsure of this new Victoria, who had suddenly acquired a lush, carnal beauty. Her eyes glistened dreamily, her cheeks glowed with vibrant color, and her breasts seemed to swell out of her tightly laced bodices. True, she glowed with health, and her laughter rang out as often as ever, but Johnathon sometimes fancied that it sounded strained, and every now and then he saw a shadow cross her face, caught a glimpse of sorrow in her eyes.

It was another balmy afternoon, and Victoria and Johnathon were returning from the village, riding past fields of ripening grain and occasional cottages. The horses' hooves kicked up the dust of the road, and Victoria wondered if there had ever been a July as hot as this. The heat didn't usually bother her, but today it was making her feel suffocated. She felt dizzy, and reined in beneath a shady tree.

Not enough sleep, she told herself, wiping the sweat from her brow with a lace-edged handkerchief. She had passed the night in Phillipe's bed, and he had been wild for her, taking her once, twice, three times. *"Say 'please', Miss Larkin . . ."*

"Victoria, did you hear me?"

Startled, Victoria looked at Johnathon, who

was watching her with concern. It irritated her, this worried expression he had been wearing of late, his high forehead wrinkled beneath the smooth golden wings of his hair, his brown eyes always seeming to ask, *Is everything all right, Vic?*

"I'm sorry. I think it's the heat," she lied, knowing that he knew it was a lie. "Why, what did you say?"

"I said I've had a letter from Harry. He asks me to beg your forgiveness. He says he has been miserable."

Victoria sighed. Harry. She wanted to forget about Harry. She wanted to forget about everyone, for that matter—Lavinia, cousin Abigail, her father, Jamie . . . even Johnathon, who was always kind, but whose eyes mirrored the fears and doubts that she felt so keenly.

"Good," she answered shortly, the heat making her crosser than usual. "Harry deserves to be miserable. I hope he chokes on it."

Johnathon's eyes looked at her, sorrowful and steady. "He means it, Vic. And I'm not arguing that he was not horrible to you, but I believe he's truly sorry. He would never have done such a thing had he been sober."

Victoria looked away from Johnathon's puppy-dog eyes, across the fields of grain that shimmered in the sun to the rolling green hills. For a moment, she longed for home, where everything had been so simple.

"You don't understand," she said at last. "I will never forgive Harry. I thought that he was my friend, Johnathon, and he bloody well insulted me. He thought to buy me, Johnathon, as if I were a doxy that he could take home for a few crowns. He offered me a carriage, a little house—"

"And what did *Monsieur le Marquis* offer you, Victoria?" The words were soft and low, but they struck Victoria with the force of a blow.

She turned on Johnathon with hot rage, shame and defiance staining her cheeks red, her eyes hot.

"Don't you ever speak to me like that! What do you know of it, what right do you have?"

Fairfield swallowed, his cheeks flushed. He avoided her eyes. "No right, I suppose, but that I am your friend." He paused, and for a second there was a glimmer of tears in his eyes. "And I had hoped for something more, Victoria. I care for you very much, and . . . I would never have insulted you by making you my whore."

Victoria felt sick. Her stomach twisted. It was true, wasn't it? Despite all the tender words that passed between her and Phillipe, the bare, ugly fact was that she was his whore. Damn Johnathon, damn him for saying it, for flinging it in her face. She fought her tears, biting her bottom lip hard.

"I'm not his whore," she whispered. "He loves me, Johnathon. He told me so."

Johnathon's brown eyes darkened, his hands tightened on the reins. "He did, did he? That was damned nice of him, wasn't it? And while he told you of his love, did he make any reasonable, decent offers? Has he offered to marry you, Vic?"

"He may," she cried, knowing that she was trying to convince herself, as well. "He may. He hasn't offered for Lavinia yet, has he?"

Johnathon looked at her sadly and pushed a strand of honey-colored hair from his forehead. "I pray that you're right, Vic. But I'm afraid that you'll be hurt. The French are much more sophisticated about such things, more jaded than we English. Words of love spoken between the sheets are a game, part of the fun, part of the chase. If you believe what a man says to you in the heat of passion, you're sure to be hurt."

Victoria felt sick, ashamed and embarrassed that Johnathon would speak to her so frankly. He was wrong, he must be. Why was he saying these terrible things to her, hurting her like this? Johnathon moved to her, as if to take her hand to comfort her, and the sadness in his gentle face was more than Victoria could bear.

"Go to hell," she cried, pulling her horse away from him. "Leave me alone! Don't ever say such things to me again. I don't want to think of it, I don't want to hear it. I love him, don't you see? And I know that he loves me. I won't have you soil it with your pious lectures!"

"I pray to God you're right, Vic," he repeated simply, looking as if he had been slapped.

Victoria kicked her horse into a gallop and left him on the road, staring sadly after her.

By the time she reached the cool, dark sanctuary of her room, she was miserable with heat and confusion, dizzy with the ugly words that had been hurled at her.

She retched into her chamber pot, then pulled the heavy blue curtains tight against the glaring sun, and lay across the cool sheets of her bed, and slept.

Phillipe St. Sebastien was, to his great dismay, in love. There was no longer any point in denying it, even to himself. If Victoria had been enchanting in her blushing innocence, she was doubly so in her newfound sensuality. Her green eyes shone secrets at him by day, her body twined to his each night as if it had been made to fit him. Her husky voice whispered words of love in his ear, as sweet and delicious as honey; and when he slept, her words haunted his dreams.

It was after such a dream that he came to the realization that he could not marry Lavinia.

Damn the château, damn Christianna and her bills, damn France, if he must, he would have Victoria. He would take her to the Auvergne, to the mountains and the ancient castle, and if the accursed timbers of the roof caved in on them, good. He would die happy.

He felt as if a great weight had been lifted from his shoulders, as if he had been reborn, and when he saw Lavinia at breakfast, he told her that he would be leaving soon, and thanked her for her hospitality.

She waited, her blue eyes fastened expectantly on his face, for the proposal she was sure would come. When it did not, she excused herself with ice-cold courtesy and retired to her room.

Phillipe felt only a quick pang of conscience through his joy, then blessed, utter relief. He sought Victoria, only to be told that she was riding with Fairfield.

With his heart as light as it had been since he was a child, he retired to the library to await Victoria.

The library was cool and quiet, the walnut wood gleaming in the sun. Phillipe settled himself in a wing chair and picked up a slender book that lay on the table, a ribbon lying across the open page. He wondered if Victoria had left it there, and when he read the words of the poetry on the page, he was sure that she had.

> Come live with me and be my love
> And we will all the pleasures prove
> That hills and valleys, dales and fields,
> Or woods or steepy mountain yields.

Yes, Victoria had left this for him, he was sure, and left her ribbon on the page. He took the piece of sky-blue silk and tucked it in his pocket with a smile. Perhaps tonight he would offer it back to her, with his mother's emerald ring tied to the end. He imagined the look of shock on her face when he would put it on her slender finger and tell her that he would have no other but her.

A deep cough startled him and looking up,

he saw Lord Cecil Harrington standing in the doorway, his ample girth clothed in his well-worn riding clothes, his ruddy face examining Phillipe with suspicion.

"*Bon-joor*, as you would say," Lord Cecil greeted him, in his lamentable accent, but the slight lift of his gruff brow was at odds with his lighthearted greeting.

"Sir," Phillipe returned uneasily; and his wariness increased as the earl closed the heavy door behind him and settled his heavy body in the chair next to Phillipe's, regarding him with a suspicious eye.

"Well then," Cecil began uncomfortably, and stopped to clear his throat. He raised a knowing brow at the book in Phillipe's hands. "Poetry, eh? I shouldn't wonder."

Phillipe was feeling distinctly uncomfortable, but he simply raised a brow at the earl's piercing scrutiny.

Lord Cecil's jaw wagged as if he were secretly laughing. "Oh, you're a cool one, aren't you? Comes from being French, I suppose. That bothered me from the beginning, by Jove. But Lavinia would hear none of it. I daresay the ladies find you irresistible, dashing, with your foreign ways."

Phillipe thought it wise to remain silent.

"All right, then, let's be blunt. Lavinia has come to me, shrieking like a fishwife. Says that you are leaving without asking for her. Not that I mind. I never cared for the idea of a bunch of French in-laws, but Lavinia is very put out."

"I'm sorry," Phillipe answered, trying to compose his features. "I never intended to hurt Lavinia, but I find—"

"Never mind that. You found that she is spoiled, petty and willful. You found that beneath her pretty face is a very unattractive spirit. I'm not blind, sir, though some around here seem to think I am. I'm not here to argue about my daughter's character, or lack of it. I want to know, my fine young man, what you intend to do about our Miss Larkin."

Phillipe sat as if he had been struck dumb, and the old earl looked very pleased with himself.

"That's right, Miss Larkin. I'm not blind, or stupid, and damned little gets by me. I know that she loves you, I know that you've bedded her, and I want to know what you intend to do about it. If you haven't thought about it, you'd better start, by Jove. The girl was left under my roof a virgin, an innocent; and you with your pretty voice and fine looks made short work of that. The girl may be poor, but she is a relative, and by God—"

Phillipe's blue eyes narrowed. "You misjudge me, sir. It is not my intention to seduce her and be on my way. I adore her, and I intend to marry her."

Lord Cecil leaned back in his chair, looking very surprised, and very amused. "You do, do you? By Jove, Lavinia will be angry, won't she? You know what this means, don't you? I shall have to buy her sixty new gowns, and send her to Bath."

Phillipe smiled in utter relief. "I'm sorry, sir. I hope that my change of heart won't cost you too much."

Cecil waved an indifferent hand. "Nonsense. Now go moon about, or write a sonnet, or whatever it is that young men in love do. And I hope to hear an announcement before morning."

"So do I," Phillipe agreed warmly. "With all my heart."

He tactfully avoided Lavinia for the rest of the day and spent the afternoon packing and organizing his belongings. He declined to go down to dinner, and had a helpful footman deliver a note to Victoria, telling her to expect him at ten. *Please*, he wrote as an afterthought, knowing that it would make her laugh.

The clock in the music room was just striking ten when he made his way across the landing at the top of the great marble staircase and heard the tense voice of Halliwell, the butler, speaking to someone in the empty hall.

The voice that replied was frantic, excited, and Phillipe realized that the speaker was answering in a confused jumble of French and English. The words that floated up to him caused him to stop.

"*Cherche* . . . to find St. Sebastien . . . please hurry . . . *horrifiant* . . . *désastreux* . . . *une foule de populace* . . ."

Phillipe felt an unholy sense of foreboding and quickly descended the staircase, his heels rapping a sharp staccato over the smooth marble in the dark foyer.

He saw a harried-looking Halliwell trying desperately to calm a man in servant's livery, a man he recognized as the valet of his friend Etienne DuBay, who owned the shipping company in London that Phillipe had invested heavily in.

"It's all right, Halliwell; I believe that this caller is for me," he called quickly, and Etienne's valet turned towards him gratefully as he slipped easily into French. "Please, what's happened? This disaster that you speak of, what is it? Etienne? The business?"

The man stared at Phillipe, and drew a deep breath, and Phillipe saw that he had traveled hard, the dust from the roads covering his pale face. The man wiped the sweat from his brow with a trembling hand before he answered.

"No, my lord marquis, it is worse, much worse. It is France."

Phillipe felt the sickening foreboding creep over him again.

"The revolutionaries have taken Paris. The boatloads of *emigrées* have begun to arrive in London, they are telling horrible stories . . ."

The exhausted man stopped at the sight of the marquis's set, white face, the ice-blue eyes. *Tell him easily*, Etienne had said, but there was no easy way to say it.

"They have freed the prisoners from the Bastille, the mobs have taken the streets, they are marching on Versailles. They ... they are slaughtering aristocrats, arresting them by the hundreds ... they say that the streets of Paris are red with blood."

Phillipe felt sick with horror. "My sister ... Christianna."

She was there in the palace with the royal family. What would the mob make of her, with her proud face and pretty silks, bearing the infamous St. Sebastien name, the name of one of the most depraved and hated men in the kingdom, thanks to Phillipe's whoreson grandfather. They would not be kind to her, Phillipe feared. Evidently the messenger of the ominous news agreed, for at the mention of Christianna St. Sebastien's name, he bowed his head and crossed himself, a quick prayer on his lips.

"A lovely girl, monsieur, I'm sure they will be merciful to her."

"*Merde*," Phillipe replied contemptuously. "I am sure they will not." He felt as if his blood had turned to ice. The quiet foyer with its soaring ceilings echoed his words in a nightmarish way.

"Stay here," he ordered the manservant. "I'll collect my things and return to London with you. If there is a way to bring her out, I'll find it."

He left the shaken man in the silent hall and went rapidly to his room, trying to fight the fear that was rising in his chest.

Amy Elizabeth Saunders

Christianna, the last member of his family, the black-curled cherub who had consoled him in the long, empty days of his childhood.

When they told him that his mother had died, he had crept to the nursery, a grubby, heartbroken ten-year-old, and had lifted the sleeping baby from her cradle and held her against his heart. His tears had fallen on her fat baby cheeks, on her dimpled arms, on her silky black curls. He told her not to be frightened, that he would always take care of her, and she had stared trustingly at him with round blue eyes, a dimpled fist in her mouth, as he wept.

"I won't lose you," he whispered furiously. "I'm coming home, piglet."

Home to what? He wondered, but the answer was immaterial. He was going to do whatever he could; he wouldn't turn his back on the last member of his family.

How odd, he thought, that what had begun as one of the happiest nights of his life should have turned into a nightmare.

He seized a pen and paper from the writing table in his barren room and began to write hastily, the emerald on his finger flashing in the candlelight.

Ma chère Victoria,
Forgive me for leaving so suddenly, but I have just received word of a disaster in Paris. A mob has taken the city, and they are apparently slaughtering the aristocracy in cold blood. I know that

242

*you, who love your brothers so dearly, will under-
stand the reason for my departure—Christianna
is there, and if she still lives, I must bring her out.*

*I hope that these are wild rumors, and that I
may return to you within days, but I know not
what to expect.*

*Do not doubt me, I will return. Wait for me, I
beg of you.*

*Keep this letter well, and if you doubt me, read
this—you are my heart, my love, and the day I
return, I would have you marry me . . . please. The
château be damned, Lavinia be damned, I will
have you for my wife.*

*If you have need of money, I will leave instruc-
tions with Etienne DuBay, of Harmon Street,
London, to advance you as much as you need. I
know that you will say, money for what? But I
will rest more easily knowing that you are pro-
vided for.*

*Already I long for you, remember me in your
haphazard prayers, and keep yourself well until I
return. I love you.*

He blotted the ink dry, traded his shoes for
his well-worn riding boots, and shouldered his
trunk easily. A feeling of unreality surrounded
him as he made his way through the quiet hallways of Harrington Park, as if this were all a
dream and he would soon awaken.

As he descended the staircase, a passing maid
caught his eye, vaguely familiar, with dark curls
escaping from beneath her white cap. He

caught her arm, and she pulled back in alarm at the sight of his stark, white face, his glittering eyes. He pressed Victoria's letter into her hand.

"This letter," he said swiftly. "It must be taken to Miss Larkin, without delay. See to it."

Mutely, the girl nodded, her eyes round.

"*Merci*," he said hurriedly, and continued down the stairway.

The girl watched curiously as he spoke to the waiting servant in the foyer, and he and the man exchanged indecipherable foreign words by the front door before leaving.

After a few moments, there came the sound of horses' hooves on the gravel drive, fading into the distance.

Slowly, the maid turned and began up the stairs, staring curiously at the hastily folded paper in her hand. In a few moments, she entered her mistress's bedchamber and extended the intriguing letter towards the girl in the bed.

"What do you want, Daisy?" Lavinia snapped. "I made it quite clear that I don't wish to be disturbed."

"Oh, yes, m'lady. But I thought that this letter might interest you a bit—seeing as how the Frenchman wanted me to take it to Miss Victoria. Without delay, he said."

Lavinia's eyes shone coldly, her face still. She sat up in her bed and held out an imperious hand. Daisy handed the missive over obediently, and watched as her mistress scanned the words, bright red spots staining her cheeks.

"It's just like I thought, isn't it, m'lady—they're lovers, aren't they?"

"Shut up, Daisy." Lavinia's lips tightened, her hands trembling with suppressed rage as she read Phillipe's declaration of love, his proposal of marriage.

"What does it say?" the irrepressible Daisy queried.

"It says that Miss Larkin is a whore," Lavinia spat, her voice bitter. She crumpled the paper in a shaking fist and handed it to Daisy. "Burn this. Right now, in front of me, and don't mention it to anyone."

The maid went to the empty fireplace and lay the paper on the grate, hesitating a moment before she touched a lit candle to it.

Lavinia left her bed and put her beribboned dressing gown over the gossamer white of her nightdress. "Don't sit there, stupid. Come and do my hair. I have a little call to pay on my sweet cousin."

Daisy looked at Lavinia's cold, angry eyes reflecting the already dying flame, and was very glad that she wasn't Miss Larkin.

"I'm sorry we're not going to France, m'lady, and that's the truth," she commiserated, picking up Lavinia's hairbrush. "That would've been grand, it would."

Lavinia's rosebud mouth tightened, and she examined her flawless complexion carefully in the mirror. "Shut up, Daisy," she repeated.

Daisy, after a quick look at Lavinia's cold eyes, shut up.

* * *

When the knock sounded on the door, Victoria's heart leapt, and she felt the blood rush to her cheeks.

"Wait, wait," she whispered to Mary. She dropped her white wrapper to the floor and, shamelessly clad in her undergarments, rushed to her bed and reclined in what she hoped was a seductive pose. "There—how do I look?" she whispered, stifling a laugh.

Mary blushed, and covered her conspirator's smile behind her small, neat hands.

"Very wicked, miss. You'll go straight to hell, no mistake," she answered, her eyes round and dancing with mischief at the sight of Victoria, clad only in her lace-trimmed drawers and tightly laced corset, the ribbons of the corset cover untied to reveal most of Victoria's bosom.

"Hell, indeed. God forgives lovers, Mary," Victoria assured her friend flippantly.

The knock on the door sounded again, louder and more impatient.

"Well, I think it's time for me to go," Mary observed. "Try to sleep a little, miss, and I'll see you in the morning."

"Thank you, Mary, and good night," Victoria whispered.

Mary opened the door quietly, and her startled gasp caused Victoria to lift her head abruptly.

"Isn't this lovely?" Lavinia asked coldly, pushing past Mary. Her face was tight and cool, a sneer playing around her mouth as she cast a disgusted glance at Victoria in her half-naked state. "How charming you look, Miss Larkin. But I'm afraid that your whorish tricks are all in vain. Your gentleman friend won't be joining you, tonight . . . or any other night."

Victoria resisted the impulse to cover herself. Her heart began to thump against the stiff corset, her eyes narrowed like a cat's, and she raised herself on one elbow. "What do you want, Lavinia?" she asked shortly.

Lavinia took her time about answering. She moved around the room, touching the hairbrushes on the dressing table, the bottle of violet-water, the silk fan from Phillipe with its painted pastoral scenes and fragrant sandalwood spokes.

"I came to bring you a message. From Phillipe."

Victoria felt her stomach clutch. Her pulse raced frantically, and she felt like a trapped rabbit, but she forced her voice to remain calm.

"I don't believe you," she answered at last, her eyes traveling from Lavinia's graceful, white-clad figure to Mary, still with her hand on the door handle, her small, round face still with fear.

Lavinia laughed, a shrill, unpleasant sound. "How can our clever Miss Larkin be so stupid?" she asked mockingly. "I shall tell you. You overplayed your hand. You thought that he would marry you, didn't you?"

Victoria swallowed, unable to speak, frozen with shock.

"Good heavens, Miss Larkin, did you really think I didn't know about this? How very stupid of you. Of course, if Phillipe wants to tumble a few peasant girls, it's of no concern to me— though I wish he'd shown more taste."

Victoria began to move forward slowly, her heart pounding, blood roaring in her ears. "You're lying, Lavinia. Get out."

"Of course you would like to think so," Lavinia snapped. "But it's true. And he's gone, Miss Larkin. Gone. He said that you were very amusing, but he's bored with you, and he's left. I'm meeting him at Bath, and we'll announce our engagement there. He felt a little sorry for you. He thought it would be cruel to announce his betrothal in the same house where you . . . well, did what you common girls do, so easily."

Victoria's chest hurt, her eyes burned. "Get out," she repeated, but this time her voice quavered slightly.

"Certainly, I shall," Lavinia replied, a hard smile playing on her full mouth. "And by the way, I'll expect you to have made plans to leave by the end of the week. I don't think I would like to look at my future husband's cast-off whore every morning. It would quite put me off my food. But you may want to make arrangements to leave as soon as possible. I should hate to write to your poor father and tell him the whole sordid story. What would your precious brothers say, I wonder, if they knew that you spent your summer as a Frenchman's whore?"

Victoria clutched the smooth wood of the

bedpost, gripping it until her knuckles turned white. "I'll go," she said, her voice low and shaking. "But hear me, Lavinia—if you say one more word to me, I shall hurt you."

Lavinia saw the glitter in the green eyes, the coiled tension in Victoria's body, and turned to go. She stopped at the door and turned to Mary, who was crying quietly, her small hands clutched in her white apron. "You, of course, are dismissed immediately. You'll have no references from this house. I expect you to be gone by tomorrow."

Lavinia cast a cool smile at Victoria. "One week," she repeated, and left, closing the door softly.

Victoria looked at Mary's woebegone face and felt guilt, guilt such as she had never known. She tried to speak, and could not. Her head felt light, her ears rang. Her stomach lurched violently, and before she could stop herself, she fell to her knees, dragged the chamberpot from beneath the bed, and was miserably sick.

Her stomach emptied itself again and again, till she felt as if she were choking. Hot tears filled her eyes and rolled helplessly down her face, and her breath came in pained, strangled gasps.

She felt Mary's cool hands on her brow, heard Mary's voice making soft, comforting noises, and when her body quieted, Mary helped her to bed and pulled the soft blankets over her, where she lay shivering despite the warm evening.

"She's lying, Mary, she must be. Please, go see where he is, go check his room, please."

Mary wiped a tear from her face with a shaking hand, and nodded. Poor Miss Victoria, who was always so kind and funny, and now looked like a deer in a trap with her eyes so big and dark. Mary wiped her tears on the edge of her apron and went in search of the marquis.

Her search did not take long.

"He's gone, all right. His room is bare, not a note or anything. I had it from one of the footmen that another Frenchman came for him, and off he went. We have problems now, miss."

They both sat on the rumpled blankets of Victoria's bed, whispering in the quiet night.

"And me sacked," Mary added miserably, "and no references. I can't very well go home. Things are so crowded there, and not enough to go around. Mum can't feed another mouth."

Victoria felt a fresh stab of pain, and she longed for home, where the hollyhocks and larkspur would be blooming and the red roses would be climbing up the thick walls of the house, twisting with the ivy.

"Come home with me, Mary. There's room, and food aplenty, and the boys will love you as much as I do. There's more than enough for one more."

Mary looked solemnly at Victoria's pale face, with the dark red curls hanging around it and her grieving eyes, and hated to say it.

"But will there be room for two more, miss?

Because there's more than just you and me to think of, no mistake about it."

Victoria looked blank. "What are you talking about, Mary?" she demanded curiously; and was horrified when Mary began to cry quietly.

"Oh, miss, what do you think? What with you so tired, and twice today you've been sick. There's a baby on the way, a baby! You're in a terrible way, miss."

Victoria was frozen with shock. A baby. She couldn't have a baby. "Oh, no, Mary, you must be wrong. I can't have a baby."

"Oh, yes, you can," Mary argued, "unless you think they grow under cabbage leaves. Think, miss . . . when did you last bleed?"

Victoria was shaking her head, a sense of horror descending on her. "Oh, Mary . . . oh, Mary . . . what will I do? I can't go home—Father would die, and Jamie . . . oh, no. And Gareth would take my head off for being so stupid . . . Oh, good Lord, what have I done?"

She cried, hard choking sobs, bitter tears that soaked Mary's shoulder and ran into her hair.

Mary made soothing noises and calmed her as best she could. "There, miss . . . there . . . we'll think of something. You're not the first girl that's been caught, and you won't be the last."

"No, but I'm the bloody stupidest," Victoria choked. "What do girls do when they're in a fix, Mary?"

Mary thought of a village girl who had tried to abort her own child and had died, bleeding quietly to death in her bed, and shuddered. "They go away until they have the baby and then they go home," she offered at last.

Victoria wondered if this were a nightmare. "And the babies? What happens to the babies?"

Some girls killed their newborns, Mary had heard, but that was horrible, unthinkable. "The babies go to an orphanage, or to a relative . . . a married sister . . . an aunt . . ."

"I haven't got any of those," Victoria answered miserably, "except for Cousin Abigail. What do you think, Mary?" she asked, a note of hysterical laughter in her voice. "Shall I go to her and say, 'Dear cousin, I'm so sorry, but I seemed to have slept with your daughter's husband, and would you mind raising the baby?' "

Mary reached out a calming hand and laid it firmly on Victoria's wet cheek.

"I'll take it," she said calmly. "I'll take your baby, miss."

"Oh, Mary, how? You're in worse trouble than I. You have no living, no home . . ."

"I'll find a living," Mary stated firmly. "And so will you, as long as you can work. I've a bit of a nest egg put by, and we can live on that when you're too far gone to work. And if there's room and food at your house, we can go there after the baby comes. And you can say that it's mine. We'll say . . . that I'm a widow."

Victoria stared in shock at Mary's calm, resolved face. "But . . . but what if the baby looks just like me?"

Mary considered. "We'll say I had a red-haired husband. That's why I grew so fond of you. You have a look of him."

"But what of Abigail and Lord Cecil? And my brothers, when they write . . . not that they write often . . . but where shall we go to find work?"

"London," Mary replied. "My sister Meg says there's lots of work in London, and good wages. As for the rest, we'll have to work that out, and carefully. This is sticky, no mistake about it. But you're clever, miss, and I'm not stupid; and we'll think of something, you can bet on that."

Victoria's head swam, her thoughts tumbling wildly one over the other. Phillipe was gone. She was going to have a baby. She was running away to London to have a baby. Alone. No, not alone, with Mary. She looked at Mary, with her round, dear face and her dark brown eyes that looked so calm—Mary would do all this for friendship, Mary would help her, Mary would raise her baby for her . . .

"Oh, God, Mary . . . you're a better friend than I deserve."

"Nonsense," Mary replied resolutely. "I just want to get a look at those handsome brothers of yours. Now, what shall we tell Lady Abigail?"

They sat together on the high four-poster bed most of the night, whispering, inventing and discarding plans, and crying together, until the candles sputtered and died in the candlestands and the cold, gray light of morning began to fill the room.

And Victoria, numb with anguish and sick with fear, began to live the greatest lie of her life. Her heart twisted with shame, and she cursed Phillipe St. Sebastien with every breath.

Chapter Thirteen

Four days later, in answer to a pleading-sounding letter from their sister, Gareth and James Larkin arrived in the village of St. Stephen's. She had asked them to meet her at the inn in the village, but when they crossed the well-traveled innyard and entered the large public room, with its dark wooden benches and familiar smells of ale and food, she was not to be seen.

"What in the hell is going on, Gareth?" James asked quietly for the hundredth time since Vic's letter had come.

Gareth cast an impatient glance at his younger brother. "Likely, nothing, you dolt. She's just not here yet. Sit down and have a pint and leave off with your worrying. Here," he added, "look at this." He nodded his head towards a buxom serving wench, sending his most charming smile towards her, and the girl sparkled delightedly at the two tall, broad-shouldered young men as she approached.

"What can I bring you?" she asked, her dimpled smile promising more than drink as her eyes flitted back and forth between them.

"Two pints. Did you know," Gareth asked, leaning forward, "that your eyes are bluer than the sky?"

James rolled his eyes as the girl fluttered her lashes, the color in her cheeks deepening. "And cheeks like roses too, I expect," he added, with an impatient look at Gareth. "Actually, we're here to meet our sister, Victoria Larkin. Have you seen her?"

The girl looked at him in surprise for a moment before answering. "Why, you *are* her brothers, aren't you? Not to be rude, but I never would have guessed. I mean, now that I look at your faces, there it is, plain as day, but just from the look of you . . ."

"Is she here, then?" Gareth asked, thinking what a pity it was that such a pretty girl was so thick. Who wouldn't know that they were Victoria's brothers at first look? Especially Jamie, sitting there with Victoria's cat's eyes and fine bones?

The girl's eyes traveled over them curiously, over auburn heads and sun-bleached white shirts, sturdy breeches and worn riding boots.

"Well, yes, she's been here for the better part of an hour, waiting."

James looked pointedly around the empty

room. "Where is she?" he asked slowly, as if he were talking to a child or an idiot.

The girl took umbrage, her pointed nose lifting. "Well! You could hardly expect me to put a lady in the common room, with all the trash that blows in here. She's waiting in a private room. Ladies like that, they see a little drinking or the wrong sort of fellow, or hear rough men swearing, and they get all aflutter, so we just put them in a private dining room. Come on, then."

James and Gareth exchanged confused glances as they followed the girl across the room.

"I think she's talking about someone else," Gareth muttered to James.

James raised a brow at the maid's back. "I don't think she's very bright," he whispered back.

"Here we are," the girl announced, knocking lightly on a heavy door and dropping a curtsy as it opened. "Are these the gentlemen you were expecting, miss?" she asked, her deferential voice very different from the saucy tone she had greeted Gareth and James with.

Victoria had heard them approaching, and just had time to give Mary's hand a quick squeeze and draw a deep breath before the door opened. It took all her self-control not to jump out of her chair and throw her arms around her brothers.

"Yes, thank you, Suzanna," she replied quietly. "That will be all."

James and Gareth entered the room slowly, staring at her, she thought, as if she had grown a third head, as if they had never seen her before, as if they didn't know her.

Maybe they don't, she thought, swallowing the rising lump in her throat.

"Good Lord, Vic. Is that you?" Gareth demanded, his face blank with shock as he took in the slender girl with the elaborately arranged curls, the delicate gown of yellow silk with its seeming miles of embroidery and ribbons, the dainty mitts on her pale hands.

"Oh, Gareth," Victoria said, a catch in her voice. "Oh, Jamie . . ." She rose from the stiff chair she had been sitting in, and tears stung her eyes as she held her arms out to them and was crushed in their arms;—rough, comfortable arms that smelled of fresh air and clean hay, and of home, and for a few moments she forgot why they were here, so glad was she to see them. How good it was to hear their soft country accents . . .

"We've missed you, Vic—"

"Bloody hell, is there steel in this dress, Vic?"

" . . . been worried like the devil since we got your letter—"

"Why is your hair stiff? Is that glue in your hair?"

" . . . don't even look like your grubby little self—"

Over Gareth's broad shoulder, Victoria caught a glimpse of Mary's round face, her eyes worried.

"Don't be silly," she laughed, firmly wiping the tears from her eyes, avoiding Jamie's eyes as she waved to the empty chairs that surrounded the round, dark table, its polished surface reflecting the sunlight from the window. "Sit down, and I shall tell all."

Gareth held her hands tightly in his as they sat. James moved more slowly, his eyes taking in every detail of his sister, who looked like a porcelain doll, her familiar green eyes fluttering nervously, avoiding his stare.

Gareth turned to Mary, smiling his brilliant smile. "Hello, are you Mary? Vic has written to us about you. Will you sit down?"

Mary bobbed a prim curtsy. "No, sir, that wouldn't be right. May I fetch something for you, miss?" Her eyes met Victoria's for a moment, the message clear. *Go ahead, get on with it.*

Victoria hesitated, and bit her lip before speaking, her voice carefully light and breezy. "Oh, yes, Mary, bring something nice. None of that horrid ale. Goodness, Gareth, how silly of you to ask Mary to sit down—I'm afraid you've shocked her."

Good, Mary's eyes told her, *very good.* Playing her role, Mary bobbed another prim curtsy as she left the room.

Victoria drew a shaking breath, avoiding Jamie's and Gareth's shocked faces. *I sound like Lavinia,* she thought. *Good. This will throw them.* She clasped her mitted hands together and smiled, false and bright. "Well, where do I

259

Amy Elizabeth Saunders

start? I've had such fun this summer that I hardly know where to begin. I've been to parties, and balls, and met the most wonderful people. And Lavinia and I have convinced her parents to take us to Bath . . . it's really the only place to be right now. And do you know what happens in September?"

Oh, bloody hell, they're looking at me like I've gone mad.

"Let me guess," Gareth said slowly. "Hmmm . . . What happens in September? Mayhap . . . the evil fairy that cast a spell on you waves her magic wand and you turn back into our sister?"

James said nothing, his eyes boring into hers, searching.

Victoria's laugh was strained. For a second she almost faltered, but she plunged ruthlessly ahead. "No, don't be silly. It's much too important to joke about."

"You're getting married," James said suddenly. "Is that it, Vic? Is that why you've asked us here?"

Her smile shattered like broken glass, her heart ached beneath the filmy lace of her fichu and the stiff stomacher of her gown. She steeled herself and laughed again, as if it were a fine joke. *Steady*, she told herself.

"No, Jamie, nothing like that." *Lord help me.* "It's this—I want to go to London in September. Cousin Abigail so wants me to, and I've been invited to so many balls and receptions already that I should hate to say no. And Lavinia says it is so gay, and we may go to Lord Cecil's hunting

260

lodge in Scotland for the New Year. It's a castle, you know. And I do want a season in London . . . Harry . . . my friend Harry says that I shall take society by storm." The words echoed in her mind, and she wanted to weep, but she smiled prettily at her dumbfounded brothers.

"Please," she added, and even that simple word hurt to say, memories of Phillipe rushing through her mind like waves of pain.

How prettily you say please, Miss Larkin. I should like to hear you say it again.

"What's wrong, Vic?" James asked quietly, leaning across the table towards her.

Don't break, she told herself fiercely. To her relief, Mary returned then, bringing a bottle of wine and three glasses, and Victoria was able to collect herself while the wine was poured.

"I do want to go to London," she repeated. "Please, Gareth, say that I may. I shall die of boredom if I have to go home, and Lavinia will have all the fun of the season. I couldn't bear rotting away on that . . . silly farm all winter, when I could be going to operas, and plays, and balls. Please, please, Gareth . . ." The tears that stood in her eyes were genuine, her words completely false.

Gareth looked sadly at her and set his wine-glass down sharply. He stood and went to the window, where he looked out at the bustling innyard before he spoke.

"Vic, if you want to go to London at the end of the summer instead of coming home, fine. But don't lose yourself in all this . . ." his hand

261

waved vaguely at her delicate gown, her carefully dressed hair, "this fuss and finery. You've changed, little Vic. Maybe you've finally grown up, become a lady. I thought it was a fine idea when we sent you, but now . . . I don't like it, Vic. I think I liked you better before." His voice was heavy and sad.

"Go to London and play at being a fine lady, if you must. But don't forget where your home is, and your family. And don't forget that we love you."

Victoria's relief was obvious. It was done. She was safe, and they would never know that she was a fool, a stupid, pregnant fool. Better that they think her a shallow, vain fool.

"Now," she exclaimed brightly, "tell me everything that's happened since I've been gone. And don't look so sad, I shall write you every week or two. Talk to me, Jamie, what do you think? Do you like my gown? Aren't I elegant now?"

Green eyes met green eyes.

"Just like a china doll," Jamie answered, his voice mocking and bitter. He raised his glass towards her and drank the wine in one swift gulp.

Victoria wanted to cry, but she forced herself to smile and chatter until she said she had to get back, that there was a ball at the Lawrence's, but how good it had been to see them.

They hugged her almost gingerly when they left, their faces closed and disappointed, and it took all of Victoria's strength not to cry out the whole, ugly story. Only the thought of their reactions kept her from spilling her tears.

She clung to James tightly as she made her farewells.

"I miss you, Jamie. I miss you terribly."

James drew back and fixed her with a long stare. "That," he said quietly, "is the first honest thing you've said since I walked in the door."

Victoria dropped her eyes, and when she raised them it was with a smile, a smile so forced that it hurt. "Don't be silly, Jamie. I'll be home before you know it."

He gave her a look of disgust. "Write," he called over his shoulder as he left, "if you can find the time between your balls and parties and fittings for new gowns. And if you ever decide to come home to 'that silly farm,' scrub the paint off your face and get yourself home."

Only when she heard the sounds of their horses' hooves on the road did she cry, lonely, bitter tears onto Mary's small shoulders.

"There, miss. Everything will come right," Mary assured her soothingly, but Victoria felt that nothing would ever be right again.

It was much easier lying to Cousin Abigail and Lord Cecil, even with Lavinia looking on, her blue eyes mocking Victoria down the length of the dinner table.

"I've had the most exciting letter from home," Victoria announced. "Father has planned a trip to Italy, and he wants me to come home immediately. Isn't it wonderful? I've always wanted to travel."

Did Lord Cecil look suspicious? No, it was her imagination.

"My dear, Italy," Cousin Abigail replied. "How very sudden, but how thrilling. And so beautiful. Cecil and I went there on our honeymoon, didn't we, Cecil?"

"It's a dirty place," he commented, raising a gruff brow. "Lots of fountains, I'll give it that. Nothing like England."

"I know it's very sudden," Victoria went on, looking away from her roast beef, which was making her feel a little queasy, "but Father just read of some Roman villas that are being excavated, and you know how enamored he is of the Romans. And it's a great opportunity for me."

"Yes, it is," Abigail conceded. "And how like Matthew, to go chasing about after Roman ruins. Are you all going? Your brothers as well?"

"I'm not certain," Victoria answered carefully, "but I'll write to you, of course."

"Italy," repeated Abigail dreamily. "How thrilling. My dear, do you have proper traveling clothes? We must have some things made for you . . ."

Victoria laughed. "Oh, no, there really isn't time. There's a coach leaving tomorrow morning, and I'd like very much to be on it. I'm so anxious to be home and spend some time there before we leave."

"That's a fine idea," Cecil agreed. "You stay close to your father and brothers, my girl. And keep away from Italians. Wily folk, those Italians."

"Oh, Cecil," Abigail sighed, "one can very hardly avoid Italians when one is in Italy. And I'm sure that Victoria will be very well taken care of. Must you really leave so soon, Victoria? I have so enjoyed your company this summer. I hope you have been happy here."

"As happy as I've ever been," Victoria answered wryly. And as miserable. She avoided Lavinia's gaze.

"Well," Abigail said. "If you're leaving in the morning, there's a lot to be done. All of your things must be packed, and we'll have the carriage brought around for you in the morning. I shall hate to see you go. Seeing you here reminded me so much of Elizabeth. She would be very proud of you, you know."

Victoria managed a sickly smile and turned her attention to her dinner.

The next morning, Victoria and Mary were driven to the innyard in the elegant Harrington carriage. Victoria's eyes were hot and dry as she looked back at the house, its white columns gleaming in the pink light of dawn, the surrounding trees echoing with birdsong.

I won't cry, she told herself fiercely. *I'm done with tears. It's time to get on with it.* She gave Mary a brave smile and turned her eyes to the road ahead, towards London.

Chapter Fourteen

London, 1789

Mary clung tightly to Victoria's arm as they made their way through the crowded streets. The throngs of people jostled and bumped against them—dandies and pickpockets, honest merchants and saucy maids, beggars and barristers, all rushing, it seemed, as they went to and from their various businesses.

The noise of the streets was almost deafening, and vehicles crowded the streets, an endless procession of everything from fine carriages to homely farm-carts.

A window above them opened, and without warning the contents of a chamberpot splattered on the walk in front of them. Victoria swore under her breath, stepping around the foul mess, lifting her skirts carefully.

"I'll give you this, miss," Mary grumbled. "This is the dirtiest place I've ever seen in all my life, no mistake about it."

Victoria laughed, but there was little humor in the sound. "When I get home, I'll never complain about the pigsty again. Look, Mary, an apple seller. Do you think we can afford some?"

Mary checked the meager contents of her pocket. "Only just. We've got to find work today, miss, or we'll be on the streets."

God forbid, Victoria thought, kicking a rotting pile of garbage out of her way. Three weeks they had been here, and though the inn they were staying at was far from luxurious, it was costing dearly, with extra charges for clean linens and warm water. And despite Mary's five long years in service, nobody would hire them, without references.

It seemed as if they had walked a thousand miles since they had arrived, from the tree-lined streets and squares of the wealthy West End to the fish-scented pubs and wharves, and every day to the Royal Exchange, where wanted-for-hire notices fluttered from sign posts, asking for wet nurses and ladies' maids, hack drivers and cartwrights, seamstresses and gardeners.

But nobody, it seemed, aside from the overdressed madames who lay in wait for rosy-cheeked country girls, was interested in hiring them.

"Here we are," Victoria announced. "Petticoat Lane. Now we'll get some money, Mary."

What the real name of the East End street was, Victoria didn't know. It had been renamed at some point in history as a tribute to the many sellers of used clothing that gathered there every day to peddle their wares.

Victoria pushed firmly through the crowded marketplace, eyeing the various stalls, wishing she had time to look through the used books.

The raucous voices of the cockney merchants sounded harsh and shrill to her country-bred ears, like the cry of seagulls, as they cried and singsonged their pleas and enticements to the passing crowds to stop and buy.

"There," Victoria said firmly, pointing at a stall that offered second-hand finery, silks and satins fluttering in the warm, sea-scented breeze. The man that presided over the display was a comical-looking figure, no taller than Mary. As if to make up for his considerable deficit of inches, he wore no fewer than seven hats on his head, one atop the other, a mountain of multicolored ribbons and ostrich feathers above his round, wrinkled face.

Mary regarded this wizened figure doubtfully. "If you say so, miss."

Victoria made her way resolutely through the crowd and stopped before him. "Look," she said without preamble, and deposited on the table before him a bundle of clothing.

The man whistled in admiration as his skilled

fingers ruffled through the offered gowns, his practiced eye admiring the rich embroidery of the roses on the pink silk gown, the taffeta lining and Venice lace of the daffodil-colored one, the fine seams and gossamer fabric of the white, the heavy crumpled satin of the green sash.

His faded eyes moved curiously to the waiting girls before him, the elegantly dressed redhead and the smaller girl in maid's uniform behind her who watched him with round, suspicious eyes.

"Down on yer luck, are you?" he asked sympathetically. "Come to sell yer pretties? Well, look no further, m'lady, old Timmo will give you the best prices in London."

"And the biggest pile of crap you ever want to 'ear," added the merchant to his right as she sorted piles of rags into bundles.

Victoria laughed out loud. "What sort of prices, Timmo?" she asked, shamelessly giving him her prettiest smile.

"Ah, up from the country," he observed shrewdly at the sound of her husky voice. "Roses in yer cheeks and the hay still in yer hair. You've come a long way, Roses."

Victoria smiled again. "Please, Timmo, how much will you give me?"

"For the dresses?" he asked with a wink. "One quid."

The rag seller next to him snorted.

"I'm not stupid, and you'll not rob me," Victoria answered sharply, her fear and tension showing at last. "These cost thirty times that, new, and I need the money."

The old man heard the fear in the husky voice and looked at the emerald eyes more closely.

"All right, Roses. I'll level with you. Aye, these are fine things, worthy of a duchess, but I've a living to make. I'll give you a pound each, and I swear upon me mother's grave, you'll get no higher price anywhere."

The rag seller snorted again. " 'E never even 'ad a mother, the motherless son of a bitch."

Mary's cheeks flamed, and Victoria laughed again as old Timmo turned on his disagreeable neighbor, the pile of hats on his head swaying precariously. "Now see 'ere, you! Don't you go off on my mother in front of the ladies. Roses 'ere is a duchess and not used to language like that—"

"I'm not anything of the sort," Victoria protested feebly, but old Timmo had made up his mind.

"And better no mother at all than a doxy with a mattress strapped to 'er back," he finished in a self-righteous tone. "Now, let's get back to business," he added, picking up the rose-colored gown and spreading its skirt across the piles of silks, worn velvets, and lace that covered his table.

"Give them a fair price, Tim." The voice had a ring of authority in it, and, startled, Victoria turned to look at the speaker.

For one heart-stopping second, she thought

it was Gareth, so alike were the men in height and coloring. But no, it was just the waves of auburn hair that made her think so. This man's face was leaner and harder, his eyes a steely gray. He smiled at Victoria, a knowing look in his eye.

"Give them six, Tim," he ordered quietly, and to Victoria's shock, Tim meekly counted six pounds into her hand, his watery eyes showing his disappointment.

"Ye're a 'ard man, Steel," he sighed. "A 'ard man indeed."

"Don't take on, Timmo," the man replied, his deep voice showing his London origins. "Consider it your good deed for the day."

Victoria wondered who this man could be whom the wily old merchant obeyed so readily. Not gentry, by the sound of his voice, but the elegant frock coat and breeches of dark gray were of good quality, and a large diamond sparkled in the snowy cravat at his throat. He smiled at her scrutiny, his teeth even and white.

"John Steel, at your service," he said, his eyes moving over the finely wrought face, the moss green eyes, the red curls that hung down from beneath the wide-brimmed straw hat.

Unsure, Victoria nodded. Was it her imagination, or did the passing crowd give him more room than they did everyone else? Yes, it was so, and several people nodded or touched the brims of their hats respectfully as they passed.

"And now that I've done you a good turn, you'll have lunch with me," John Steel announced, taking her arm in a possessive way.

Victoria pulled her arm away and lifted her chin. "I'll not," she replied. "I didn't ask for your help, and though it was kind of you, I'll thank you to leave me alone."

Mary was gripping her hand, her eyes wide and startled.

John Steel looked surprised that she should refuse his offer, and then he smiled, a slow, lazy smile. "So you didn't ask for my help," he agreed. "And I suppose you'll be telling me you don't want it if I were to offer more."

"That's right," Victoria answered, her voice as cool and haughty as Lavinia's had ever been. "Good day, Mr. Steel."

She took Mary's hand firmly and began to pull her through the crowd, away from the arrogant Mr. Steel. To her dismay, he followed them.

"Funny thing," he said persistently, "your not needing my help. From what I hear, you do. How long have you been in our lovely city, now, duchess? Three weeks, is it?"

Victoria stopped in her tracks and stared over her shoulder at the man. How in the devil did he know that?

"And you've not found work," he added, affecting a sad tone. "At least, not honest work. And from what I hear, you've said no to half the brothel-keepers in the city. You're too spoiled or stupid to move to cheaper rooms,

273

and now you're selling the clothes off your back."

Victoria's eyes narrowed. "How the hell do you know so much?" she demanded, her voice strong and clear even though her heart was beating rapidly.

He smiled. "I know everything that happens around here," he answered simply. "I own a full half of these streets, and what I don't own I may as well. Not much gets by me. I know, for instance, that your little friend had her money lifted out of her pocket not more than ten minutes ago while you were admiring a basket of apples."

Mary's small hand disappeared beneath her apron, and her eyes grew even rounder as she realized that the gray-eyed man spoke the truth.

"Do you want it back?" John Steel asked with a teasing grin.

"Bloody right we do," Victoria answered evenly, fury rising in her chest.

"Calm down, duchess, I didn't nick it. But I know who did. Come sit down and have a bite to eat and rest your feet, and I'll get the money back for you."

Victoria hesitated.

"You've walked a far ways," he added kindly, and again Victoria saw his resemblance to Gareth, "and I'll bet you haven't eaten yet today. Come and take a load off your feet, and I'll get you your money back."

"All right," she conceded, ignoring Mary's

imploring tug on her sleeve. "But after that, we'll be on our way."

"As you wish," he answered calmly. He made no attempt to take her arm again, and Victoria followed him across the crowded street and into the dark doorway of a pub, her stomach growling at the smell of fresh-baked bread and roasting meat. To her surprise, he walked through the crowded room as if he owned it and taking a key from his pocket, opened a heavy door at the back of the room, gesturing to them to follow.

"Don't be a coward, Victoria," he said as she hesitated.

Had she told him her name? No, she was sure of it. A stab of fear caught at her heart, but he tossed her a merry, teasing look over his broad shoulder. Again, a look of Gareth.

She followed him, Mary's hand clutching her sleeve.

Mary, who had been expecting to enter the den of Satan, breathed a sigh of relief as she saw the room—a clean, comfortable dining room, nothing more, with sunlight streaming through the lace curtains at the windows, a comfortable rug on the clean floor.

"Please, sit," he said pleasantly, and did so himself, tipping his chair back and fastening his admiring gaze on Victoria again.

"Now see here," Victoria began. "How do you know my name? And how long we've been here, and that we're looking for work?"

The heavy door behind her opened

abruptly, and a serving girl entered, golden curls showing beneath her snowy cap, and a fair amount of bosom on display. The look she she gave Victoria and Mary was less than welcoming, but her smile beamed readily at John Steel.

"What are you needin', sir?"

"Nothing for me, Rose, but get some lunch for my friends, will you? And perhaps some tea. Oh, and find young Jack Beal and send him here at once."

Rose disappeared through the door, casting an envious glance back at Victoria and Mary.

John Steel leaned forward and smiled into Victoria's eyes.

"Now, to your questions, Miss . . . ?"

Victoria did not supply her last name, and that seemed to amuse him.

"All right, then. I know your name, and where you're staying, because I like to know everything that happens in this city, and whether you know it or not, a lot of people are interested in you. Namely, a lot of brothel keepers."

Victoria stared in disbelief, and Mary's cheeks flamed with horror.

"There you are at the Exchange every morning," he went on, "looking for work, and finding none, spending less on food each day, and they're watching you. Pretty girls fresh from the country, ripe for plucking. Mother Thomas, Long Anne, Mrs. Jessop—they're keeping an eye on you, taking bets as to how long you'll last. They gave a week from the time you started selling your fine feathers before you were on the street."

Victoria felt sick. Rose entered the room, bearing steaming plates of roast chicken and bowls of soup, a loaf of fresh bread, and to Victoria's delight, a bowl of ripe peaches. It had been a week since she had seen so much food, and all of it fresh and good.

Mary regarded the bounty before her with suspicion, but Victoria took a peach and savored it in her hand for a moment. It smelled of clean country air and trees in quiet orchards, and home. She bit into it happily, and swallowed before turning suspicious eyes on her auburn-haired benefactor, who was watching her with pleasure.

"How do you know so much about Mother Whatever-her-name-is, and Long Anne, and whoever else you said?" Victoria demanded, not satisfied with the answers she was receiving. "Who are you, God's recording angel?"

John Steel looked very taken aback, and then laughed. "Nothing of the sort. Actually, duchess, I own the establishments that those women run, so you might say I have a personal interest in what happens to you."

Victoria almost choked on the bread she was eating. Mary cried out softly, sure that she was in the presence of Satan himself, and that poor Miss Victoria was certain to be fetched off to the nether regions immediately, for all her sins and lighthearted blasphemies.

John Steel laughed at their horrified reactions. "Don't worry, duchess. If I'd wanted you to work in one of my houses, you'd be there now. I'd have had you taken off the street and drugged, or blackmailed. All it would take is my word, and it'd be done."

The fresh bread and peaches tasted like dirt in Victoria's mouth, and she wished she had never come to London. John Steel's eyes were on her, calm and knowing.

"But like I said, I'm interested in you. What are you doing here? Running away, I figure, with your maid. And somewhere, someone must be looking for you. Those things you were selling didn't come cheap. They were quality, my girl, and so are you. Things can go hard on your type when you're on your own with nobody to foot your bills."

Was there a threat in the words? Victoria felt sick, but she swallowed hard and lifted her chin. She took the six pounds Tim had given her from her pocket and counted five of them onto the table.

"There. Take it back. Tim would have paid me one, and that's what I'll take. I don't think I want your help, Mr. Steel. I thank you, but it's time for us to go."

She rose with a great show of dignity and went to the door, Mary fluttering behind her like a small, frightened bird. Her hand was on the doorknob when Steel spoke.

"I wouldn't do that if I were you. I'm offering to help you, and I don't like having my offers rejected. You can sit down and listen to me, or I'll say the word in the right ear and you'll find yourself in Newgate by tonight."

Victoria turned on him, her face pink with rage, trembling with fear and anger. "Newgate? What in the bloody hell for? I've done nothing to be jailed for!"

"You don't need to, sweet. I only need to say that you tried to rob me. I line the pockets of every constable on these streets—at least the ones who don't owe me. Sit down."

Victoria sat, genuinely frightened.

"Don't look at me like that, duchess. I've no great desire to see you in prison, or on your back in a whorehouse." He stood and stretched lazily, smiling at her fear as if this were all a superb joke. He walked to the window, lifted the curtain, and peered out into the alley before turning back to her. "I'd like to keep you for myself. You'd be safe, and rich. You could do a lot worse, you know. And," he added with a toss of his auburn head and a flashing grin, "I don't see as how you have much choice, do you?" His smile faded as Victoria reached calmly onto the crowded table and picked up the sharp knife that lay beside the bread.

"Don't be stupid, duchess; what in the hell do you think that—"

Victoria threw the knife with a skill born of years of practice, and it stuck in the wall next to his hip, quivering. Before he could release his sharply drawn breath, she had another knife in her hand.

The green eyes that met his were cold and unflinching, the pale face set.

"If I have to throw this one, I'll take your balls off," Victoria said bluntly. "And don't think I can't, or won't. I'm not a whore, Steel, not for you or any other man. And if I go to prison, I'll be no worse off than I am now." Out of the corner of her eye she could see Mary, tears running down her round face, horror in her dark eyes, and the sight enraged her.

John Steel stared at her, his face cold and angry, his gray eyes narrowing. Despite her outward bravado, Victoria felt her knees trembling, her heart beating hard against her ribs. And then, to her shock, John Steel threw his head back and laughed, a great booming laugh that filled the room, his white teeth showing.

Victoria remained frozen, her hand gripping the knife.

"God's teeth," he finally exclaimed, wiping a tear from his eye, "you really are something. I never expected that, not in a million years. Where the hell did a girl like you learn to throw knives? Damn the whorehouse, you could be working in a fair, with a skill like that. All right, duchess, I give up. If you want honest work, I'll find it for you."

Victoria didn't move as he returned to the

table and sat, tipping his chair back on its back legs, smiling at her.

"Oh, put down that knife. Listen, there's a woman up the street that owes me. She runs a bakeshop, a good one, and she's looking for a girl, but I think she'll take two if I ask her. Long hours, and hard; and I think you'd have more fun in my bed, but if you're bound to sweat for a few piddling shillings, so be it."

Victoria hesitated, her eyes searching Steel's now merry face for any hint of deceit, but she saw only laughter, and admiration.

"And what do I owe you," she asked carefully, "should we accept?"

He smiled again. "Not much. How about the pleasure of your company every once and again? No tricks," he added hastily, as Victoria's eyes narrowed. "Just let me call on you, or take you to a play or something like, every now and then. Let me woo you like one of your country swains. You're something else again, duchess, and good things are worth waiting for."

"You'll wait a long time," Victoria answered bitterly. "I'll be honest with you, Steel. I'll not trust a man again, not as long as I live. I'm tired and I'm angry, and I'm carrying a child. You were right, I've run away from my family, and I intend to have my baby and go home as if nothing happened; and I will. If you think I'll stay here in this filthy, ugly city a moment longer than I must, you're wrong."

He sat quietly, his eyes moving over her

slender figure. "How far gone are you?" he asked at last.

"About two months," Victoria answered evenly.

He appeared to consider this. "Well," he exclaimed finally, "that gives me till March, doesn't it, to change your mind? All right, sweetheart. Why don't you and that little pigeon there eat up, and then we'll take you around to Mrs. Leigh's and see if we can't find you some work. I'm not usually a patient man, and men have died for less than throwing knives at me, but I'm willing to forgive and forget. I like you, duchess."

Victoria granted him a grudging smile. "Good," she answered, grabbing for a peach. "I'd hate to think what would become of me if you didn't. But if you think you're going to charm me onto my back, don't hold your breath. I'm done with all that."

John Steel chuckled, his eyes moving over her tilted eyes, her full mouth, the glowing skin of her rounded cleavage. "Somehow I doubt that, duchess. You look like a woman that was made for it. You'll feel differently after you whelp that pup. Was the father a nobleman?"

"Don't ask me," Victoria said, her heart twisting with pain. She could picture Phillipe too clearly, his dark, glossy hair, his blue eyes shining at her with a loving glow, his elegant hands touching her cheeks softly. "Never ask me about him again. He's gone, and it's all done. I don't want to ever think of him again."

Steel's eyes were piercing as he filed away the information.

"Done," he agreed. "Now eat up, and we'll get you some work and find you some decent rooms, and I'll bet that in nine months you'll have forgotten the bastard's name."

Victoria smiled, a bitter smile. "No, I'll never forget, and I hope I don't. I've learned my lesson, and I don't intend to forget it."

If John Steel thought differently, he said nothing of it, and at that moment the door opened and the golden-haired serving wench entered with a ragged-looking urchin at her side.

"Well, Jack," Steel greeted the frightened looking lad, "it seems that you picked the wrong pockets this morning. Give the ladies back their money."

Mary's coins, looking very meager, appeared in the grubby hand.

"God 'elp me, Steel, I din't know they was friend of yours, or I'd a never—"

"That's all right," Victoria answered quickly, pitying the trembling little lad. "It's all taken care of now, Jack, and I'm not angry, really."

"I am," John Steel replied coolly. "You're not to be picking pockets, Jack, it isn't your job. I need you for better things, my boy. You're the best boy I have for sneaking in coal chutes and between fences and open windows, and there's more money to be made in the houses of the gentry than in the pockets of country girls. See that you don't forget it. I've bought you out of Newgate twice, but the next time you're caught picking pockets, I'll let you hang."

Victoria was horrified at the callous words, but the boy seemed to take it in stride and thanked John Steel as if he were bestowing a great gift.

She finished her food, watching John Steel with suspicious eyes, wondering what she had gotten herself into and what manner of man this Steel was, and if he could be trusted to keep his word.

What choice do you have? she asked herself sternly. *Where else will you go?* And there was Mary to think of, and the baby. And if they found honest work, they were better off than they had been before. And then, when this was all over, they could go home, where she wanted to be more than anywhere else, where the orchards were full of apples and the kitchen ripe with the smell of cooking blackberries and roast chicken, and the breezes carried the warm scent of hay through the air.

For a moment she closed her eyes and was there; and then she was back, sitting in a private room with a hardened, dangerous man who was about to lead her into the sewage-scented streets of London.

"All right, Mr. Steel. Let's go meet this Mrs.

Leigh and see what she can do for us." Her voice was firm and decided, her chin at a resolute angle.

John Steel smiled with pleasure. He knew exactly what Mrs. Leigh would do—work them hard from dawn till dusk every day in the blazing heat of her bakeshop, and for pennies a day. The rooms that they could afford on such meager earnings would be nothing short of squalid; and there he would be, good John Steel, to fetch this rosy-cheeked lass in a fine carriage and take her to beautiful places and buy her pretty things.

And it wouldn't take too long, he thought, before this haughty, knife-throwing vixen succumbed to his sympathetic charms. Who was she? The daughter of a country earl, perhaps. He would find out, he was sure, with his connections. There might even be a bit of gold in that, if certain people wanted certain things hidden—and in John Steel's experience, the gentry usually paid well for that sort of thing.

As for the baby, that would be dealt with when the time came. She could shed a few tears for the untimely death of the little bastard, and he would willingly dry her tears.

"Very good, duchess," he said agreeably. "To Mrs. Leigh's we go."

The brilliant smile and auburn sheen of his hair were so like Gareth's that Victoria smiled back. "Stop calling me that—my name is Victoria."

"Victoria," he agreed happily.

Victoria felt, rather than saw, Mary's disapproving glare, and she sent her a comforting smile as they followed John Steel back into the noisy, stinking streets. She tipped her head back for a minute to feel the sun on her face, looking past the grimy buildings, past chimneys that poured black coal smoke over the blue sky.

Unbidden, unwanted, the thought came to her mind: Phillipe, where was he, and did he ever think of her?

Chapter Fifteen

Paris, 1789

In a back alley in Paris, off of one of the narrow cobblestone streets that twisted their dark paths through the city, at a back table of a dark barroom, Phillipe St. Sebastien sat, his face shadowed by the light of the smoking candles.

He did not look at all like the man who had left England only four months before. The fine laces and velvets of the elegant aristocrat were gone, replaced by the rough, somber clothing of an ordinary citizen. Beneath the loose, rough shirt, the St. Sebastien emerald hung on a leather cord, cold against the skin of his chest.

The nonchalant grace and easy movement that had marked him as a member of the despised aristocracy were gone, too. He moved

Amy Elizabeth Saunders

with a dangerous tension, the watchful, careful movements of a man whose life was in constant danger. His face was thinner, his eyes bore dark circles, his cheekbones were sharp, almost gaunt.

He drank heartily of the wine served to him, not even tasting the cheap, sour quality. In this city, once so beautiful and now so evil and dangerous, he was grateful for whatever small luxuries he could afford.

He looked around the dank and gloomy interior of the bar, the sort of place he would never have come only a year ago, and he thought, as he always did, of Victoria. He wondered if she was at her father's farm, in the sweet English countryside that seemed so far away, so peaceful, as if it were another world.

Outside, in the cool October night, Phillipe could hear a group of drunken students walking by, singing the "Marsellaise," the song of revolutionary Paris. To Phillipe, it was a song of death, a song of waistcoated gentlemen and carefully coiffured ladies imprisoned in the Conciergerie, a song of gutters running with blood, a song of tumbrils carrying innocent men, women, and children to their executions.

The heavy door to the bar opened, and the man Phillipe had been waiting for entered the smoky, grease-stained room. He was a small man, wiry and dangerous-looking, clad in the loose pants and stocking cap that was the uniform of the French *révolutionaire*. Spying Phillipe, the man smiled, showing stained and broken teeth, and signaled the barkeep to bring him wine. He sat next to Phillipe and slurped noisily at his drink before speaking.

"I have brought the information you were seeking, citizen."

Phillipe thought that the man's eyes were like those of a snake, watchful and dangerous, and he was silent as he laid a precious gold coin on the dark wood of the table between them.

The man drank again, making no move to take the money. He seemed to enjoy stalling.

"I wonder," he said at last, showing his broken teeth, "what this girl is to you, that you pay so well to have a letter taken to her. It's dangerous work, smuggling letters to an *aristo*."

Phillipe's answer was sharp and short. "You've been paid well. Tell me what you know."

Again a smile, cynical and knowing. "I did not give the girl the letter, citizen."

Phillipe was frozen with cold, murderous rage. For four long months he had been living like a criminal, in squalid lodgings and under assumed names, carefully laying coins in the hands of dangerous and shady men, trying to get a letter to Christianna, who was being held with the royal family at the Tuileries. And this man who worked in the stables and was a trusted member of the revolutionary party had charged him heavily.

"Because," the man explained, a watchful glow in his eye, "she is no longer there."

Phillipe's face gave away none of his emotion,

and he forced himself to speak carefully. "Where is she?"

"Where do you think?" the man asked, finishing his wine with a swift gulp. Oh, yes, he was enjoying this. "On October third an order for her arrest was carried to the Tuileries; and I'm sorry to say. . ." The man signaled the barkeep, pointing at his empty glass.

Phillipe was steeling himself, ready for the worst. He had seen what happened to the hated aristocrats unfortunate enough to be arrested; their blood had spattered his shoes in the gutters, he had seen the heads of youthful acquaintances hanging from lamp posts. He had seen pretty Gabrielle De Lambelle's head, impaled on a pike, paraded through the streets of Paris, her golden hair of which she had been so vain floating around the bloody stump of her neck.

"She escaped."

The words hit him with the force of a lightning bolt, and Phillipe sprang forward, gripping the man's shirt in tense hands.

"Where is she? Is this true? Swear that you don't lie."

He realized that people were staring, and released the man, who gave him something between a smile and a sneer.

"Oh, it's true all right, though where the stupid *aristo* is now, who can tell? Good luck to her; she needs it." He stood quietly, his eyes fixed unpleasantly on Phillipe. "And good luck to you 'Monsieur Blanc.' " He laughed, making no secret of his disbelief of the name. "Perhaps

290

you, too, might consider leaving Paris suddenly. I do not think anyone even vaguely connected to the St. Sebastien family will be safe here much longer."

The warning was obvious, the threat taken.

"I thank you, citizen, for your help," Phillipe replied coolly. "I'll take your words into consideration."

He waited until the man left, and made his way back to his rented room above the bar.

Wasting no time, he began to pack his meager belongings immediately. If he was here in the morning, he would be arrested, that was certain. The wild hope that he had felt throughout the day, waiting for a message from Christianna, was rapidly turning to despair.

Christianna had escaped—but to where? She could be lost in the twisting labyrinth of the streets of Paris, streets ruled by bloodthirsty mobs. She could be anywhere, she might be arrested, she might have fallen into unscrupulous hands, she could be dead.

A sense of hopelessness descended on him, and furious at his own helplessness and despair, he hurled his bundle of clothing to the filthy floor and sank onto the narrow pallet that served as his bed.

He didn't know how long he sat there, his face buried in his hands, and for the first time since he was a child, he found himself praying; not the formal prayers he had been taught by the old priest at the château, but a desperate, fervent litany of his own anguish, his head

291

bowed on clenched fists, whispering in a harsh, broken voice. "Don't let her be dead, dear God, don't let her die. Where do I go, where am I to begin, how will I know where to begin . . . ?"

There was no answer, of course, only the twisting, bleak pain of black depression that descended on him. None of this could be real, he thought, this ugly little scene—the once proud nobleman divested of his fine clothing and estate, head bent in frantic, hopeless prayer in an evil-smelling, flea-ridden room.

"It's hopeless," he whispered aloud into the darkness.

There was a sharp noise, a light rattling sound, and Phillipe tensed as he lifted his head, looking towards the door, expecting to see a ready pistol, an angry revolutionary demanding his arrest.

There was nothing.

Relief spread through his body, and he laughed, a short, harsh bark. *My nerves are getting the better of me*, he thought, and stepped forward to make sure that the door was bolted. He felt something beneath his foot and stepped back, looking at the floor.

There on the greasy, filth-covered floorboards lay his mother's emerald ring, reflecting the light of the sputtering candle from its green depths.

He reached for the thin leather cord that he wore around his neck, wondering how the jewel had worked itself loose; but the cord was still knotted firmly, and picking up the ring, he saw that the band was intact, solid. He frowned, turning the stone in his hand, wondering how such a thing could happen.

The ring felt warm in his hand, the stone's steady gleam seemed almost alive, the golden ivy filigree that twined around the setting reminded him of the ivy that grew over the ancient mausoleum of the Château St. Sebastien, like unkempt green curtains, and he thought of how, as children, he and Christianna had played there, comforted rather than distressed by the presence of their dead ancestors encased deep within the stone walls.

She was there.

The thought entered his head with a sharp, certain clarity. She would be there waiting for him, where no one else would think to go. An image flashed into his mind, vivid and clear, a picture of Christianna, her thick, black curls loose on her back, rosary beads sparkling in her fingers, her head resting against the statue of the Virgin that adorned their mother's tomb.

As suddenly as it had come, the image was gone.

Phillipe raised his head, his heart hammering a swift, hard drumbeat against his chest. He wondered if he was going mad with hopelessness, with fear. His breaths were hard and quick, his scalp tingled, gooseflesh covered his well-muscled arms.

For a moment, the emerald in his hand seemed to glow. "No," he whispered, "this is not madness. This is truth, and she'll be there."

Amy Elizabeth Saunders

He took a last look at his mother's emerald before securing it deep into his pocket, tied in a knotted handkerchief, and gathered his possessions into a tight bundle. It was well over two hundred miles to the Auvergne, and if he couldn't find a horse, he would have to steal one. It was a long journey under the best of conditions, and these were not the best. He would have to travel stealthily, and by night, avoiding towns where he might be stopped and asked for papers. Simply leaving Paris would be tricky, he knew.

He took a final, quick look around the shabby room, the narrow pallet, the sputtering candle.,

"*Merci, Dieu,*" he whispered. He made the sign of the cross quickly and walked out into the dark streets of Paris, his mind already in the snow-dusted forests of the Auvergne.

Chapter Sixteen

March, 1790

Victoria pushed her way through the crowded alley that was now her front yard, kicking away the piles of rotting fish left out by the shop beneath the rooms that she and Mary shared.

She hated bloody fish, hated the sight, hated the smell, hated everything about it. When she got home, she would never eat fish again. She would just sit in the sun, eating fresh apples and pears, and she would be so happy. And she would never, never come to London again.

It was one of those gray and dreary days, the clouds and smoke darkening the sky as if it were evening instead of morning, the fog covering everything with a cold, wet mist, the gutters full of last night's rain and today's garbage. It was just the sort of day that Victoria hated, like too many days she had known since coming here.

She pulled her cloak closely around her heavy body, shivering in the damp chill, stopped to give a penny to a beggar child, and made her way slowly to the market corner where the news-seller waited.

The news-seller looked pleased to see her, smiling above his half-penny papers.

"You're soft-hearted, that's what you are," he greeted her, indicating the filthy little vagrant vanishing into the crowd, Victoria's penny clutched in his grubby hand. "And that ha'penny was meant for me, I'll be bound."

Victoria laughed at the man's morose expression. "It was," she admitted.

"Damn. And now you'll be wanting your news for free. I don't make much money that way, Miss Vickie."

"I don't imagine you do," she agreed. "But what of France?"

She had heard the news of the revolution not long after her arrival in London, and had been following the stories in the news-sheets ever since. She tried to stop herself, but she read the gruesome stories over and over, hoping for any word of Phillipe.

She tried not to imagine him with his hair shorn, in prison, kneeling before the guillotine. No matter how many times she had cursed him, she couldn't bear to think of him dead.

Her baby moved heavily in her belly, and she wrapped a protective arm around her swollen body and tried to concentrate on the news-seller's raucous voice.

" . . . and that the royal family 'as been prevented from makin' an escape, and are now under 'eavy guard." The man shook his head in disbelief. "They don't sound any brighter than our King Georgie, bless him anyway. Even if he is a bloody halfwit."

Victoria laughed at the man's assessment of his sovereign. "And that's all the news of France?"

"That's it girl, and a damned sight more than you paid for. Say, John Steel was looking for you earlier."

Victoria rolled her eyes toward the heavy, gray skies and blew a damp curl out of her face. "Isn't he always?" she asked impatiently. "I knew that as soon as I lost my job he'd be around like a drunk to a wedding."

The news-seller looked shocked. "You've been sacked? Whatever for?"

Victoria patted her round stomach. "I'm too big to work. Too big, and too tired. It's just as well. Mrs. Leigh wasn't an easy woman to work for, and the baby will be coming in a month, and then I'm going home."

The man looked puzzled. "I 'eard that you were staying, that you were going to stay with John Steel."

Victoria rubbed her cold hands together. The familiar cold, wet dampness of the street was seeping into her worn shoes, and she was anxious to be about her business. "You heard wrong. Well, I best be off. Thank you for the news."

"Go on then," the man answered, rubbing his red nose. "I've got a living to make, you know."

Victoria made her way up the street, elbowing her way through the crowded market. She stopped at the used-books table, but it was too cold and wet to linger long. She was never told to quit reading or buy the book, as most customers were, and after a while she had learned that this was because John Steel had expressed an interest in her, and nobody wished to anger him.

Oh, he was handsome enough, and took her and Mary to see wonderful things—a play once, and the Tower of London, and the majestic cathedral of Saint Paul. He had begun to keep his distance as her body began to thicken, and Victoria had noticed him watching her like a cat watches a mouse.

She had told him a million times that he was wasting his efforts, that she was going home with her baby, and he had smiled in an arrogant way and said, "We'll see." Harmless words, but they made her worry.

She and Mary lived a frugal life in their shabby room. They had managed to cheer the room up, with the purchase of some good, second-hand finery—a faded red shawl with heavy fringe that had seen better days but was still rich and warm in color, a slightly cracked teapot with a pattern of painted violets.

They had purchased a used, worn copy of

The Travels of Lemuel Gulliver, and Victoria had
read it out loud to Mary over the dreary winter
nights. They sat in front of the fire, the coals
blazing in the small but brightly polished grate,
laughing and marveling at Gulliver and his ad-
ventures, losing their melancholy in the pages
of the book.

And while Victoria read, Mary would sew tiny
gowns and bonnets, precious little embroidered
things that Victoria held with a mixture of joy
and sorrow. To her great surprise, she no longer
dreaded the baby's coming, she was anxious
for it, and longed to see the face of this small
stranger that she carried within her. She found
herself talking to her great, round belly, laying
her hands upon it as if the baby could feel her
touch.

As much as she longed to be home and safe,
she dreaded the day when she would put her
baby in Mary's hands and become nothing
more than "Aunt Victoria" to her own son or
daughter. Mary said that perhaps, when the
child was grown, they could tell him.

"And won't it be a fine thing," Victoria had
said, laughing despite herself, "if you should
get married and your husband will find you a
virgin, Mary? What lie can we tell then?"

Mary had blushed with horror and stammered that she hadn't thought of that, and she
was sure that she didn't know, that they'd have
to worry about that another time.

Poor Mary, Victoria thought as she passed
Mrs. Leigh's bakeshop. There she was, behind

the windows that seemed to glow with warm light onto the foggy street, loading another tray of buns onto the counter, her round face red with the heat and the sharp pace that her employer demanded she keep.

Victoria waited in the wet street until she caught Mary's eye and gave her a quick wave before she moved on towards the stall where old Tim was still hawking his finery.

Today Tim had wrapped a bedraggled fur around his neck and was wearing at least three embroidered waistcoats, besides his usual stack of four hats, their bedraggled plumes dripping around his wrinkled face.

"'Ello, Carrots," he shouted gaily at the sight of Victoria. He reached out and tugged on a damp red curl that was escaping from beneath the battered brown brim of Victoria's bonnet. "Look at that," he ordered the peddler to his right, tugging at the curl. "That's a warm sight on a cold day, bright as sunshine."

"I've brought you something, Timmo," Victoria told him, pulling a bundle from beneath her cape.

"Wait, wait," the old man protested, pulling her around the stall and offering her a battered chair. "Sit down there, Carrots, and take a load off. You ought not to be walking so much, in your shape."

Victoria took the chair gratefully, easing her aching back against the hard slats. "Thanks, Tim, I need a rest. Do you want to see what I've brought?"

The man was peering anxiously at her thin, white face, the dark circles beneath her eyes. Was it in December that he had stopped calling her Roses? There was nothing of roses about Victoria's face now, it was a tired, worried face, a look of sad resignation in the green eyes.

She lifted up the dress that she had worn so long ago, the day she had first seen Phillipe. The blue and white stripes were as bright as a summer sky, the heavy white lace rich and clean-looking, reminding her sharply of the life she had known before coming to this place. Had it only been last summer?

"Listen, Carrots . . ." Victoria was startled at Tim's hushed, secretive voice, and she leaned closer to the worried old face. "I ought not to tell you this, and God 'elp me if anyone should 'ear us . . . but . . . well, word is, if you try to sell anything, we're to tell John Steel, and right smart. Orders."

Victoria's eyes narrowed, and she felt a strong misgiving. "Why do you suppose that is, Timmo?"

Tim looked nervous, as if he had said too much. "God help me, that I don't know, and don't ask me. You're not to know, 'e said."

Victoria nodded, trying to control her fury. "Damn him," she snapped. "Always watching me, breathing down my neck, as if he bloody owned me. It's none of his damned business what I sell, for whatever reason."

"Please, Carrots, keep it down," Tim pleaded earnestly. "I don't want any trouble. Look, I'll give you a bob for the bloody dress, and you go home and get off your feet like a good girl."

Victoria stared at him in indignation, John Steel momentarily forgotten. "A bob, Tim, for that! It was twenty, new."

"Aye, but it's not new now. 'Ave pity, Carrots, I'll starve if I pay you more—"

"Not if God strikes you down for a liar first," Victoria retorted. "Give me two, Tim. You know you'll sell it for four, at least."

Tim handed her the money without further argument, which surprised her. "There. And don't be buying books with it. Put it aside for a rainy day."

Victoria smiled brilliantly as she struggled heavily to her feet. "Thanks, Tim. You're a darling."

"Now you'll be robbing me blind, I suppose," he grumbled. "I'll have to hide, Carrots, next time I see you coming. Now get home and eat. Those arms of yours are like sticks, and your color ain't good. Get those bloody roses back in your cheeks."

"Maybe later," Victoria answered, pocketing the money with one hand and rubbing the aching small of her back with the other. "Right now, Timmo, I'm off to give John Steel a piece of my mind."

The old man hopped up and down like an enraged child. "Damn! What are you trying to do, girl, get yourself killed? Give over, Carrots, even you can't push Steel too far. Me and my mouth," he added dismally as Victoria tossed him a careless smile and turned to go.

Tim sighed heavily, and then noticed two blowsy-looking girls eyeing the used finery on his table, and rushed to help them, waving a pair of white silk shoes with glittering buckles for their approval.

"Look at this, look at this, I bought these off the daughter of a duke down on her luck. I could charge you four, I should charge you three, but for only two shillings they're yours. Look at those 'eels, barely been worn . . . ."

Victoria considered stopping by Mrs. Leigh's to tell Mary where she would be, but that meant an extra walk two blocks in the wrong direction, and she was tired, and her back and feet were aching; so she pressed on, past the shop windows that glowed with light in the foggy day, past the crowded, grimy buildings, past the already drunk collection of wretches drinking gin on the corner, to the large building, unmarked by signs but known to many, that housed John Steel's gaming hall and offices.

It also, she knew, housed a good many blowsy jades who plied their trade on the third floor, but at this hour of the morning the girls would be sleeping and nobody would be about except for Steel and a few of his cronies, tallying the take from the night before.

By the time she lifted the heavy door-knocker and banged it loudly, a slow, cold rain was falling, and Victoria was as wet and out of sorts as the proverbial wet hen.

The butler who opened the door looked more like a brick wall than a proper servant, Victoria noticed, but she followed him through the quiet gaming rooms, where the dark felt-covered card tables, rich draperies, luxurious patterned carpets, and elegant chairs contrasted sharply with the poverty of the streets outside.

The lumbering servant knocked respectfully on the polished door of Steel's office before opening it. Just as Victoria had suspected, Steel was there with a dangerous-looking assortment of cronies, the air thick with pipe smoke, a comfortable fire blazing in the grate, and an immense pile of money on the table before him.

"Victoria!" His smile was smooth and bright. "Good, I was expecting you, sweetheart. Gentlemen, will you excuse us, please?"

"Gentlemen" was going a bit far for that crew, Victoria thought privately, but she nodded pleasantly as the men filed out of the room obediently. If any of the men resented having their business interrupted, they gave no sign of it.

As soon as the door closed, Victoria dropped heavily into the nearest chair, sinking gratefully into its well-upholstered depths. Her eyes closed briefly as she sighed, and when she opened them, Steel was smiling coolly into her eyes.

"I'm angry, John."

"I could see that, love, when you walked in. You've been sacked, I hear. What a shame," he added, looking as if he didn't think it was a shame at all.

"That's not why I'm angry," Victoria snapped. A drop fell off the brim of her sodden bonnet, and she untied the brown ribbons impatiently, the silk singing between her fingers, and dropped it to her lap. "I'm angry at you."

Steel examined her carefully, his gray eyes giving away none of the disgust he felt at the sight of her swollen body, the great roundness of her belly so sharply at odds with the thin wrists and drawn face.

"For not interfering and forcing Mrs. Leigh to give you back your job? That wasn't the deal, my girl. You agreed that once you were hired, you'd sink or swim on your own. Damned stubborn of you. You could be living easy, if you'd just—"

"Live with you," Victoria finished bluntly. "Well, I won't. Not now, not ever. I've told you that a million times, and I won't change my tune, Steel. You're a handsome man, and a rich man, but that's not enough. You know how I feel."

John Steel said nothing, simply watched her.

"Damn it," Victoria exclaimed impatiently, "I'm tired, Steel. And now I can't even sell my own clothes without someone reporting to you."

"Who told you that?"

"None of your damned business!" Victoria cried out, at her wit's end. "You just don't listen, Steel. I'm tired of being watched, tired of being

Amy Elizabeth Saunders

followed. I'm tired of hearing people say, 'There goes John Steel's woman.' And I'm not, I never was. And now I hear that I'm not going to leave London—and I am, John Steel, I am, so fast it'll make your head spin. I've had it, do you understand? I'm tired of you, and I've lost my patience."

Victoria was trembling with rage, twisting her damp bonnet in her pale fingers.

John Steel rose slowly and reached out to brush a damp red curl off of her cheek. Wondering if she had gone too far, Victoria glanced nervously up at him. His face was calm, almost too calm, his gray eyes cold. A muscle twitched in his jaw before he spoke.

"I'm losing my patience too, Miss High and Mighty Victoria Larkin—if that is your real name, which I doubt. I've been very kind to you, I've invested a lot of time in you, and I've put up with crap from you that I'd take off no man."

Victoria flinched at the suppressed anger in the cold voice.

"And whether you're aware of it or not, I've spent a lot of money trying to find out who you are, and where you come from, and who the father of that brat is."

Victoria's face burned. "That's none of your damned business."

Steel's hand gripped her shoulder. "Ah, but that is my business, my dear. Blackmail is very profitable, and I daresay that you've a rich dad or lover somewhere that would pay dearly for my silence."

306

Victoria was startled, and then she laughed, long and hard.

"Oh, Steel, how did you ever get so rich, being so thick? Blackmail my father . . ." She choked with laughter. "Do you want payment in sheep, or used ink bottles? Or do you want it in honey? Our farm makes the best honey in the village, you know." Victoria wiped her eyes on the shabby cuff of her sleeve. "Or were you going to blackmail the father of my child? That's even better. He wouldn't marry me, Steel, because I had no money, and he was almost destitute. All he had was a title, and a rotting castle in France, and if he's still alive, he won't even have that. I understand that French titles aren't worth a lot these days."

Victoria stopped laughing abruptly at the sight of Steel's face.

He had tried so hard for so long to charm her and impress her with his better qualities that she was apt to forget who he was—a hardened criminal, the king of the London underworld, a man whose word was law. He was a man who prided himself on his charm and cunning, and this was one of the more expensive mistakes he had ever made.

His eyes were as deadly as a snake's. "Are you done?" he said at last. Victoria knew that she had gone too far.

"I'm sorry, John, I didn't mean to laugh, and I'm sorry that you've wasted your money on this blackmail thing and now you've got nothing to show for it."

"Nothing," Steel repeated. "Nothing, my girl, except you."

"You don't have me, Steel," Victoria answered quietly. "And you won't. I'm sorry, but you lose."

It was the wrong thing to say. The muscle in his jaw twitched again, and he walked to the door with an elaborate show of calm.

"Jim," he called, and the enormous manservant who had led Victoria in appeared.

"Miss Larkin will be staying with us for a while. I'd like you to show her to a room—downstairs, please."

Victoria struggled to her feet as gracefully as she could. "Bloody hell, Steel, I am not staying here. Have you lost your mind? You just can't keep me here against my will. I won't stand—"

"Shut your bloody mouth." The words were as sharp as a cracking whip, and Victoria shut her mouth.

"Now, Miss Bloody Farm Girl Larkin, who thinks what she has between her legs is too damned good for John Steel, shut up and listen to me. I've shown more patience with you than I've ever shown with any man or woman on God's earth, and you've pushed me too far. Acting like a damned duchess with your fine airs and treating me like some country Jack. I've paid a lot, in a lot of high places, for any word of who you are, and where you came from, and I'm out a lot on this deal. And the time has come for you to pay up."

"I haven't got anything, Steel," Victoria cried

pathetically, "and you know it." He had never spoken to her so crudely, she had never seen him so angry, and it frightened her.

"You've got your body," he replied bluntly. "It's not worth a tinker's damn now, but I can keep you here until it is. And then, my girl, you can either work for me or in a room upstairs . . . and I don't think you'll like the work I find for you there."

Victoria knew that her situation was hopeless, even as she rushed to the door. The giant servant, Jim, caught her easily, and if anyone heard her screams of rage and fear as she was hauled to the dark basements of the building, they didn't respond.

Chapter Seventeen

Phillipe arrived at the Château St. Sebastien in the cold light of dawn. He had not wanted to go through the village in broad daylight when he might be recognized by an old servant, or anyone that had a good eye and long memory. But the village had been silent, with an eerie Sunday morning silence, and only a shivering dog had marked his coming with a timid growl.

Though the effects of the revolution had not been so violent in the countryside, he had passed many burned-out ruins of country estates and castles, and there was certainly no reason to think that his own home had fared better.

The cold winds of March blew his wool greatcoat around his lean body, his black hair blew long and unkempt around his face, the cold air of the mountains biting his cheeks and ears.

When he caught sight of the château, the sky was pink and clear behind it, standing proudly on the horizon, the dark gray stone echoing the darker silhouette of the mountains behind it.

It was a ruin.

A few charred beams were all that remained of the ancient timbered roofs, and there was no sign of life anywhere. A peculiar numbness settled over him, and he made the remaining walk up the hillside like a man bewitched, too tired and defeated to be upset.

The ancient iron gates were down, the St. Sebastien coat of arms that had been forged in them hundreds of years ago still showing beneath a light dusting of snow.

He walked across the bricks of the courtyard, watching the dry snow blow over them, and into the blackened hole where the great doors to the castle had been. He stood in the doorway, trying to digest the sight of the blackened stone walls where there had once been rooms, the blackened timbers where there had been ceilings, criss-crossing the vast, cold, brightening sky above. The stone staircase of the great hall climbed into nothingness, wind whistled through the empty arches that had held the precious stained-glass windows.

Phillipe walked through the empty shell, his boots crunching over the rubble and piles of cinders. Here had been the great hall, over there the chapel, there the sunlit salon where Christianna had practiced her violin, and somewhere above, the window a hole to the sky, had been the bedchamber where his father had died, and then his mother.

Could it have been only two years ago that he had stood in that room, watching his dying grandfather? In his memory, his grandfather mocked him from the bed.

Would you like to save your château, Grandson? This crumbling old whore of a castle that you love so much?

"There's nobody here but ghosts now."

Phillipe whirled around at the sound of the voice, his heart in his throat, but instead of the apparition he expected to encounter, he saw only a small boy, his shabby coat and scarf moving in the wind, his dark eyes regarding Phillipe with interest.

"How do you know I'm not a ghost?" Phillipe asked after a moment, glad of human company in this empty place.

"A ghost wouldn't walk up the road to get here," the child replied, somewhat scornfully. "I saw you from our cottage," he added, pointing a mittened hand in a vague northward direction.

Phillipe remembered a small cluster of cottages outside the castle wall where a number of servants had lived.

"What is your name?" he asked, coming down the stairs and going back towards the door. The child fell easily into step beside him as they walked out into the sunlight, his worn boots echoing over the snow-dusted stones of the courtyard.

"Paul," the child replied simply. "My grandmother used to work here a long time ago. Then it burned. I play here now sometimes. I'm not afraid of ghosts."

Phillipe smiled at the words and took a last look at the castle behind him. "No, Paul, I'm not either. What is your grandmother's name?"

"Annette. She was a nursemaid to the girl who used to live here, before she went to live with the queen. There's no queen anymore. Did you know that?" The child's round cheeks were bright and red with the sunshine and cold wind, his eyes sparkling and brown.

Phillipe nodded seriously. "Yes, I've heard."

The boy stared at him closely for a moment and tugged his knitted cap down around his ears. "Are you Phillipe? The brother?"

Phillipe was startled for a moment. "Yes, how did you know?"

"You look like her. Your sister."

Phillipe's heart began to beat faster, hope swelling in his heart.

"She's staying with my grandmother. Do you want to come with me and see if they're awake? She sleeps late, my grandmother says, because she's a lady."

The shout of joy that rose from Phillipe's throat echoed off the empty walls and rose to the sky, where it disappeared into the blue expanse.

Phillipe turned to the startled child next to him. "Do you know what I'm going to do, Paul? I'm going to go and fetch my sister, and do you know where I shall take her? I'm going to take her far away, across the sea on a big ship, to England. It's warm there, and green, and peaceful. And do you know who lives there?"

The child shook his head, his eyes wondering.

"The most beautiful woman in the world. She has eyes greener than leaves, and a voice that sounds like honey, and hair like autumn; and I'm going to marry her." Phillipe tried to remember the last time he had wanted to laugh with joy.

"I like the part about the ship," Paul said. "Aren't you angry about them burning your castle? Your sister said you would be angry."

Phillipe did laugh then. "No, I'm not angry. Who wants a castle when they could have a girl with red curls and green eyes?"

"Me, that's who," the child answered soberly, wiping his nose on a heavy sleeve. "I play here and pretend that it's mine."

They walked past the fallen gates on the narrow road, little more than a path, that led to the cluster of stone cottages.

"Do you know what, Paul?" Phillipe asked quietly. "I used to play here and imagine that it was mine. And then it was, and I didn't want it."

Paul looked at Phillipe as if he doubted this. His small, heavy boots trudged along beside Phillipe's larger, better-made ones.

"Who does it belong to now?" he asked at length.

Phillipe looked back at the towering walls, the craggy battlements. "France, some would say. Or ghosts. But I think it's still mine."

"Will you live there?"

"With the ghosts?" Phillipe asked lightly, feeling better than he had in months. "No. I'm afraid they'd keep me awake at night, howling and dragging their chains."

"I wouldn't be afraid," Paul informed him.

"No? Then why don't I give it to you? And you can keep it for me, in case I ever want to see it again."

The boy's red cheeks grew redder, his eyes were brilliant. "Really? And I can play there whenever I want?"

"Whenever you want."

The child broke into an excited gallop, and then stopped abruptly. "Do you think the ghosts will mind?"

Phillipe smiled. "No, but France might."

"There's our house," the child said excitedly, "and it looks like they're up. Come on, monsieur, don't you want to eat?"

Phillipe watched Paul run for the battered door, and followed at a slower pace.

The door of the cottage opened with a swift bang, and there was Christianna, dressed in the worn, dark clothing of a peasant, her face thinner and smaller than he remembered.

She cried out at the sight of him and ran towards him, stumbling over the rough ground.

They held each other for a long time, and Phillipe was surprised to find himself crying, his tears falling onto the top of Christianna's glossy black head.

She felt small and thin, her bones as fragile as a child's, and when at last they stood back to look at each other, he saw that she had changed.

Her blue eyes looked too large for her angular face, and there was a bitter tightness about her full mouth. She looked as if she had suffered, as if she knew grief.

"How did you get here?" he asked.

She looked away for a moment, wiping her tears on the back of her hand. The shawl around her shoulders was a rough knitted affair, and he remembered the cape of heavy velvet she had been wearing the last time he had seen her, the dusty lilac satin of the lining.

"Peasants," she answered at last in a vague voice. "A peasant brought me here." She said nothing for a few more moments, and then began to speak and cry at the same time, choking on her words as they tumbled out. "Oh, Phillipe, take me away from here. The whole country has gone mad, and nothing has been right. I've been so frightened, Phillipe, I can't sleep, I've gone without food, and there was nobody, nobody anywhere. I want to go away, I want to be rich again, I want to feel safe . . ."

Phillipe pulled her shoulders against him and tousled her black curls. "We're going, piglet, we're going. Today, if you like. I'll take you to England, and I shall introduce you to the most wonderful girl in the world. You can play your violin at our wedding, if you like."

She paled for a moment. "I . . . don't have it, Phillipe. They . . . took it from me."

Phillipe nodded, watching her small hands twisting in the fabric of her wool skirt.

"They took everything . . . they . . . they smashed mother's picture . . . they . . . they took everything. Let's not think of it," she ordered abruptly. "Tell me of England, Phillipe. Tell me about your betrothed. Is she beautiful? Is she rich? May I have some new clothes, and a fine house?"

"She's beautiful, and she laughs all the time, and I love her more than anything in the world," Phillipe answered. "And as soon as we arrive in London, you shall have some pretty gowns. Shall we go in out of the cold, piglet? It looks as if your nursemaid is waiting."

Christianna laughed, a brittle laugh, and Phillipe wondered if laughter felt as unfamiliar to her as it did to him.

"Oh, Phillipe, I'm so glad to be leaving this place. It's so cold here."

"We'll be in England by May," Phillipe promised, "and everything will be wonderful. By the way," he added, "I meant to have a word with you about your bills. I hope I really don't have to pay for that ermine-lined cape. And I really think your hairdresser is overcharging you."

She looked at him as if he had lost his mind, and then saw that he was joking. She laughed almost happily, staring at him, both of them thin, haunted-looking, clad in clothing that their servants wouldn't have worn.

"I don't think Monsieur Antoine will mind waiting a little longer, Phillipe. Business is bad these days. After all, who will go to a hairdresser who has no head?"

There was a bitterness in the careless words that tore at his heart, and he took Christianna's hand gently as they walked towards the cottage together, the last Marquis St. Sebastien and his pretty sister who had been the toast of Versailles.

Chapter Eighteen

Victoria surveyed her prison dismally. The only window, high up on the wall, had been boarded over long ago, and the door was firmly bolted. There was a narrow cot against one wall, a cracked chamber pot beneath, a pile of papers and rubbish next to the door. That was all. The dark, stone walls were damp, the floor was filthy. Water puddled in one corner, and the whole room smelled dank, like a cellar that was seldom used.

She kicked at the door furiously, though she knew that no one would hear. She succeeded only in stubbing her toe, sharp pains shooting through her foot.

"Damn you to hell, Steel," she whispered, enraged at her predicament. She wondered how long she had been here. Hours, maybe. Except for the single candle that Steel had left her, no light reached the room, and no sound. She wondered how long he intended to keep her here, and if there were some way that she could convince him to let her go.

The sound of the bolt lifting off the door caused her heart to race with fear and hope, but it was only Jim, Steel's giant lackey, bringing her a tin tray of food.

"Well, it's nice to know I won't be starved," Victoria commented wryly, examining the plate of chops and potatoes.

The silent man replaced the almost gutted candle and handed her a sheaf of papers—the day's news sheets. "Steel says you like t' read," he said with what might have been a smile, or a grimace.

"How very kind. I also like to walk about and breathe fresh air. I don't suppose he's made arrangements for anything like that, has he?"

"No, nothin' like that," the huge man replied with no trace of humor, leaving the room. The door closed solidly behind him, and she could hear the bolt dropping.

"Bugger you, too," she shouted at the door. She knew it was childish, but it made her feel a little better. She sank to the narrow cot with a heavy sigh, trying not to think about how dirty it was.

She wondered if Mary had returned home from work, and if she was worried. She wondered if anyone ever came down here, aside from Steel and the taciturn Jim. And she tried with all her might not to cry, to remain calm and clear-headed.

She should have been hungry by now, but the fried chops and potatoes were making her stomach turn. There was no knife on the tray, of course, nothing that could have served as a weapon.

She lay on the cot, resting her back, and the baby moved heavily inside her, a familiar, comforting feeling.

"Don't worry, little fat thing," she whispered. "We'll be fine. I'll think of a way to get us out of this. And in just a couple of months, we'll take you to see your uncles." Or would they? she wondered.

The minutes dragged by, the candle burning lower. Victoria thought she would go mad from the silence, from waiting, from fear.

"We may as well read the papers," she said aloud. Did all pregnant women talk to their bellies? Well, she did, and if it made her feel better, she would go on.

Her fingers ached with the cold as she picked up the first paper, rolling heavily to her side and drawing the candle closer. Stupid paper, full of fashion and gossip about the high-born of the city.

Has Lord D. gambled too heavily? Has the Prince of Wales forsaken his latest mistress? What twice-married duchess will soon make it thrice? Has the newly made Duke of R. returned to the flock of admirers surrounding Lady Lavinia H., after she cast him off only last season?

For a moment it didn't register, and then Victoria sat straight up, heedless of her aching back and cumbersome belly.

"Lavinia," she whispered. And Lavinia H. It was still Harrington, not St. Sebastien. And the Duke of R., why, it must be Harry, the newly made Duke of Rutledge. Phillipe had not married Lavinia, he hadn't, and Lavinia had lied to her.

"Oh, God almighty," she cried out, throwing the papers to the floor. Where was he, then? What had really happened?

She returned to the door and beat on it till her fists hurt.

"John Steel! Let me out, do you hear? Somebody, please, let me out! Please!"

She sank to the floor, almost crying with frustration, tired and cold. Childishly, she kicked at the tray Jim had left her on the rickety stool, and swore when it fell, the hard metal hitting her foot, making her grimace with pain.

Damn! She wanted out of here, it was cold and stank of rotting wood and mold. She tried the boarded window again, but it was too high to reach, and the stool was not tall enough to be of help.

Determined not to sit helplessly, she dragged the iron cot across the small room and climbed up on it.

The boards covering the window were wet with moisture, slick with mold, and she shuddered at the dark green that stained her hands.

Was it her imagination, or did the wood give slightly when she pushed on it?

"It's rotting," she said aloud, fresh hope rising. She climbed down from the cot, grabbed the tray her ruined dinner had been on, and smashed it furiously against the boards, thanking God for the dank air and constant rain of London.

She pushed and smashed and worked at the boards until sweat poured down her face and her arms ached. Splinters embedded themselves in her fingers, but she worked on, tears of rage and frustration welling in her eyes more than once.

By the time she had pushed the weakest board away, and could see the dark alley that ran behind John Steel's gaming hall, the candle was half burned. There was still plenty of traffic on the streets, to judge by the sound, so it couldn't be too late. In the rooms above her, John Steel's gaming hall and bawdy house would be full of people enjoying their evening's debauchery.

The space she had opened would never allow her through, and she knew she would have to work quickly to get out before someone came to check on her.

It was at least another hour before she had opened an entrance large enough to permit her cumbersome body through, and her hands were sore and bleeding where the rough wood had caught them.

Getting her heavy body from the cot to the window required more effort than she had thought, and the window was a tight squeeze, the rough edges of the broken wood scraping against her side, catching at her heavy cape. Her heart pounded with fear and exertion as she heaved herself onto the damp stones of the alley, the sound of rats scurrying away frightening her almost as much as the fear of discovery.

Only when she climbed to her feet and saw that there was nobody in sight did a thrill of freedom rush through her.

She tried to run, but it was too much effort, and a sharp pain lanced through her side. A steady rain was falling, and she wished she had her bonnet, lying forgotten on the floor of her former prison, as she pulled the hood of her cape around her head.

Once on the street, fear of discovery gave her speed, and she moved with surprising swiftness.

But where to go? She didn't dare go back to the room that she and Mary shared, for there was nothing to stop Steel from going there and taking her back, and she wasn't about to underestimate his ruthlessness again. And yet, there had to be some way to get a message to Mary . . .

"A penny, miss? 'Ave you a penny for an orphan?"

Startled, Victoria looked down to see one of the countless beggar children that haunted the streets of the East End, two enormous eyes gazing at her from a grimy face.

"Yes," she answered, and was surprised that her voice shook. "Yes, I have a penny . . . please, what's your name?"

"Danny, miss," the child replied warily.

"Are you clever, Danny? Can you keep a secret?"

"Can you pay?" the boy returned cagily.

"Oh, yes," Victoria assured him, almost laughing with relief. "Four pennies, and more if you can do this . . . . Do you know where Addly's fish shop is, one street over and down?" To her relief, the child was nodding. "There is a room right above the store, the stairs are off the alley. Run there and ask for Mary Atwell, can you remember that? Mary Atwell. Tell her to leave as fast as she can, and go to . . . go to the coffee house by the theater, where we had chocolate with John. Tell her to take all the money and a change of clothes, that she won't be going back. Can you remember all that?"

"It's a mouthful," Danny answered doubtfully. "Let's see. Above the fish shop, Mary Atwell, tell 'her to go to the coffee 'ouse where ye had chocolate with John. And bring money. Is 'at right?"

Victoria almost cried with relief. "Yes, that's it. But if there's anyone there, say nothing. And tell her to give you a sixpence, that Victoria said to. And here . . . here are your four pennies. Will you run before you forget?"

A broken, gap-toothed smile appeared. "You can bet on it. Will she give me a sixpence, truly?"

"Truly," Victoria echoed with an encouraging smile. "Go like the wind, Danny."

And I will too, she thought as the child broke into a run down the dark street, *for I'll not be anywhere near the East End, when John Steel finds me gone*.

The streets of West London were broader and cleaner than those she had left behind, the crowds thinner, the people better-dressed. Victoria was faint with cold and hunger, and the blazing windows in the dark streets had a strange, unreal quality.

She had never seen this part of the city by night, for she and Mary liked to stay inside after dark, the door of their room bolted against the many dangers of the London streets. She wondered if she would be able to recognize the coffee house that they had been to so long ago, in the days after they had first arrived in the city, when she was still slender and agile, and John Steel a jolly friend, showing two country girls the sights.

She looked up at the elegant façade of the King's Theatre as she passed, a few richly dressed patrons waiting for their carriages, and wanted to laugh as she thought of the last letter she had mailed to Jamie.

Dear Jamie, Tonight we are going to see 'Don Giovanni' at the King's Theatre, and Cousin Abi-

*gail has bought me a new gown, peacock blue.
London is so very fine . . .*

A sharp pain seized her, and she stood still, a
hand to her side, before moving on. Two well-
dressed young men rushed by her, their carefully folded cravats white against their dark
great coats, their expensive walking sticks clattering along the pavement.

" . . . brandy in my coffee," one was saying,
and " . . . good to have something warm," the
other answered.

Something warm, Victoria thought longingly, forcing her feet to move. It would be
warm in the coffee house, and dry, and she
could sit and wait for Mary. Her hands were
numb, and she was shivering uncontrollably. It
would be nice to drink hot chocolate and forget
about everything— forget that she was alone in
the city, that she had no job and very little
money and nowhere to go. She hoped the beggar child had gotten the message to Mary, and
that they could find a room for tonight, somewhere far from John Steel.

The warm, rich air of the coffee house surrounded her like a blanket, a fire crackling
cheerfully in the fireplace, the dark tables shining in the light.

Victoria felt dazed, light-headed, and she
didn't even notice the eyes that fastened on her,
the only unescorted woman in the crowded
room. She sank heavily into the nearest empty

chair, gathering her cape tightly around her middle to hide her girth, and closed her eyes, inhaling the rich smells of roasting coffee and cooking food. The chatter of the room buzzed in her ears, the words making no sense.

"Are you all right, miss? Can I get you something? Are you meeting someone?"

Victoria saw a concerned-looking waitress bending over her, a pair of worried blue eyes fastened on her face. *Do I look that odd?* she wondered, forgetting her stained cape, her bleeding hand. What had the young woman asked? The words made no sense, they were jumbled. She tried to speak, and could not. To her horror, her hands began to shake.

"Are you all right, miss?" the woman repeated, staring at the very white face, the huge green eyes dilated as if with pain or fear.

The words seemed to come from very far away, echoing in her aching head. *She thinks I'm mad*, Victoria thought. *How odd, what on earth is wrong with me?* She tried again to speak, and could not, and the waitress was saying something, who knew what. Victoria tried to stand, to leave, and the dull pain in her back turned into a fierce, fiery arrow that gripped her, shaking her, pulling her down.

Her heavy hood fell off her head as she gripped the back of the chair, but the chair didn't help, she was falling, and for a moment every eye in the room was fastened on the sight of her, her hair twisting and corkscrewing down her back, brilliant red reflecting the fire, as her body spiraled down to the floor.

She could hear the waitress crying out, and then, oddly, someone was calling her name.

As if through thick glass, she saw Harry and Johnathon rushing towards her, Harry's fat face and Johnathon's thin one, both shocked and worried, and they looked so funny, so funny.

The last thing she heard was her own laughter, high-pitched and far away, and then another pain seized her, and the darkness rushed up to claim her.

The handsome carriage emblazoned with the coat of arms of the Duke of Rutledge raced through the streets of London, the hooves of the horses clattering on the wet, dark streets.

Inside the carriage, the swaying lantern showed the rich leather and deep blue silk interior, warmed by a small charcoal brazier. Johnathon Lester, the fifth Earl of Fairfield, and Harry Winston, the newly made Duke of Rutledge, still in the finery they had worn to the opera that night, were bent over their barely conscious passenger.

"Good God, Johnathon, what can have happened? How did she get here?" Harry's plump face was flushed with worry, and he slapped ineffectually at Victoria's pale, cold hands, trying to revive her. "What's wrong with her? Is she ill? Is she dying?"

Johnathon laid his slender fingers to Victoria's throat, reassured by the warm pulse, rapid but steady.

"She's not ill, she's pregnant, you jackass. Stop slapping at her hands and look at them, Harry. She's been working with them, and hard, too."

Harry stared at his friend, his eyes growing rounder. "Pregnant? Did you do this, Fairfield?"

Johnathon lifted his golden head abruptly. "Harry, if I had done this, do you really think that Vic would be wandering the streets in the rain and fainting in public places? If I didn't know how stupid you are, I'd call you out for suggesting such a thing." He untied Victoria's cape as he spoke, pushing the wet, brown wool from her shoulders. Her eyelids fluttered, and she looked at him in complete confusion.

"Vic? Are you all right? It's Johnathon, and we're going to take care of you."

For a moment she seemed to smile, and then her face tightened with pain, a frightened cry rising from her trembling mouth.

"Can you speak, Vic? Is it the baby?"

The red hot pain subsided, and blissful exhaustion beckoned her. She opened her eyes, and smiled at Harry's question. She tried to give him a shove, but the effort was too much, and her hand slid back to her side.

"Of course it is, you great booby," she answered, and her voice sounded very small and soft. Another searing pain wrenched the smile from her lips, and her spine arched, she bit back her cry.

"Is it?" Harry demanded, his voice rising in panic, staring at Johnathon, who was holding both of Victoria's hands and making soothing noises. "Is it the baby? Do you suppose it shall fall out here?"

Johnathon looked appalled. "Damn it, Harry, I don't know much about it, but I'm relatively certain that they don't just 'fall out.'"

"We can only hope not," Harry added anxiously, staring with horror at Victoria's swollen abdomen.

Victoria thought she might have laughed if she had not been so tired. She had never been so tired, never in her life, and she wanted just to sleep, someplace warm. It all seemed like a strange dream, that one minute she was locked in a damp, basement room, and then out on the rainy streets, and now in a bouncing, silk cocoon of a carriage. She wished she could be warm, her teeth chattering, her legs shaking with the cold.

"Take off your coat," Johnathon ordered Harry, "and help me get this wet cape off of her. God knows how long she's been wearing it, it's soaked."

Harry in his agitation managed to hit his head on the wall and hit Johnathon in the head with his elbow, so eager was he to comply.

"Hold on, Vic," Johnathon whispered, tucking the voluminous folds of Harry's violet blue frockcoat around her. "Just a few more minutes."

Victoria heard the soft words, felt the warm velvet around her shoulders, and drifted into a sea of darkness illuminated by lightning flashes of searing, tearing pain.

The liveried footman and butler of the elegant house on St. James Square stood frozen in shock when they opened the door, the footman nearly dropping his candle at the sight of their fashionable young master struggling under the load of a very pregnant young woman, whose red curls fell wildly around her still, white face.

"Don't stand there staring," Harry shrieked with rage. "Let us in, you fools."

They swiftly stood aside, and stammered "good evenings" in reply to Johnathon's more polite greetings as the two young men staggered past with their awkward load.

"Watch it, Harry, don't drop her . . . . Mind the stairs, Harry . . . . Watch her head now, you've almost banged it on the railing . . ."

Harry stopped dead in his tracks, puffing up with indignation. "You're so damned good at this, Fairfield, why don't we put her back in the carriage and take her to Fairfield House?"

Johnathon took a deep breath before answering.

"Harry," he said patiently, "I've been your friend for most of my life, but if you don't quit twitting around and get poor Vic upstairs and into a bed immediately, I won't even bother to call you out. I shall shoot you right through your thick head right now as we stand here."

"Good God," Harry remarked anxiously.

Victoria writhed, her face contorted, and she let out a strangled cry.

"What the hell are you waiting for?" Harry shouted at the horrified butler and footman, who were watching from the bottom of the stairs. "Prepare Auntie Augustine's room, or even Mama's, you fools."

The two servants ran past them in their haste to open the doors and light the room.

Harry and Johnathon deposited Victoria in the rococo splendor of the great bed, and Johnathon began pulling her wet shoes and stockings from her cold legs.

She saw the room through a red haze as the pains came closer and closer together, Johnathon's calm face and Harry's terrified one bending over her. There was yellow silk on the walls, a portrait of a round-faced woman with owlish eyes. She felt as if her back were breaking, and she moved frantically, her head tossing, trying to escape the pain that knifed through her.

And then, a blissful respite when she could breathe, and the pain subsiding to an aching, low throb.

"Mary," she whispered, and it was hard to say the words. "Please ... Mary will go to the ... the coffee house ..."

"Mary, from Harrington Park? Don't worry, Vic, I'll send someone for her right away."

She felt the next pain before it came, and

shook with the agony of it. Oh, the pressure, the hard, biting force against her spine. She cried for Mary, for Mrs. Hatton, for her mother . . .

Then the moment's ease that she knew would follow.

"Johnathon . . . I'm sorry . . . I think the baby's coming . . ."

Her eyes closed, she floated in the wrenching pain, she was being split apart, she would die . . .

Harry lost what little composure he had and reached across the bed, seizing the lapels of Johnathon's frock coat. "The baby's coming!" he shrieked. "Good God, Fairfield, the baby's coming!"

Fairfield slapped Harry's terrified face firmly. "Stop screaming, you jackass, you're not having it, Vic is. If you want to be useful, go and get a woman."

"A woman," Harry repeated, looking about the room as if one were hiding there. "A woman. Of course."

He ran from the room, his shoes thumping heavily down the hall.

Johnathon bent over Victoria's writhing body, gently stroking the damp curls from her clammy brow. "Don't worry, Vic, Harry's gone to fetch someone, and everything is fine."

Harry's footsteps came thumping back up the stairs, and he bounded into the delicate yellow room, dragging a terrified scullery maid by the arm.

"A woman," he announced breathlessly.

Johnathon closed his eyes and prayed for patience before speaking.

"Not that sort of woman! Damn, Harry, how did you manage to reach this advanced age without thinking! We need a midwife, an older woman, someone who knows something about childbirth, not a twelve-year-old scullery maid! Think, you idiot!"

Harry looked crestfallen.

Johnathon removed the diamond pin from the snowy lace of his cravat and offered it to the girl. "Do you see this? Fetch me a doctor or a midwife, and it's yours."

The girl's eyes widened and sparkled, and she ran from the room.

Victoria screamed, an animal sound of pain that terrified both men.

Harry took a lace-edged handkerchief from his pocket, and mopped his face with a trembling hand.

"Get over here," Fairfield ordered, his words short and sharp. "And remember, if you faint, I'll shoot you. Here, take Vic's hand and hold it. Yes, I know it hurts, she's in pain. Now take care of her hands, and do whatever I tell you, and leave the rest to me. *Don't look, Harry*— remember, I have to shoot you if you faint. Oh, God, poor Vic . . ."

When the scullery maid returned some minutes later, leading a black-robed physician, Harry and Johnathon were sitting in the dainty wing chairs that graced the room. Wrapped in the soft white folds of one of Harry's shirts was Victoria's daughter, sleeping against Fairfield's heart.

They beamed at the doctor like proud grandparents, while Victoria slept an exhausted sleep.

"She's beautiful," Mary whispered. "Just beautiful, miss. And so tiny . . ."

Victoria stroked the baby's silken cheek, marveling at her perfection. The miniature face was perfectly peaceful, the rosebud lips exquisitely silken, the black hair that covered the perfect head like the down of a new chick.

"She's perfect," Victoria agreed, lifting a miniature hand on one finger, thrilling at the sight of the tiny fingers, the smooth pink nails. A tear of joy splashed on the baby's face, and Victoria and Mary both went to wipe it away at the same time, and laughed at each other, both of them with happy tears in their eyes.

Mary settled back into the yellow brocade of the wing chair that she had moved next to the bed, dimpling with pleasure as she surveyed the silken luxury of the room.

"Who'd have thought," she remarked, "that we'd end up here. I was that scared, miss, when the boy came to tell me to meet you. Oh, and when you weren't there, I thought I would die of fright . . . . Do you suppose that John Steel will find us here?"

Victoria smiled as she laid the baby on the soft bed next to her and leaned on one elbow to watch her, the dark lashes on the silken cheeks, the soft, even rise and fall of the tiny chest.

"No," she answered Mary, loath to disturb her happiness with any unpleasant thoughts. "He would never think to look for us here. And even if he did, I don't think that even John Steel would want to cross a duke."

Mary smiled happily. "No, I guess he wouldn't, at that. Oh, this is lovely, no mistake about it."

"No mistake," Victoria agreed, snuggling into the lavender-scented linens.

There was a gentle knock on the door, and Harry's round face peered anxiously in at them. "May I come in, Vic?"

"Of course you may," Victoria cried. "Would I deny entrance to the best midwife in London? Come in, Harry, and see how lovely she is."

Harry entered the room timidly and looked down at the sleeping baby. "She's damned small, isn't she?"

"She's perfect," Victoria argued. "Just a little early, the doctor said."

Harry touched the baby's hand with a plump finger, a diamond sparkling in the light that streamed in through the windows. "Yes, she's perfect. What will you name her, Vic?"

"Gabrielle. Gabrielle Elizabeth, after both her grandmothers."

Harry looked uncomfortable. "Have you seen him, Vic? Phillipe, I mean. Does he know?"

Victoria's face paled. "No, not since July. Have you, Harry?"

"Well, once. I saw him on the street a day or two after the news of the revolution came through. He was with Etienne DuBay; do you know him?"

Victoria shook her head soundlessly.

"Etienne owns a shipping company; he deals mainly in antiquities, paintings, furniture, things like that. Apparently, Phillipe has money invested with him—"

"Yes, yes, I remember. Go on."

"They were arguing. Phillipe wanted money to go to France, and Etienne was calling him a fool, said that he'd never get out alive. Told him that no damned castle was worth a man's life."

Victoria nodded, looking down at the sleeping baby, whose black hair and blue eyes were so much like her father's. Mary said that all babies had blue eyes, but Victoria knew that they wouldn't change.

Harry went on, "Phillipe said the bloody castle could go hang, that it was his sister he was concerned with, and he had to get her out; and Etienne said that he was a madman, and Phillipe said that Etienne should go to hell, and a lot of that sort of thing. I didn't speak to him," Harry added hastily. "After all, the last time I saw him . . . well, I had behaved very badly, Vic." His face flushed red, and he didn't meet Victoria's eyes. "Am I forgiven, Victoria? I never meant to hurt you, you know."

Victoria smiled at the downcast face, the unhappy words. "I think you redeemed yourself last night, Harry. Forgive and forget."

Harry breathed a sigh of relief, and watched Victoria as she leaned over the baby. "Do you hear that, Gabrielle? Your father went to France to save your auntie, and then he will come home to us."

Harry bit his lip, not wanting to reveal his true feelings. If Phillipe had intended to return, he would have been back by now. London was full of *émigrés*, all telling the same stories of the mob that ruled France. They killed aristocrats, ruthlessly and efficiently. If St. Sebastien had attempted anything as foolhardy as trying to rescue his sister, he had probably lost his head some time ago.

Fairfield entered the room, followed by a footman struggling beneath the weight of an elaborate cradle draped in soft blue silks.

"Here we are," he announced. "And I've been around to your rooms and fetched all the baby's clothes and your things. They're not to go back there," he told Harry firmly. "I won't have my godchild living in squalor. It's not healthy. If they can't stay here, Harry, we must buy them a house."

"Oh, but you can't," Victoria exclaimed. "You've already done so much; and as soon as we can, we intend to go back to Middlebury."

Johnathon looked up at her from where he was fussing with the silk hangings around the cradle. "Yes, Mary told me your plan. But, Vic, I think you need more time. Give yourself a year before you turn the baby over to Mary. You know it will break your heart to do it, even living under the same roof. At least this way you can have her for your own for a year."

Victoria thought she could have resisted any other argument in the world.

"Of course we will keep you here in London," Harry declared. "I shall find you a nice townhouse, Vic, and we will visit you often. She's my godchild too, you know, and I ought to have some say about it. After all, I did deliver her. With a little help from Johnathon, of course," he added hastily as Fairfield lifted his golden head indignantly.

"Please, miss," Mary chimed in. "You don't want to wean her too soon."

"It's not as though we can't afford it," Johnathon added.

"All right, all right," Victoria capitulated. After all, Harry was a duke, and Johnathon an earl, and they could afford it. And she had no desire to turn Gabrielle over to Mary so soon. And it was for the baby. "But only a year, at most; and then I'm going home."

By the end of the month, Harry had installed them in a townhouse on a fashionable tree-lined street, and he and Fairfield showered them with pretty clothes and useless gifts. As soon as Victoria had regained her strength, they began escorting her to balls and plays and operas, until her life began to resemble the false one she had written about in her letters home.

Spring was in the air, and Gabrielle St. Sebastien was blooming like a rose.

Chapter Nineteen

Etienne DuBay looked up from the papers that covered his desk and rose so quickly that he spilled an ink bottle.

"*Bon Dieu*, St. Sebastien! You're alive! And Christianna—I never thought to see you again. I've asked every *émigré* I've seen, and no one had seen you. Sit down, sit down for God's sake, and tell me where you've been." Nowhere pleasant, that much Etienne could see. Phillipe St. Sebastien had acquired a lean hardness about him, his blue eyes bright and wary in his tanned face. He looked like a man who had learned to fight, and win.

Phillipe laughed aloud at the disbelief on his friend's face, and they embraced before they sat.

"And little Christianna . . . how pretty you are. Tell me, how did you manage to help her escape from the palace, Phillipe? When did you arrive? Would you like a drink?"

Phillipe stretched his legs as he settled into the comfortable leather chair and glanced around the clutter of Etienne's office fondly, catching the view of the wharves of London outside the window, the empty masts of ships in the sun.

"Yes, brandy if you have some. We arrived in London this morning, and Christianna has been at the dressmakers ever since. I hope my money is turning a good profit, or I'll be in debtor's prison by tomorrow."

Etienne smiled at his friend. "Oh, business is good, very good. Every *émigré* that arrives has something to sell—paintings, jewels, whatever they could get out. It's a pity to make money on the misery of France, but better me than someone else. Tell me, how did you manage to get Christianna out?"

Phillipe glanced at his sister, whose face was set and closed, a pretty mask that he had been unable to penetrate. She had not spoken of the revolution since the first day he had seen her, but she cried out in her sleep, screaming of blood and hunger.

She looked up, fixing Etienne with brilliant blue eyes, and cast him a dimpled smile. "What do you think of my new gown, Etienne? Phillipe thinks it very silly."

Etienne smiled, his eyes darting from Christianna's brittle smile to the warning lift of Phillipe's brow.

"It's very pretty, mademoiselle," he answered at last, his eyes moving over the stripes of lavender and pink, the matching jacket, the silk flowers on the fichu and the wide-brimmed hat. "You are as sweet as May herself."

Christianna looked pleased and tossed her black curls.

Phillipe leaned forward, his eyes blazing with curiosity. "Etienne, do you remember before I left I told you of my intended? Victoria Larkin? Has she been here, has she written? I left instructions for her to do so if she had need. Has she?"

The smile froze on Etienne's face. "No, Phillipe, the charming Miss Larkin has had no need of your money."

"I'm not surprised," Christianna exclaimed with her light laugh. "From what Phillipe says, she is a paragon of virtue, a goddess among mere mortal women . . ."

"Shut up, piglet," Phillipe said pleasantly. "But you've seen her, she's written you?" What the hell was wrong with Etienne? Phillipe wondered.

Etienne looked damned uncomfortable. He raked his hand through his dark curls before answering. "I've seen her, yes, but not met her, Phillipe."

Something was wrong, very wrong. "Damn, Etienne, what news of Victoria? Is she in Middlebury, or still with her cousin's family?"

"Neither," Etienne finally answered, meeting Phillipe's eyes. "If all accounts are to be believed, your little country girl has done very well for herself. She has a very lovely house of her own, on Hanover Square. I myself saw her only last week, at the theater. She looks very . . . well taken care of. What hair she has, St. Sebastien! No wonder you were so enamored of her. She was all in gold silk, and she glittered like the sunset. I understand that the Prince of Wales is pursuing her, but she won't give him the time of day. She's quite the girl of the moment, you see. She appeared in public for the first time only two months ago, and already has society at her feet . . ." Etienne's voice trailed off at the sight of Phillipe's face.

"I'm sorry, Phillipe. She never called on me, never wrote to ask of you . . ."

Phillipe was frozen with shock. It had never occurred to him that Victoria would not wait. He sat perfectly still, thinking of the countless days he had longed for her, the nights he had dreamed of her as he made his stealthy way through the horrors of the revolution, sleeping in forests, in rude rooms, once even in a pigpen. And all the times he had been longing for her golden laugh, and wry wit, and her soft, white skin, she had been fluttering around London like a butterfly in gold silk. Her own house! On Hanover Square, no less!

"Who has been . . . taking care of her so well?" Phillipe asked at last, his voice like ice.

Etienne thought he would rather not answer, but there was little help for it.

"Well, that depends on who you listen to. Half the rumors say it's the Duke of Rutledge, half say the Earl of Fairfield, some say both."

Phillipe rested his forehead on the palms of his hands before speaking. "The faithless little bitch."

Nobody answered. There seemed little to say in the face of such grief. Christianna's eyes were round with horror.

"Where did you say her house was?" Phillipe asked, rising abruptly to his feet.

"Hanover Square. Damn, St. Sebastien, don't do anything foolish, will you? Listen, I've something to talk to you about. I need your help— I've a position open, and it pays well—"

"I'll take it," Phillipe answered, his words bitter and sharp.

"Listen first, Phillipe. It's in New Orleans, on the other side of the world. The *émigrés* are going there at an amazing rate—"

Phillipe turned to go, straightening the lapels of his new black frock coat. "I said, I'll take it. The sooner I'm out of London, the better." He turned and began to walk from the room.

"The ship leaves in four days," Etienne called after him, but that information didn't appear to faze Phillipe.

Christianna half rose from her chair, her small hands gripping the arms. "Phillipe! Phillipe! Where are you going, Phillipe? Come back here! You said we were done traveling, you that it was all over! Phillipe—"

Etienne went to the frantic girl quickly, laying a hand on her arm. "Let him go, Christianna. He'll be back."

Her face was tight with fury, and she stamped her foot. "He has dragged me across a country and a sea, and he told me we would stay here, that I could rest! I'm tired, Etienne, and I don't want to travel anywhere. Even New Orleans. Especially New Orleans! I don't even know where New Orleans is!" And with those words, she burst into loud tears.

Etienne, who was well acquainted with the irrational behavior of the noble expatriates, many of whom were suffering deprivation and hardship for the first time in their spoiled lives, took the black-haired girl into his arms and made comforting sounds, while she raged against the brutality of her brother, who was going to take her away from the first dressmaker she had seen in months.

Victoria and Mary left the fan-maker's shop in the bustling Royal Exchange and stepped out into the May sunshine, Mary carrying a bundle of gaily wrapped parcels, Victoria holding the sleeping Gabrielle, the child's bonneted head comfortably resting against her shoulder.

"Is that everything, Mary?"

Mary smiled as she consulted the list in her hand. "Let's see. Paper, and ink . . . your fan . . .

violet soap . . . gloves . . . yes, that's all. We need to go round to the dressmaker's, and that's it."

Victoria smoothed the skirts of her new dress, printed in a floral pattern of lavender and mint. "Good. I'm anxious to be home, and to feed Gabrielle. Shall we walk or hire a hack?"

"Hire a hack," Mary returned, eyeing the crowded streets with obvious disapproval. "We'll have more to carry when we leave the dressmaker's. I wish you'd let the duke buy you a carriage."

"There's no need," Victoria explained. "And it's so expensive to keep horses in the city. Harry and Johnathon have done so much already. A hired hack is good enough for me."

"There's one," Mary announced, gesturing at one of the many hired carriages that crowded the bustling street. "Step lively, miss. Mind your shoes," she cautioned as they stepped off the curb.

The driver left his seat to help them into the worn interior of the carriage, his eyes admiring Victoria, her slender figure laced into the well-made gown, the lavender ribbons that fell from the straw cartwheel hat mingling with her long curls.

"Where to, ladies?" he asked, doffing his battered hat.

"Madam Alard's, please, Cornhill Road," Victoria answered. "And will you open the windows, please? It's a shame not to enjoy the air on such a day."

"They're stuck shut," the man replied cheerfully. "No elp for it, m'lady."

"Shall we get another hack, miss?" Mary asked.

"No, don't be silly," Victoria laughed. "It's a short enough drive, Mary. How spoiled we're getting," she added as the driver closed the door and the coach lurched into the busy streets. "And don't tell me it's for the baby. That seems to be the answer to my every argument these days."

"Aye, we're spoiled," Mary agreed, "and it's glad I am of it."

Victoria laid her cheek against the top of Gabrielle's head, breathing the soft baby scent of her skin. She never tired of watching this marvelous child who looked so much like her father.

How luxurious life seemed, compared to the past few months. How wonderful it was to feel safe, and cosseted; and how good it was that spring was here. And tomorrow, if the weather held, Harry and Johnathon were going to take them on an outing to the country.

What a pleasure it would be to see green fields and blossoming trees, to smell the clean air. Almost, she thought wistfully, like going home.

"Are we here already?" Mary asked curiously as the carriage lurched to a stop. "Fancy, miss, it seems as if we hardly started."

The door swung open, and Victoria froze as she found herself confronting the deadly-looking barrel of a pistol.

"Good morning, ladies," John Steel greeted

them, leaning into the carriage. "Ah, shopping, I see. How lovely."

Victoria's arms tightened around her sleeping child, her eyes felt dry and frozen, her heart was lodged in her throat.

John Steel swung himself easily into the carriage, his auburn hair shining in the sun, the pistol resting easily in his hand, and reached out to close the door behind him. "Drive on," he called to the coachman, and he smiled like a cat as the carriage began to roll. He settled comfortably on the seat opposite the two terrified young women.

"So this is the brat, is it?" he asked, almost pleasantly, gesturing at Gabrielle with the pistol.

Mute with fear, Victoria nodded.

"Pretty," he remarked, tipping his auburn head to the side and surveying them through cold gray eyes. "As are you, Miss Larkin. Motherhood becomes you."

Victoria was afraid to speak, her eyes glued on the deadly pistol that he gestured with so casually.

"I hope you don't mind a little trip. I know you don't frequent the East End much these days, but we have a little business to attend to, don't we?"

"What do you want?" Victoria asked, her voice shaking. "If it's money, I'll get it, Steel."

"Of course you will. But it's more than money, you know. You made a fool of me, Victoria, and I don't like it. Not one bit. So yes, I'll get my money; but I'll have you work for it. And there'll be no sneaking away this time. Not if you want that brat to live through the night."

"Please," Victoria whispered, tears coming to her eyes. She clutched the warm baby tighter, her hand protective over the small head. "Please, John, don't hurt my baby."

"Ah, the baby. I imagine a certain nobleman might pay well for her return. You lied to me, Miss Larkin. Impoverished father, indeed. You look very prosperous, very prosperous indeed."

Mary was so still and white that Victoria wondered if she had been frightened to death.

Outside the creaking carriage she could hear the sounds of the street, the familiar noise of everyday life as the people of London went about their business, completely unaware that she was being held hostage at gunpoint inside the closed carriage.

John Steel's eyes mocked her from across the carriage. "Sticky, isn't it? You really can't do a bloody thing, can you? And I mean to make a pretty penny off you and your pup.

"By the way," he added, "which one is the father? His grace the duke or m'lord earl?"

"Neither," Victoria bit back. "They're friends, Steel. Simply friends."

"Is that so?" he drawled. "That isn't what people are saying. They say you're having it off with both of them."

Victoria flushed. "People gossip. I don't care."

Mary cried out as Steel's strong hand reached out and snaked around Victoria's neck, dragging her forward, his fingers biting into her flesh. Gabrielle let out a wail as Victoria clutched her tightly, her heart hammering.

The cold metal of the gun was at her temple, pressing hard, and she was so frightened she couldn't breathe.

"Still high and mighty, Miss Larkin?" His breath was hot against her face, his eyes deadly. "Don't be stupid. I have you, I have your brat, and I have your little friend. Every snotty word out of your arrogant mouth will go hard on them, so don't you look at me and say 'I don't care' or I will make you care. Do you understand?"

"Yes," Victoria managed to gasp, conscious only of the barrel of the gun against her skin, the crying baby in her arms.

"Good." Steel released her abruptly, and she almost fell to the floor, so great was her relief.

The carriage creaked to a halt, and when the door opened, it was facing the alley door that led to John Steel's gaming hall and house of pleasure.

"My dear Miss Larkin," Steel said amicably, "welcome to your new place of employment."

Phillipe uttered a curse at first sight of the house in Hanover Square. It was small but elegant, every graceful line speaking of expensive understatement, from the violets that bordered the front walk to the moss green draperies that showed through the tall windows. Cherry trees scattered pink blossoms across the lush grass,

Amy Elizabeth Saunders

falling on his shoulders like snow as he passed beneath them, and he swore as he brushed them off.

For a moment he considered leaving, but the urge to mock Victoria was too great. What had she said to him on that sweet summer night when she had lain naked in his arms and he had tried to explain his love of his château to her?

A castle is just a pile of rocks, Phillipe. A place is only worth something if you truly love someone inside. Love is worth more than a stupid pile of rocks that does not love you back.

Pretty words, words that he had remembered a million times, and the soft glow in her eyes when she spoke to him. He would throw those words in her face.

He knocked on the door, his eyes burning with anger.

"Thank God you're here ..." Johnathon stopped abruptly in midsentence, dark eyes widening. "Good God ... Phillipe. You're alive."

"Apparently so. I'm afraid it's probably an unpleasant surprise, isn't it?" Phillipe's words were light, careless, the sort of flippant tone that Christianna and her friend Artois used when they sat and insulted hairdressers, princes, grooms, and duchesses, with equal disdain for all of them. It was the tone of someone who takes pleasure in being unkind.

It was lost on the young earl, with his smooth, innocent brow and kind brown eyes, who waved

354

Philippe urgently into the house, speaking with unusual speed.

"No, not at all, not at all. I'm damned glad to see you, I need a level head around here. I thought it was Harry when you knocked, and I would even have been glad to see him, which shows you how bad it is. Thank God you're here. Sit down, please."

Phillipe was staring at the elegant room, the carpets as soft and green as moss, the pale wood and curved legs of the furniture, the rich, soft upholstery. On the wall was a large painting of a bucolic country scene, a thatched cottage surrounded by flowers.

This was Victoria's room, this was her house. The colors had been chosen for nobody else. And here was Fairfield, his former friend, damn his boyish face and angelic golden hair, showing him in and offering him a seat as if he had dropped in for tea.

"Is the mistress of the house available?" Phillipe asked politely, resisting the temptation to sneer on the word "mistress."

Johnathon pushed a heavy lock of hair off his forehead, the gesture tense. "No. No, you see, that's what I'm trying to tell you, and I'm going about it all wrong. Let's start here." He withdrew a letter from the pocket of his pale blue brocade waistcoat and offered it to Phillipe. "This came an hour ago."

The note was creased and dirty, the writing awkward.

I have the woman and the child. Do nothing if you want them to live.

Phillipe stared in disbelief. "Victoria?"

"It looks like it. Nobody can find them. It seems that she left with Mary and the baby this morning; and then this was under the door when I came round an hour ago."

There was a heavy thump of footsteps on the porch, and Johnathon went quickly to the door and opened it.

Harry almost fell in, in a state of obvious agitation, his face red and his wig askew. "Dear God, Johnathon, what can this mean? Kidnapping! Who would kidnap Vic, and why? And my poor Gabrielle! Victoria must be—hello, Phillipe, damned good to see you're alive—Victoria must be frantic, simply frantic. Are you sure this isn't a prank, some sort of sick joke?"

Johnathon grasped the sidecurls of Harry's white wig and straightened it impatiently. "Stop babbling, Harry, and think. Does Vic have any enemies that you know of?"

"Only Lavinia, and she didn't do it, she's having tea with Auntie Augustine this very minute. I don't think she could do such a thing and still have time for tea—"

"Of course it wasn't Lavinia, you jackass. And she doesn't even know about the baby. What about that man in the East End that Vic was running away from? Did she mention his name to you?"

356

Phillipe stared, silent, as Harry pursed his mouth thoughtfully. "No, no, she never said. Oh, good Lord, shall we find a constable?"

"No, the note said to do nothing. For all we know, the house is being watched. I say we pay, as much as it takes. What do you say, Phillipe?"

Phillipe looked from one panic-stricken face to the other, a terrible suspicion dawning on him.

"What baby?" he asked, his voice soft in the silent, sunlit room.

Johnathon and Harry glanced at each other.

"Your daughter, Gabrielle," Johnathon answered gently. "Not quite seven weeks old, and as sweet and healthy a child as one could hope for. I thought Vic was going to die when we found her, she was so thin and exhausted. She'd been working like a dog for pennies a day, and having a very bad time of it. We brought her here."

Phillipe felt as if he had swallowed glass. "I didn't know. She didn't tell me . . ."

"How could she?" Johnathon asked, "when you were gone? She said that you just disappeared without a word."

Phillipe shook his head in disbelief. "I left her a letter at Harrington Park. Who could have taken it?"

"Lavinia," chorused Harry and Johnathon in equally disgusted voices.

Phillipe wanted to weep, but he forced himself to concentrate on the issue at hand. "And this man that you spoke of, that Victoria was running away from . . . who is he?"

"We don't know, really," Harry explained, his plump hands twisting nervously. "Some character from that neighborhood she was living in, who wanted more than Vic was willing to give. Sounded like a ne'er-do-well, some sort of criminal . . . That's all we know about him."

Phillipe tried to digest all this. Victoria had a baby. No, *he* and Victoria had a baby, and her name was Gabrielle . . . . Victoria had been kidnapped, possibly by this unknown man in the East End . . . . She thought that he had abandoned her . . .

"I say we ask questions in this neighborhood that she was living in. Do you know exactly where it is? Perhaps someone there can lead us to this man."

Harry looked thrilled. "Good thinking, Phillipe."

"I know where their room was," Johnathon informed him. "I went to collect their things after the baby was born."

Phillipe rose abruptly, tossing his dark hair from his eyes. "Then that's where we start. A few discreet questions, a few coins in the right hands . . . I've learned a lot about this sort of thing in France. If you intend to come," he added, looking disapprovingly at Harry's waistcoat and jacket of brilliant embroidered birds and the diamonds on his fingers, "I'd advise you to change into something a little quieter. Discretion is in our favor."

It was agreed that they would meet at Rutledge House, where Harry would try to find
something simple in his vast closets, and from
there they would proceed to Petticoat Lane, to
the rooms above Addly's Fish Shop.

Chapter Twenty

" 'Aven't seen 'em. It's not my business. They rented the rooms, and then they was gone, all in a 'urry." The woman who owned the fish shop wiped her red hands on her apron as she spoke to Phillipe, her eyes fastened on the pile of cod on the table before her.

"Is there anyone in the neighborhood that knew her, anyone she spent time with?"

"It's not my business," the woman repeated, picking up a knife and methodically cutting the heads off the fish. Their sightless eyes stared up at him.

She was lying, Phillipe could see that. It was in her evasive eyes, her tight mouth.

He laid a pile of coins on the scarred table.

"All you'll get is fish," the woman informed

him, making no move to touch the money. "I don't know a thing."

Phillipe nodded. "Thank you. If you should happen to remember anything—"

"I won't," the woman said brusquely. "Now buy something or get out. I've a business to run, you know."

Phillipe left the shop and went back to the crowded street, where he saw Fairfield walking towards him, defeat on his boyish face.

"Nothing," Fairfield reported. "You'd think she never lived here, that no one had ever seen her. It's hard to believe . . ."

"It's impossible to believe," Phillipe agreed. "You'd think that someone would know her. Did you get anything from the woman in the bakery?"

"That she had fired Vic when she got too big to work, and that Mary had quit not long after. She claimed to know nothing about them. I think she was lying, she looked frightened."

Phillipe rubbed his forehead. "They are. They're all lying. That's good, it tells me that we're close. Where's Rutledge?"

"Having a beer. I told him to stay put and keep his mouth shut. I'm afraid he might say something stupid. I told him to sit in the pub and listen."

"Good," Phillipe said. The sea of people moved around them, pushing and jostling, the cries of the vendors and merchants rose in the twilight, all hoping to make one more sale before the market closed for the night.

"There's nothing more to be done," he admitted at last. "All we can do is go back to the house and wait for a message. If it's money they want, we'll hear from them soon enough." Though the words were calm, he was bitterly disappointed and frustrated.

He stared down the length of the bustling market, his eyes roving over the merchandise, the stacks of used books, the barrels of shoes and piles of gloves, the tarnished cloth of a gold cape fluttering from a pole, a rag seller, her wares tied in neat bundles, a wizened gnome of a man wearing at least six hats on his head, holding up a gown . . .

A gown of stripes, white and blue like the summer sky, heavy white lace falling from the shoulders, a froth of blue ribbons falling from the neck. For a moment Phillipe didn't breathe, and in his mind he saw Victoria standing in a bubbling stream, the striped skirts of the gown flung over one arm, her eyes glowing at him with indignation.

I'm Victoria Larkin, Lavinia's cousin . . .

"Come on," he said abruptly, and began pushing his way through the crowd, Johnathon on his heels.

The little man behind the stall bowed at their arrival, losing a hat off the stack on his head. "And what can I 'elp you gents with today? I've got west coats as fine as any in the city, I've got shoes and breeches fit for a king—"

" 'E's got a big load of crap, is what," finished the rag seller to the man's right.

The merchant rounded on his neighbor, fire in his eye. "Will you give over? I've a living to make, and I don't bother you!"

Phillipe lifted the dress, the blue ribbons moving silkily over his hands, the white taffeta linings whispering. "This dress, please . . . where did it come from?"

"It's a beaut," the man agreed. "Just the present for your sweetheart, ain't it? Taffety linings, sewn right in. Bought it off a duchess, I did, down on 'er luck."

The rag seller snorted. "Looked more like a tart that 'ad been down on 'er back, if you ask me."

"Now stop! What did old Timmo ever do to you that you want to devil me so? That was no tart, my Carrots wasn't. Still had the country air in 'er cheeks, sweet as roses—"

"And big as a house," the rag seller snorted in disgust, turning her ample back and giving her attention to the merchant on her other side.

Phillipe's heartbeat was moving a little faster. "This girl, this duchess, that you call Carrots— have you seen her?"

"Used to," the man replied mournfully. "Wanderin' through wif her little friend what looked like a pigeon. She don't come 'round no more. I been told she went 'ome."

The man was afraid, that was obvious. His eyes traveled quickly over the tall, dark-haired nobleman before him, then he began folding clothes, his aged hands quick and sure.

Phillipe caught the man's gnarled hand. "Please," he said, and there was urgency in his voice. "Please, do you know anything, anything at all?"

To his shock, there were tears in the old man's eyes, and the red nose became even redder.

"God 'elp me, guv'nor," he whispered, his watery eyes pleading, "it's worth my life to know nothin'. I'd like to 'elp, but people listen, and I'm afraid. Let go my hand, and shop."

The old man stepped back and threw a pile of gaily embroidered waistcoats in front of the two men who stood before him.

"See there, see there," he called loudly, "just the thing to turn a pretty girl's eye. And if you're lookin' for one, this is where you should be. Out for a night of sport, gentlemen?"

His voice dropped and he leaned over the counter, his eyes moving around the crowds like a bird. "What's that, guv'nor? A good place to spend your cash? I'd go to John Steel's gaming hall. There's a lot going on there, if you get my drift. Yes, they do say you can find anything you like at John Steel's." An almost imperceptible pause. "You might just find what you're looking for."

Behind Phillipe, Johnathon exhaled softly. The old man's rheumy eyes met theirs bluntly for a moment, and then he turned back to his table, already moving towards another customer. "See here, see here, this here coat, I bought off a duke. 'ad 'is arms cut off and couldn't wear it no more, I swear to God. I could charge you five, I should charge you four, but we'll let it go for two, and I'm robbin' myself . . ."

Phillipe turned to Johnathon, his smile bright in his tanned face. "We've found her," he said quietly. "Let's go round up Harry and decide what to do next."

Chapter Twenty-one

"You look good in a whore's room," John Steel announced, a smile of satisfaction playing around his mouth. "Very good."

Victoria felt as if she were made of ice, and she looked around the gilded cocoon of the room. The bed was draped in pink silk, pink silk covered the walls, and everywhere she looked, gilt-framed mirrors reflected her cloying prison. No windows this time, she noted wryly. As if she could leave, with Mary and Gabrielle prisoner in some unknown part of the house.

"I think I liked the basement room more," she answered at last.

"Then you should have stayed there, shouldn't you?" Steel's voice was like silk. Outside the door, the evening's merriment was beginning. She could hear the clink of glasses, the low rumble of men's laughter, the answering high, soft note of a woman's giggle.

"And just look at you," Steel added happily. "The attire becomes you very well, duchess."

Victoria's face flamed as he crossed the room and traced the outline of her breasts with his finger, his eyes like gray ice. She turned her head away, but there she was, reflected again and again in the gaudy mirrors, dressed only in a heavy corset of pale blue beaded satin, and filmy drawers that hid nothing of her body, gartered stockings tied with rosettes and ribbons above each knee.

She closed her eyes against the sight.

Steel's finger traced the upper curves of her breasts where they swelled above the tight lacing of the corset. "You must be a little friendlier, my girl. There are nine hours in a working night, and I intend that you work all nine."

Victoria tried not to shudder.

"And I damned well don't want any complaints about you. Don't even think about raising a fuss, or spilling your sorry story to anyone. You know what will happen if you do, don't you?"

Victoria tried not to think about it. She tried to answer, but her throat was too tight. She nodded mutely.

"Good. It would be a shame if something should happen to that pretty baby of yours. And don't get any stupid ideas about heroic rescues. I don't intend to let the girl or the baby out of my sight. They'll stay in my office with me until the place closes, and I have a gun. I'll use it, too."

Victoria believed him, and she ached with misery. She wanted her child, wanted to hold her in her arms, hear the small sighs and feel the warm, sweet breath against her cheek.

"Don't worry, John," she whispered. "I'll be as good as gold. Just don't hurt her."

Steel grinned and fondled her hair. "That's a clever girl. Now put a smile on your face and look lively. There's a drunk fellow downstairs, plenty of ready cash, and do you know what he's asking for? A redhead that likes it rough. Sounds perfect, don't you think?"

If I told you what I thought, you'd shoot me, Victoria answered silently, her stomach turning. She closed her eyes for a minute, offering a desperate prayer. But she knew that there would be no answer, no miracle to save her now.

"All right, John," she answered at last. "Let's get it over with."

Steel laughed as he made his way to the door. "Cheer up, duchess. At least this one won't mind if you cry a little. That sort never do. As a matter of fact, he'll probably like it. He's a mean-looking bastard."

Victoria tried to hide her fear, not wanting to give him the satisfaction of knowing how afraid she was. "Meaner than you, Steel? How ever did you manage to find such a man?"

Steel laughed. "Oh, I managed, all right, and I'll manage again. Try not to cry too much, duchess. The next fellow won't want to see a red nose."

The door banged shut, muting his laughter.

"I hate you, Steel," Victoria whispered, burying her face in her hands. "Oh, God, I hate you."

She tried to still her shaking hands, to fight the tears that threatened. *Pretend it's a dream*, she told herself, *and that soon you'll wake up*.

But the sound of the door opening was no dream, the sound of the bolt sliding into place, the footsteps that approached her, muffled on the heavy carpets.

She tried to lift her head, but found that she could not. She didn't want to look at this man, the first of many that would buy her body and use it against her will.

The footsteps stopped before her, a heavy hand touched her hair, moving through the curtain of silk that fell in her face, and she shuddered involuntarily. *Don't think*, she told herself, *don't think*.

The hand touched her cheek, the cold surface of a ring grazing her skin.

"My dear Miss Larkin. What am I to do with you? It seems that you are never where you should be. Perhaps I should just take you home to your innumerable brothers and see if they can keep an eye on you."

She *was* dreaming, she was. And what a cruel dream, that this stranger should have Phillipe's low, soft voice, his gentle touch. *Have I gone mad?* she wondered.

A gentle finger ran across her lips, and trembling, she forced herself to open her eyes, focusing on the hand that caressed her face.

It was a lean, strong hand, dark from the sun, a fine lace cuff falling over the back of it, and a glowing emerald on the finger, an emerald surrounded by delicate gold filigree in a pattern of ivy vines.

"Or perhaps I should marry you immediately and never let you out of my sight again. Yes, I think that's the answer."

Hardly able to breathe, she raised her face.

Phillipe's eyes shone at her through a haze of tears, eyes as blue as the sky, his smile brilliant and tender, his teeth white in his tanned face. And he was real, as real as anything in the room. She could see the small lines in the corners of his eyes, the dimples beneath his hawklike cheekbones; she could smell the familiar scent of the sandalwood that scented his shirt. His eyes seemed to sing to her, soft love songs of summer days.

"Well, *petite* Victoria, do you marry me, or shall I go and ask for my money back?"

Her answer was a raw cry of joy, and hope, and sorrow; and she was in his arms, shaking with laughter and choking with sobs, feeling his arms tight around her, the familiar sound of his heart beating against the broad strength of his chest, his hands moving through her hair, warm and strong.

When his mouth took hers, it was with an

anguished longing, a brilliant heat, until it seemed that their souls had touched in the soft air of their mingled breath.

"Well?" he asked softly. "Will you come with me? Or shall I have to pay for another hour? Just think what it would cost me, every hour, every day for the rest of my life. And people would say, poor Gabrielle St. Sebastien, I hear her father died in a whorehouse without a penny to his name . . ."

"Oh, God," Victoria cried. "Phillipe, he has her! John Steel has her, and Mary, and . . ."

His fingers touched her lips, covering them gently. "Hush, I know. Harry saw them go in. He's down at a card table watching the door. They're fine."

"But how will we get them out? Or me, for that matter. There's someone at every door . . ."

Phillipe took his heavy gold watch from his pocket and checked it. "We shall bring them out in exactly forty-five minutes."

Wondering, Victoria reached out to touch his heavy dark hair, barely able to believe that this was real.

"Until then," he added, "we can do nothing. Unless, of course, you think that we can amuse ourselves. By the way, you haven't said yes, yet."

"Yes. Yes, you bloody fool. Oh, good God, Phillipe . . ."

Their bodies met and melded in a heated rush, with lightning bright touches of need and joy; and when they reached the pinnacle of desire together, shattering and breaking their fe-

372

vered, hungry bliss, Victoria felt his tears against her cheek, mingling with her own.

"Whatever you do," Phillipe told her, his eyes never leaving her face, "when I say to move, do so immediately. If we are all to get out undiscovered, time is essential."

Victoria nodded, her heart in her throat, longing to hold Gabrielle, to know that she was safe.

"I hate to go out there like this," she added, gesturing to the flimsy undergarments, covered by a thin silk robe of the same blue, so sheer that it did little to disguise her. "I wish he hadn't taken my clothes."

"Don't worry, there are at least twenty girls in the room, some of them wearing less. Most of them, as a matter of fact. At any rate," he added, "I rather like it. Do you think you might wear it some other time?"

Victoria began to reply indignantly, and saw the suppressed laughter in his eyes. "Oh, for God's sake," she exclaimed, her voice shaky with nervous laughter. "You wear it sometime, if it pleases you so much."

Phillipe leaned against the door and pulled her against him, raining kisses on her face. "I've missed your laughter more than anything. Well, almost." The laughter left his face as he consulted his timepiece. "Are you ready?"

Victoria shivered, once again conscious of her flimsy garments, and of the danger of the charade they were about to enact. She thought of Gabrielle and drew a deep, steadying breath.

"Ready," she answered.

Almost immediately, a sharp rap sounded on the door. "Time's up," called a deep, abrupt voice.

Victoria nodded at Phillipe. "Jim," she mouthed silently, and he nodded back, gathering her hand in his and pressing it against his heart.

"*Je t'aime*," he whispered, and his eyes glowed when she echoed his words.

"Now," he said, taking her slender wrist in the strong grip of his fingers and opening the door with a loud bang.

Just as Victoria had expected, Jim was waiting, and he started at the sight of her and began moving his giant body through the hall.

"She's supposed to stay in 'er room," he informed Phillipe, his deep voice leaving little room for argument. "There's another customer wants 'er."

"Let me speak to the proprietor," Phillipe demanded, his voice haughty with aristocratic scorn. "Immediately, please. I wish to purchase more time."

Jim crossed his arms stubbornly, a colossus in waistcoat and breeches. "There's another customer," he repeated patiently. "And she's not supposed to leave 'er room. The boss says."

Phillipe raised a dark brow. "And what would the boss say if I were to offer him fifty pounds, and what would the boss say if he knew that you refused me?"

Victoria tried not to panic as Jim deliberated, clearly swayed by the amount.

"Aw' right," he agreed at last. "Follow me, then."

Victoria focused on Phillipe's hand over hers as they crossed through the crowded gaming room, thick with smoke and the scent of drink, buzzing with conversation. Except for a few whistles for the new girl, nobody seemed to take notice of them.

Jim knocked on the dark door of John Steel's office and waited patiently, his eyes never leaving the arrogant nobleman or the slender redheaded girl next to him. Victoria wondered if he could hear her heart beating. Her ears strained to hear inside John's office. Was that the sound of a door closing?

"Who is it?" he called at length.

"Jim. I need your say-so, here."

The door opened, and John Steel was staring into her eyes, as deadly as a snake, as composed as a gentleman in his fine, black frock coat and breeches, his neck cloth perfectly folded, every auburn hair in place.

"Is there a problem, sir?"

Victoria shivered at the veiled threat in the silky words. She felt Phillipe's hand tighten over her own.

"Not at all," Phillipe answered coolly, his face as haughty as a prince. "*Bon Dieu*, everyone is touchy around here. Why should there be a problem? No, I simply wished to purchase more time, and this . . . person refused to take my money. Fifty pounds, gold."

Phillipe glanced around the crowded, noisy room with distaste. "Do you mind stepping into your office, sir? I'm not very comfortable discussing my . . . more unusual tastes in front of an audience."

Victoria saw the light in Steel's eye when Phillipe mentioned the amount of money, and the interest that Phillipe's last statement piqued. She turned her head as his eyes sought hers, and focused on the nearest card table. Oh, God, was that Harry's broad back, his carefully styled white wig, sitting only inches away? Hardly daring to breathe, she stared hard at the floor, at the gold patterns on the worn wine red carpets.

"Please," Steel said graciously, opening the door wide and waving them in. Victoria heard the door close behind them, muffling the noise of the room outside. Her eyes went immediately to the closet door in the corner, wondering if Mary was there with Gabrielle.

Or what if he had moved them to another room? She fought the panic that flooded her, and told herself to concentrate only on the present—Phillipe sitting her in a wooden chair, taking a seat himself, stretching his legs as if he had all the time in the world.

John Steel was smiling at Victoria, almost purring with delight at her tear-stained face, her unsteady hands.

"Now, what can I do for you, sir?" he asked,

turning to Phillipe, his eyes assessing the simple but expensive clothing, the size of the sparkling emerald.

Phillipe smiled. "A lot, I hope. I'm very pleased with this girl, very pleased. I'd like another two hours, and I'm willing to pay."

Steel nodded. "I'm very glad to hear that, sir. But you see, I've already promised her to someone else, and I hate to let down a customer. Perhaps another girl?"

Phillipe raised an arrogant brow. "I don't think so. It's an awkward thing to explain, but I have somewhat specific tastes, tastes that are considered . . . shall we say, a bit depraved. And it seems, to my great delight, that this little wildcat here is also so inclined."

He patted her thigh with a lewd wink, and Victoria resisted the almost hysterical urge to laugh, so great was the look of surprise on John Steel's face.

"You don't say?" he answered at last, looking quite taken aback. The noise outside the door grew louder, there was the sound of breaking glass, and Steel's eyes darted towards it.

"Didn't you know?" Phillipe asked him. "My good fellow, this girl is a treasure! The more I beat her the happier she was. And when I clouted her with the candlestick, she simply sang . . ."

John Steel was speechless, and Victoria managed a weak, apologetic smile and a shrug.

Outside the door, a drunken, belligerent voice

was demanding to speak to the owner. Steel glanced impatiently towards it, torn between the desire to see, but unable to tear himself away from what he was hearing.

"And you know," Phillipe went on lightly, as if he were blissfully unaware of the ruckus, "I've never seen anything like that sheep imitation she does. Exquisite! I could never have imagined such a thing, myself. Could you?"

"No," Steel answered, looking at Victoria as if she had grown another head.

The voice at the door was shouting, ". . . must see him, right now, by God . . ."

"And when she started to bark, I tell you, I was so delighted that the chamberpot almost fell off my head! What a woman you have here, my friend."

" . . . and if he doesn't settle this immediately, I shall take my two hundred pounds and walk out of here!"

This last gained Steel's attention, and he took his bewildered eyes from Phillipe's face at last and looked towards the door. "Excuse me for a moment," he apologized, rising from the desk where he had been listening in growing shock.

"Of course," Phillipe agreed, standing politely. As Steel passed, Phillipe calmly drew a pistol from beneath his midnight blue frock coat and cracked the butt of the gun across the back of Steel's head.

Victoria winced at the sound of the sharp crack, and leapt to her feet as Phillipe caught Steel's body as it slid to the floor.

"He's breathing, move quickly," Phillipe whispered, handing her the pistol.

She didn't have to be told twice. She almost jumped over the wide desk in her haste to open the closet door. Phillipe was gagging Steel with his own cravat, pulling the heavy cords from the damask draperies to bind his hands and feet.

Victoria hardly dared to breathe when she opened the door and peered into the dark recesses of the closet. For a moment she saw only boxes, the shapes of draped furniture, a rack of wine bottles. And then, a movement beneath a blanket.

"Mary?" she whispered, her voice quavering.

The blanket moved, and there was Mary's round face, her eyes brown pools of fear. And in her arms, thank God, was Gabrielle, her silky dark head contentedly on Mary's heart.

"Oh, miss," Mary breathed, her eyes on the heavy pistol in Victoria's hand, "however did you manage?"

"Quickly," Victoria whispered, tears of relief pouring down her face. She had barely taken the baby into her arms and felt the warm, milky breath against her face when Phillipe spoke behind her.

"Give me the gun, Victoria. Hurry, get out the window."

He was already pushing it open as he spoke. "Are they all right? If he's harmed them—"

"No, no," Victoria whispered joyously, examining Gabrielle's tiny fingers, feeling her small, dimpled legs. "They're fine."

It sounded as if there was a fight in progress outside the door.

Phillipe half pushed Mary out the window to the alley, her face white, absolutely speechless with shock. He took the baby from Victoria so that she could follow, and then handed Gabrielle into her mother's waiting arms below.

He landed lightly next to her, the sound loud in the quiet, dark alley. "Do you see the carriage waiting on the street? Run, quickly. I'll be right behind you, and I've got the gun." His arms were around her waist, pushing her towards the carriage as he spoke. "If anyone tries to stop you, I'll shoot them."

Victoria ran, one arm clutching the baby, the other holding Mary's arm, pulling her along. Their footsteps clattered through the empty alley, and Victoria's heart was in her throat, the night air cold on her face. Every shadow seemed menacing, a potential enemy, and fear lent speed to her feet.

The carriage door was opening, and there was Johnathon, his golden hair shining in the light of the shuttered carriage lantern. He pulled them inside, first Mary, who crumbled weakly to the seat, and then Victoria, her breath coming in ragged gasps.

Phillipe nodded quickly to the young earl as he followed, pistol in hand.

"Harry was thrown out two seconds ago," Johnathon said quickly, gesturing around the street corner. "I just heard the noise. Get in, and I'll drive." The door closed silently.

Phillipe sat next to Victoria and wrapped a warm arm around her shoulders, pulling her close. "It's almost over. Are you all right?"

The carriage began moving, turning a corner sharply.

"I'm fine," Victoria answered with a shaky laugh. "But look at Mary! If her eyes get any bigger, she'll have no face left."

"Oh, miss," Mary gasped, finding her voice at last. "I never dreamed that you would come . . . it's like a dream, isn't it?"

Victoria's eyes went to Phillipe. "Yes, it's like a dream," she agreed, her voice soft and husky.

The carriage swayed to a halt, and Victoria clutched at Phillipe's arm.

"Don't worry," he told her softly. "That will be Harry." He leaned forward to push open the door, and Harry staggered in, holding his crested handkerchief to his bloody nose.

He sank onto the seat next to Mary as Johnathon started the horses up, and the carriage clattered away, down the dark streets.

"We did it," Phillipe announced, breaking into a brilliant smile.

Victoria began to cry then, leaning heavily against his shoulder, exhausted by the tension of the day, dazed by his sudden reappearance. "Where have you been?" she asked at last. "What happened to you? I thought you were dead . . ."

"I thought *I* was dead," Harry snuffled from across the carriage, "when that brute at the gaming hall decided to throw me out. I really

381

don't see why Johnathon got to drive and I had to pick the fight."

Victoria laughed through her tears. "Perhaps because you have a thicker head," she suggested wickedly, and everyone laughed with her, except Harry, who affected an offended face.

"Well," he sniffed, "that's all the thanks I get. Perhaps we should turn around and take you back."

"Oh, no," Phillipe said, pulling her tightly against him. "There's only one place you're going, Miss Larkin, and can you guess where that is?" His smile was white in the darkness, his long fingers caressing Gabrielle's silken cheek as he spoke.

Victoria touched his face, stricken by the gentle glow in his eyes as he stared at his daughter.

"Where am I going?" she asked, her voice husky and warm, thinking that if he said "the moon," she would find some way to follow him.

"To a little village called Middlebury. I understand that it's very beautiful there in the spring, and that a certain Reverend Finkle lives there. Do you think he might be willing to perform a marriage ceremony on such short notice?"

Home, Victoria thought, and she wondered if she would ever again be so happy. The lilacs would be blooming, and the apple blossoms in the orchards, and the new-born lambs would be frolicking through the green fields. Home to Father, and Gareth, and Jamie, and all the boys, and Mrs. Hatton with her chilblains and homely wisdom.

For a moment her heart was so full that she couldn't speak.

"Oh, yes," she whispered at last, her eyes brimming. "Oh yes, I should like to go home, Phillipe."

"And on the way," he added, "I'll have to tell you about New Orleans. I'm afraid that we may be forced to take a trip sometime soon."

"I'll go anywhere," she answered, "as long as you're not out of my sight again."

Mary blushed at the sight of them kissing and covered her face with her small hands, and Harry's booming laugh rang out into the night, and the coach sped on to Hanover Square, to collect the things needed for the journey.

Chapter Twenty-two

Was it the birds that woke her, calling to each other, singing their early morning songs; or was it Phillipe's hands, warm and heavy, pulling her against him?

Unwilling to open her eyes, still languid with sleep, Victoria pressed willingly against his body, warm in the cool morning air, and rubbed her cheek against his chest, wrapping her arms around his shoulders.

His hands moved over her back, over the smooth curves of her derrière, and she felt him growing hard against the curve of her thigh.

With a sigh of delight, she rolled on top of him, straddling his body, and guided him into her already damp sheath, shivering with delight at the sound of his low groan as she began to move slowly.

They made love quietly, gently, whispering tender words to each other, while the room grew brighter with the rising sun. She opened her eyes just before she reached the peak of her ecstasy, and he was watching her, his eyes glowing with lazy pleasure, his chest and shoulders dark against the pristine white sheets.

"I love you," he whispered, pulling her hips closer to his own, and moving beneath her with an almost unbearable heat.

Victoria couldn't answer, her eyes closed as the waves of heat and light claimed her, shaking her body. Only then did Phillipe seek his own release; then he gathered her against him, and stroked her hair gently.

"This is heaven," Victoria murmured. She gazed fondly around her room, finding joy in the familiar sights—the battered old dower chest at the foot of her bed, the gleaming oak floor, the simple white curtains with the sun streaming through them, the sight of the blossoming apple trees outside her window. On the windowsill sat an empty bird's nest, a souvenir of a girlhood summer long ago, filled with dried lavender and rose petals.

Oh, it was good to be home and to hear the familiar sounds. Somewhere in the house, she heard the low murmur of a masculine voice, and Mrs. Hatton's more strident tones answering. And the birds—she had forgotten how many birds there were in the spring. The trees were full of them, their songs filling the morning air.

Outside the window, a loud, rhythmic creak sounded, the sound of someone drawing water from the well, and even that discordant noise fell on her ears like music. And then, outside, a tuneless voice began to sing, in rhythm with the creaking windlass.

> "Of all the girls that are so smart
> There's none like pretty Sally.
> She is the darling of my heart
> And she lives in our alley . . ."

Victoria shook with laughter at Phillipe's pained groan.

"What is that awful noise?" he asked, his brow furrowing, his eyes still heavy with sleep.

"Oh, that's the old windlass on the well. It does need fixing, doesn't it? Somebody always means to get to it—"

"I meant the singing," Phillipe answered with a grin.

"Oh, that. It sounds like Gareth, I think. Or maybe Richard. It is awful, isn't it?" Victoria reached for her chemise where it lay tangled on the floor, and pulled it on before going to the window.

She pushed the window open and leaned out happily, drinking in the cool, sweet air of the new day, surveying the overgrown gardens and rolling green hills with delight.

"Good morning, Gareth," she called, and Gareth, lifting the heavy bucket from the stone well, smiled up at her, the sun bright on his fiery head.

"There you are, you lazy little beggar. Your baby's been awake for an hour, you know. She's down in the kitchen with Mrs. Hatton and Mary."

Victoria made a rude noise at her brother and left the window. Gareth began to sing again, his flat, tuneless voice causing Phillipe to groan and pull the blankets over his head.

"Come back to bed," he suggested, his voice muffled beneath the blankets.

Victoria laughed as she pulled a dress over her head. "Listen to you, giving orders. No, this is my last day at home, and I intend to spend it with my brothers. Why don't you get your bum our of bed and come down with me?"

"What a wife," Phillipe lamented. "I thought that perhaps when we were married, you'd become more obedient."

Victoria laughed and pulled the blankets from his head. He wrestled her to the soft mattress, causing her to shriek with laughter, and his hands fumbled in the laces of her bodice. "Turn me loose, Phillipe! I've got to go feed the baby—stop that and let go—"

"Good morning, Vic," a voice called from the hall, and Phillipe released her immediately, a guilty look on his face.

"Good morning," Victoria called, blushing,

and the voice on the other side of the door added, *"Carpe Diem."*

"Seize the day, indeed," Victoria agreed with a wink at Phillipe as she pulled her hair back with a green ribbon.

"Which one was that?" Phillipe asked as the footsteps disappeared down the hall.

"Daniel. Get up and come downstairs with me."

Phillipe smiled at her, watching the sunlight her hair with bits of gold, the graceful curve of her arm as she bent to slide her shoes on. "Come back to bed," he suggested.

Victoria laughed. "For shame," she answered, but went, and they held each other for a few minutes more.

"Phillipe," she asked quietly after a moment, "Do you really think that Christianna will be happier here than joining us in New Orleans?"

Phillipe laughed, remembering the look of horror on his sister's face when they had arrived and been besieged by the crowd of red-headed giants and barking dogs.

"Believe it or not, yes. She needs rest, and peace; and the last thing in the world she wants to do is travel. And it's only for two months. After all, what can happen in two months?"

Victoria smiled, a faraway look in her eyes. "Do you know," she asked softly, "that's almost the exact thing I said to myself when I left home to go to Harrington Park a year ago. And look what has happened."

Phillipe touched her cheek softly. "Are you sorry, Madame St. Sebastien?"

"Never," Victoria swore, looking up at him with eyes as clear and light as jade. "And you? Do you think you will always be as happy as you are now?"

"*Pour toujours*, Victoria," he whispered. "Forever."

He pulled her almost roughly against the warmth of his chest and covered her slender hand with his, feeling the cool, hard surface of the emerald against his palm.

The dappled sunlight streamed through the gabled windows, the birds sang in the trees, and the air was warm with the promise of spring.

LOVE SPELL

THE MAGIC OF ROMANCE
PAST, PRESENT, AND FUTURE....

Dorchester Publishing Co., Inc., the leader in romantic fiction, is pleased to unveil its newest line—Love Spell. Every month, beginning in August 1993, Love Spell will publish one book in each of four categories:

1) *Timeswept Romance*—Modern-day heroines travel to the past to find the men who fulfill their hearts' desires.

2) *Futuristic Romance*—Love on distant worlds where passion is the lifeblood of every man and woman.

3) *Historical Romance*—Full of desire, adventure and intrigue, these stories will thrill readers everywhere.

4) *Contemporary Romance*—With novels by Lori Copeland, Heather Graham, and Jayne Ann Krentz, Love Spell's line of contemporary romance is first-rate.

Exploding with soaring passion and fiery sensuality, Love Spell romances are destined to take you to dazzling new heights of ecstasy.

COMING IN SEPTEMBER 1993
TIMESWEPT ROMANCE
TIME REMEMBERED
Elizabeth Crane
Bestselling Author of *Reflections in Time*

A voodoo doll and an ancient spell whisk thoroughly modern Jody Farnell from a decaying antebellum mansion to the Old South and a true Southern gentleman who shows her the magic of love.

_0-505-51904-6 $4.99 US/$5.99 CAN

FUTURISTIC ROMANCE
A DISTANT STAR
Anne Avery

Jerrel is enchanted by the courageous messenger who saves his life. But he cannot permit anyone to turn him from the mission that has brought him to the distant world—not even the proud and passionate woman who offers him a love capable of bridging the stars.

_0-505-51905-4 $4.99 US/$5.99 CAN

Discover the real world of romance in these passionate historicals by Leisure's Leading Ladies of Love!

Apache Conquest by Theresa Scott. Sent to the New World to wed a stranger, beautiful young Carmen is prepared to love the man chosen for her—until a recklessly virile half-breed sets her blood afire.
_3471-9 $4.99 US/$5.99 CAN

Song of the Willow by Charlotte McPherren. When tomboy Willie Vaughn meets handsome Rider Sinclair, she vows to hang up her britches and Colt .45 and teach the mysterious lawman a thing or two about real ladies.
_3483-2 $4.50 US/$5.50 CAN

Elfking's Lady by Hannah Howell. When Parlan MacGuin takes lovely young Aimil captive, the fierce Highland leader means to possess both the beauty and her magnificent white stallion Elfking. But only love will tame Elfking's lady.
_3475-1 $4.99 US/$5.99 CAN